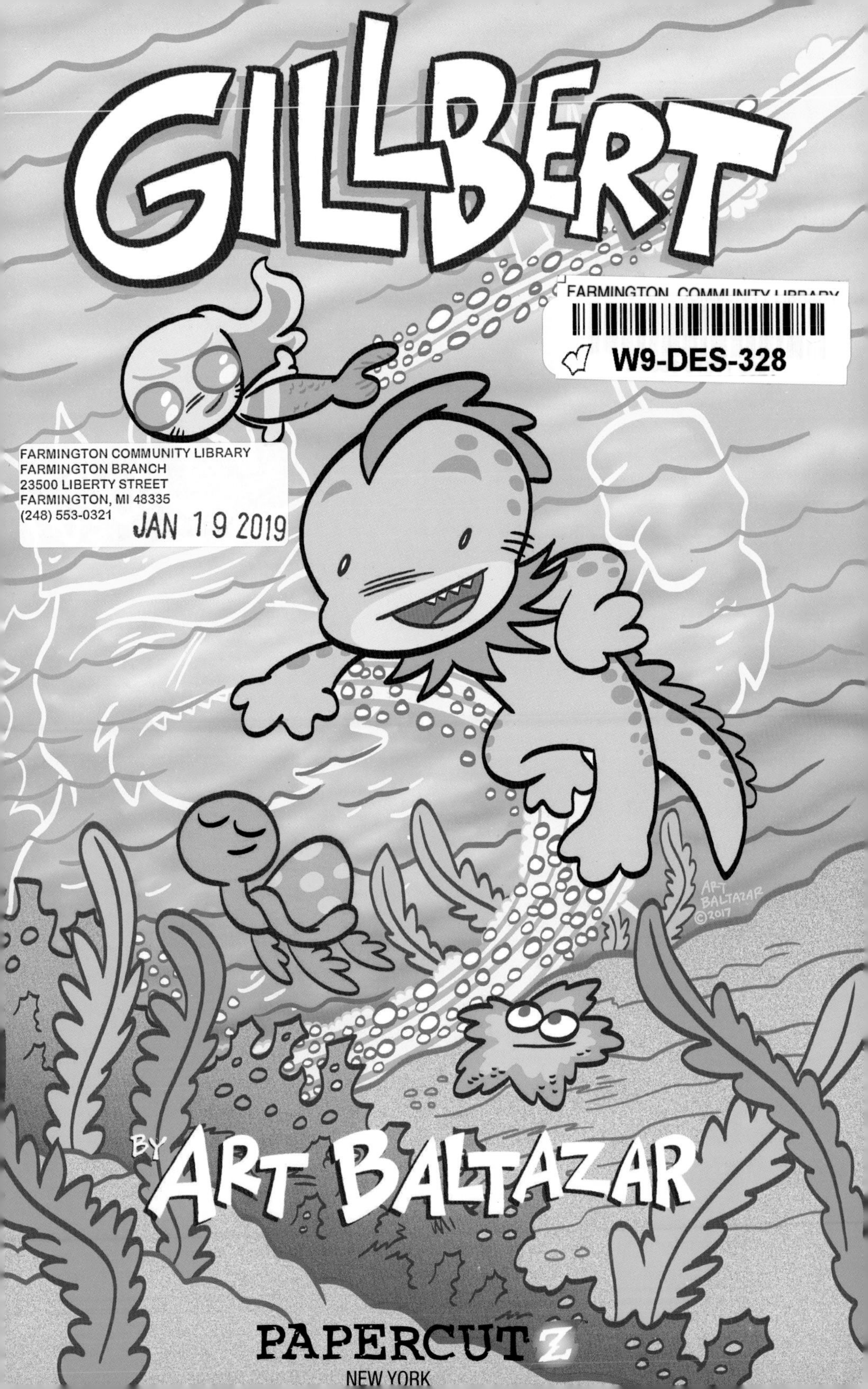
GILLBERT
ART BALTAZAR ©2017
BY ART BALTAZAR
PAPERCUTZ
NEW YORK

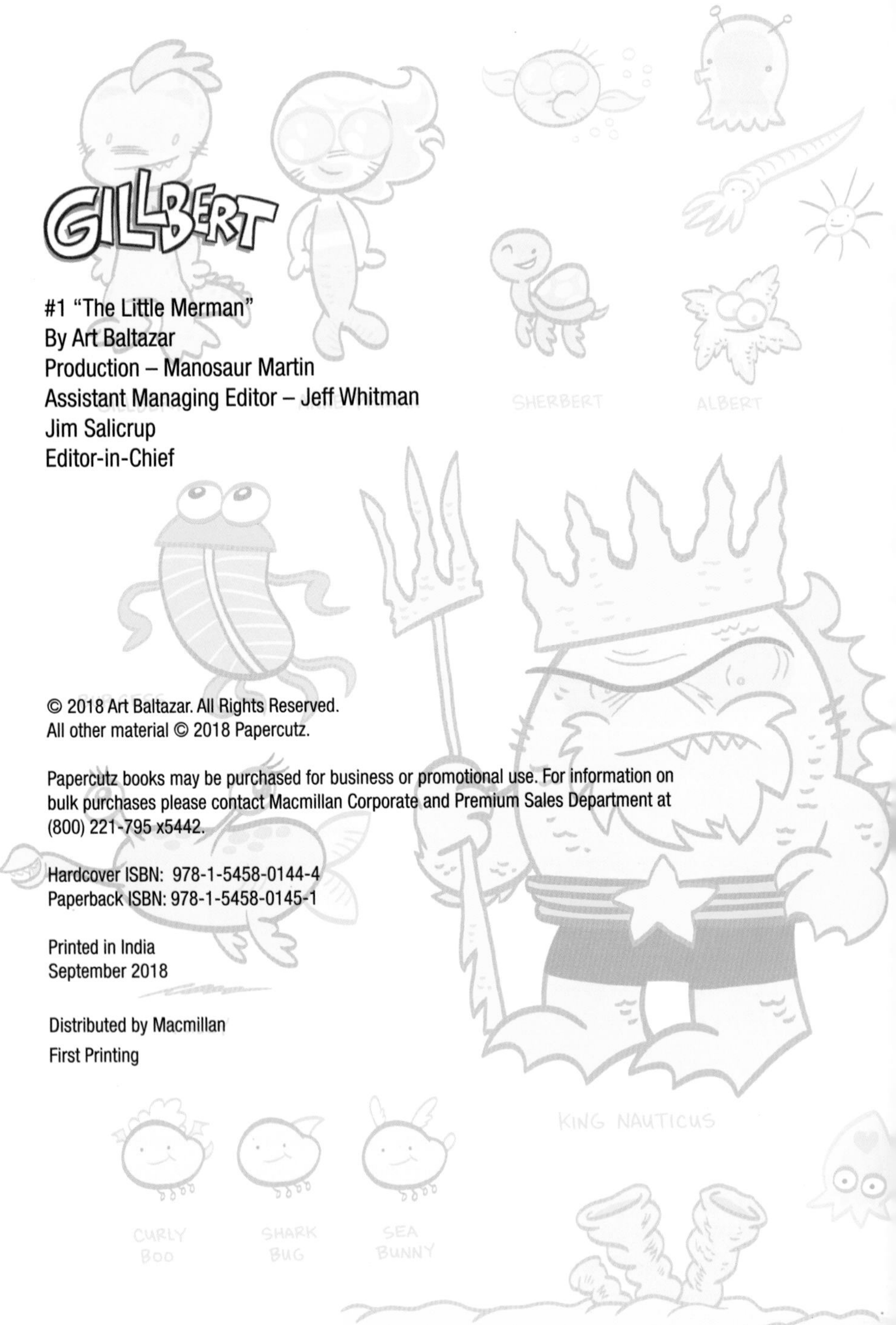
SHERBERT
ALBERT
KING NAUTICUS
CURLY BOO
SHARK BUG
SEA BUNNY

GILLBERT

#1 "The Little Merman"
By Art Baltazar
Production – Manosaur Martin
Assistant Managing Editor – Jeff Whitman
Jim Salicrup
Editor-in-Chief

Papercutz books may be purchased for business or promotional use. For information on bulk purchases please contact Macmillan Corporate and Premium Sales Department at (800) 221-795 x5442.

Hardcover ISBN: 978-1-5458-0144-4
Paperback ISBN: 978-1-5458-0145-1

Printed in India
September 2018

Distributed by Macmillan
First Printing

AW, YEAH! PAPERCUTZ PRESENTS...

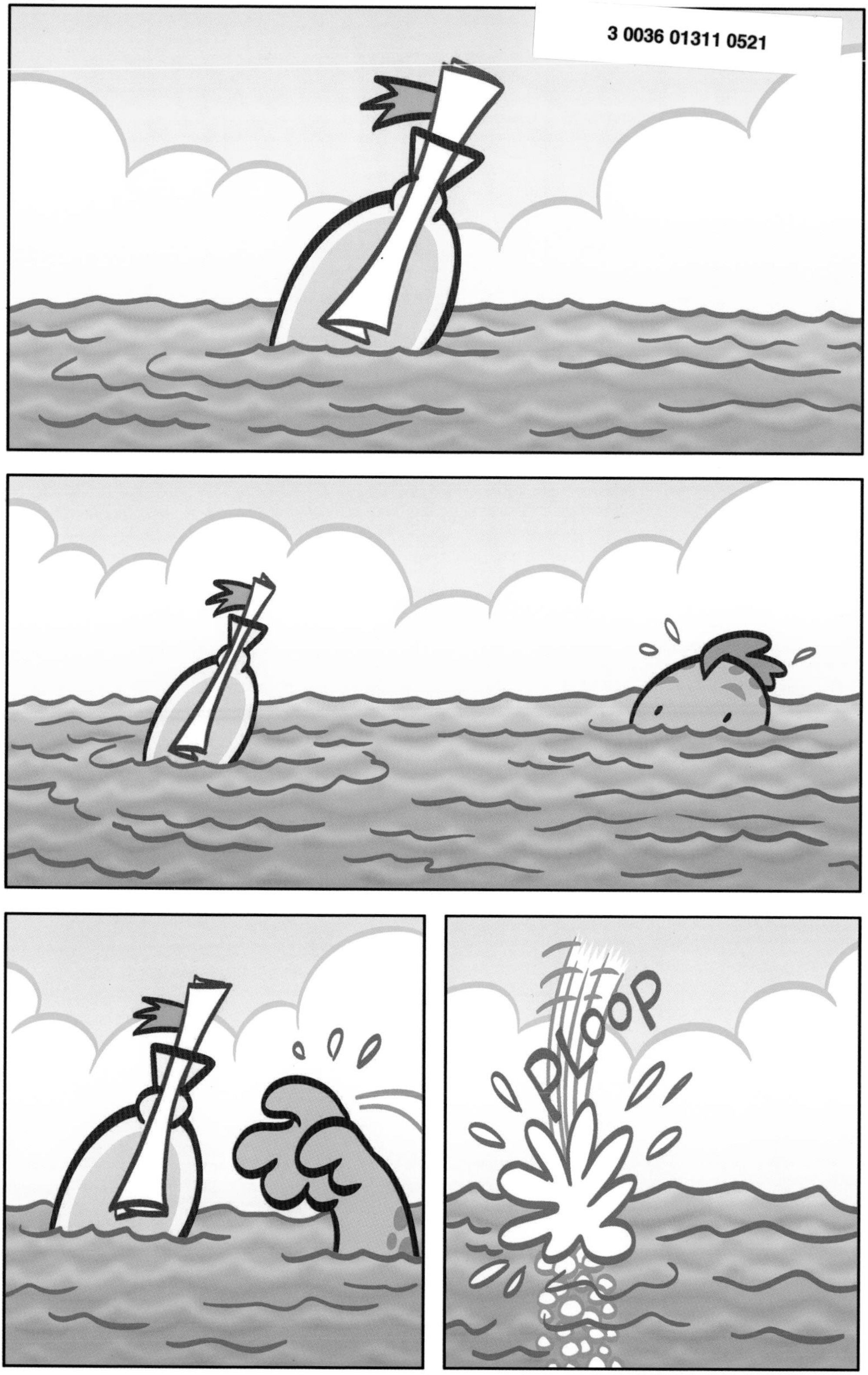
PLOOP

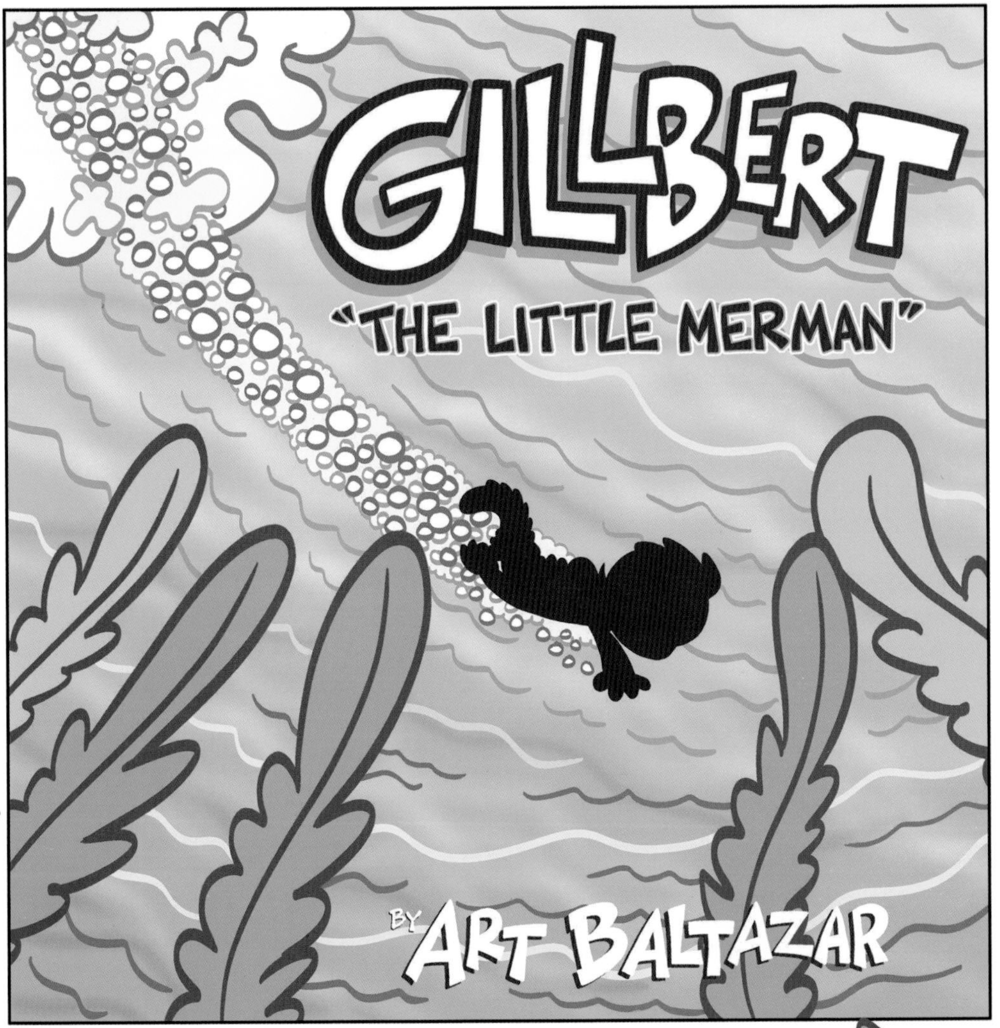
GILLBERT
"THE LITTLE MERMAN"
BY ART BALTAZAR

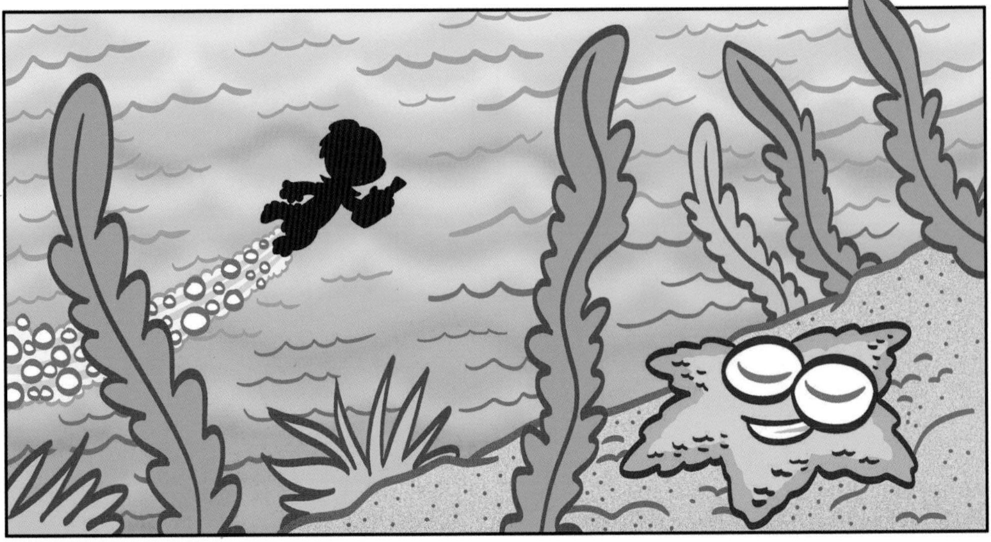

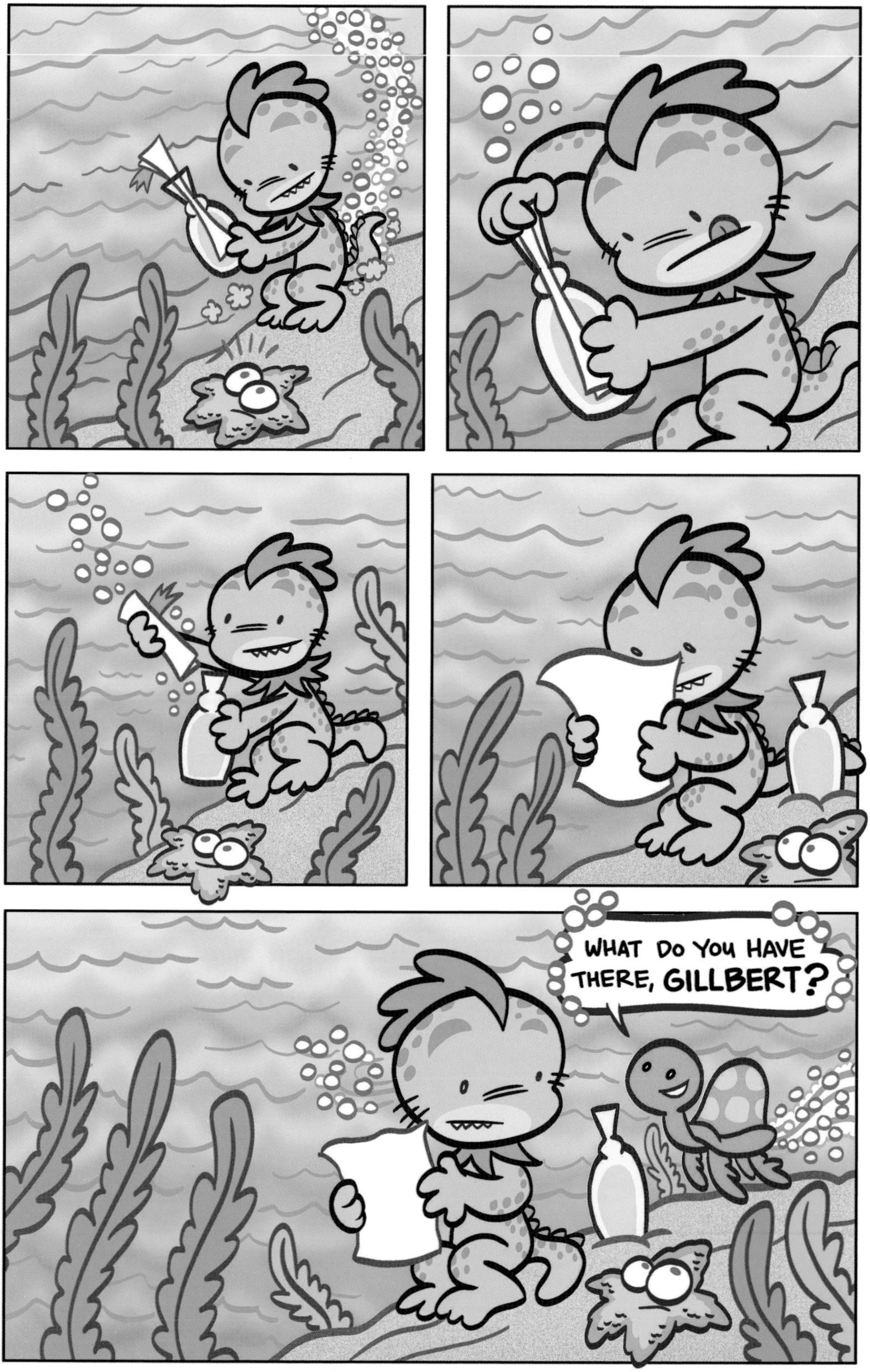
WHAT DO YOU HAVE THERE, GILLBERT?

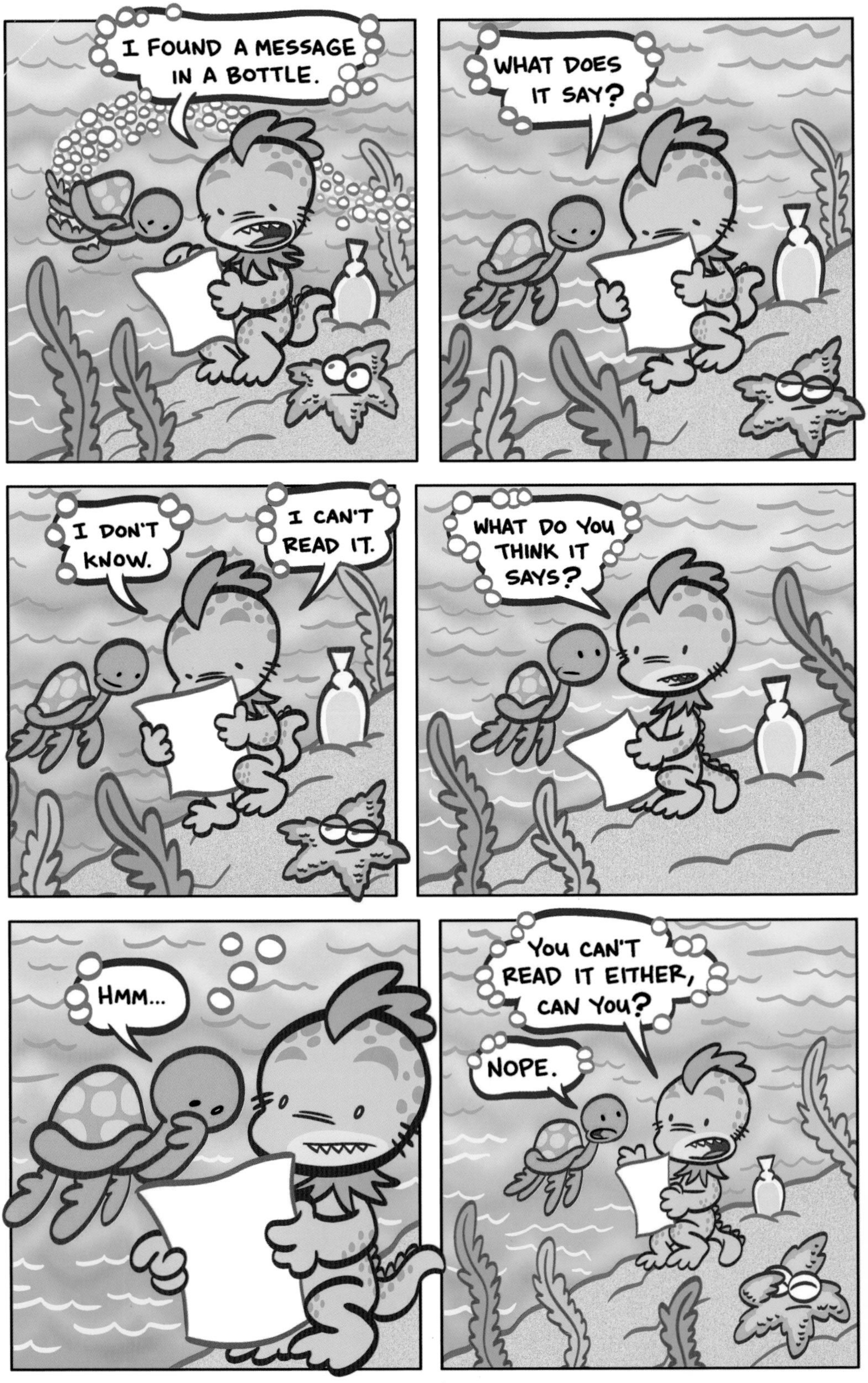
I FOUND A MESSAGE IN A BOTTLE.
WHAT DOES IT SAY?
I DON'T KNOW.
I CAN'T READ IT.
WHAT DO YOU THINK IT SAYS?
HMM...
YOU CAN'T READ IT EITHER, CAN YOU?
NOPE.

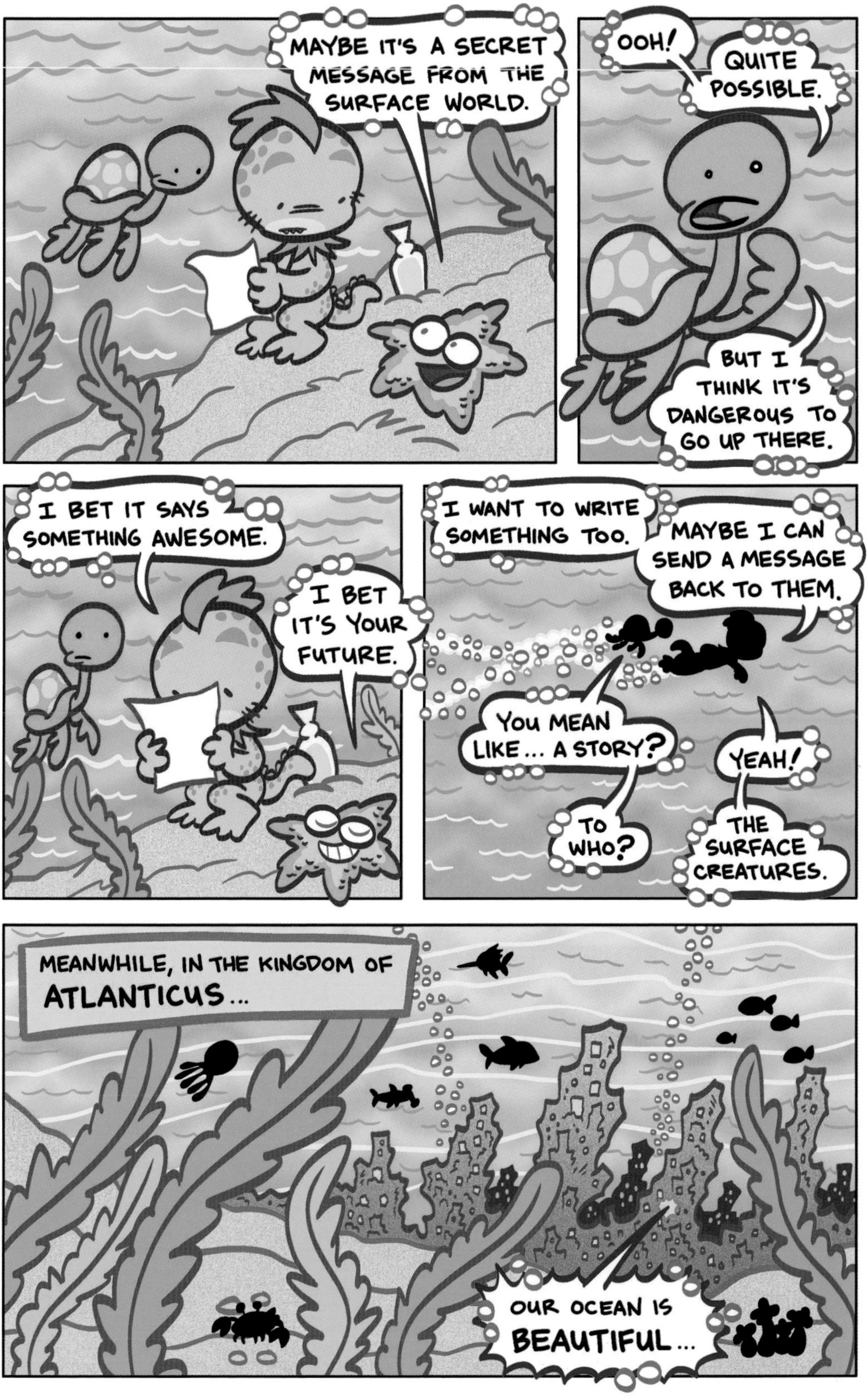

MAYBE IT'S A SECRET MESSAGE FROM THE SURFACE WORLD.
OOH!
QUITE POSSIBLE.
BUT I THINK IT'S DANGEROUS TO GO UP THERE.
I BET IT SAYS SOMETHING AWESOME.
I BET IT'S YOUR FUTURE.
I WANT TO WRITE SOMETHING TOO.
MAYBE I CAN SEND A MESSAGE BACK TO THEM.
YOU MEAN LIKE... A STORY?
TO WHO?
YEAH!
THE SURFACE CREATURES.
MEANWHILE, IN THE KINGDOM OF ATLANTICUS...
OUR OCEAN IS BEAUTIFUL...

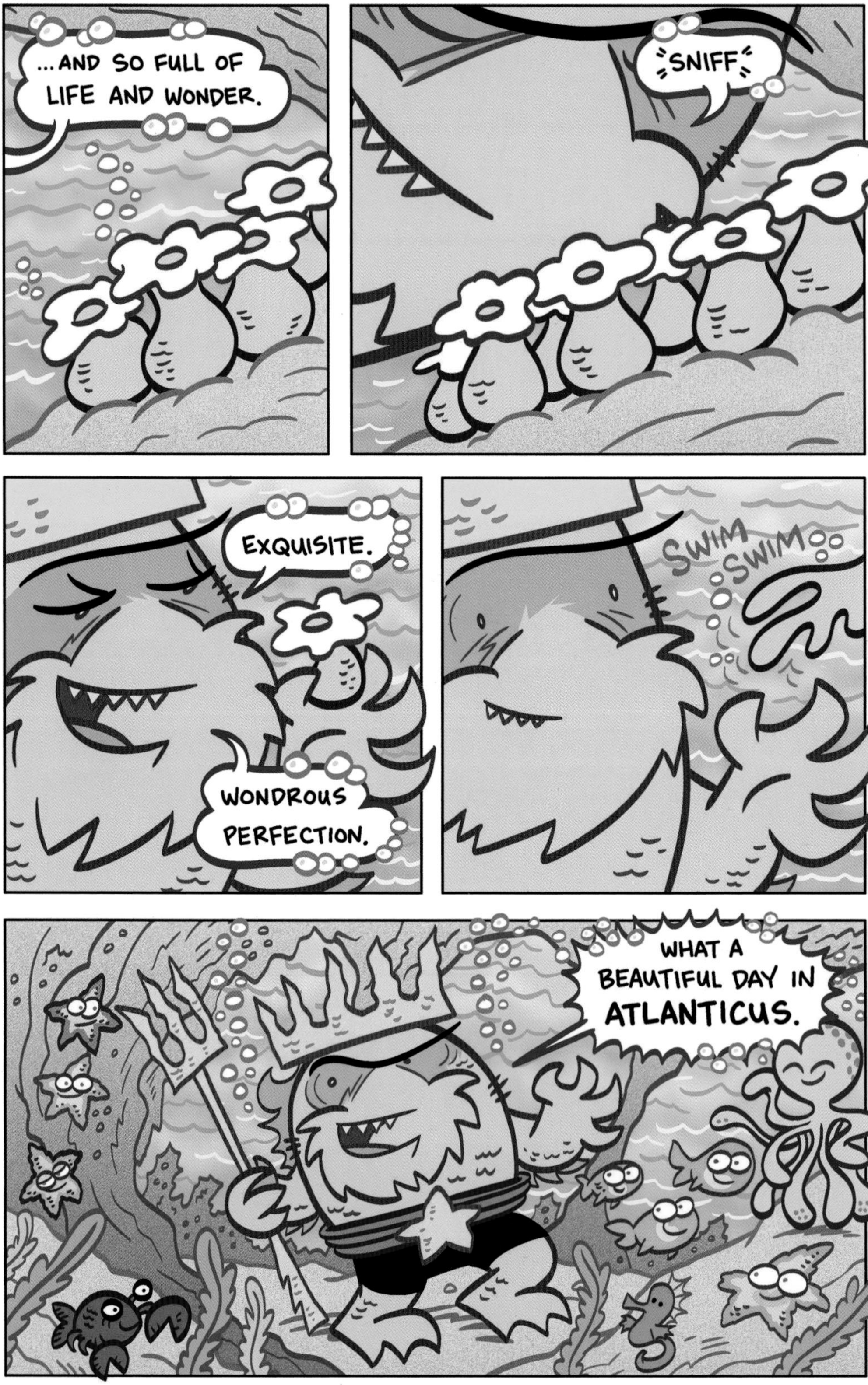
...AND SO FULL OF LIFE AND WONDER.
SNIFF
EXQUISITE.
WONDROUS PERFECTION.
SWIM SWIM
WHAT A BEAUTIFUL DAY IN ATLANTICUS.

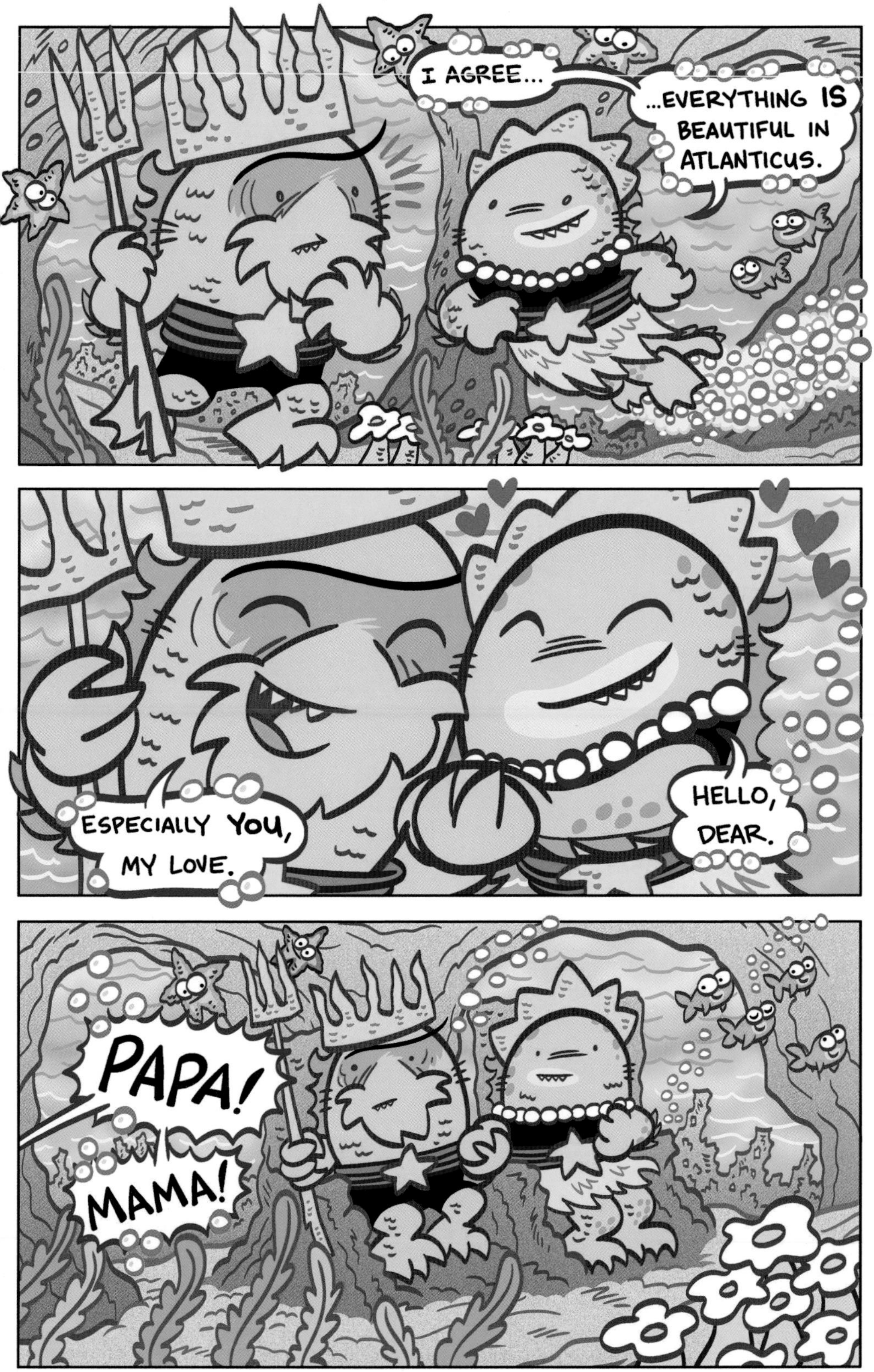
I AGREE...
...EVERYTHING IS BEAUTIFUL IN ATLANTICUS.
ESPECIALLY YOU, MY LOVE.
HELLO, DEAR.
PAPA!
MAMA!

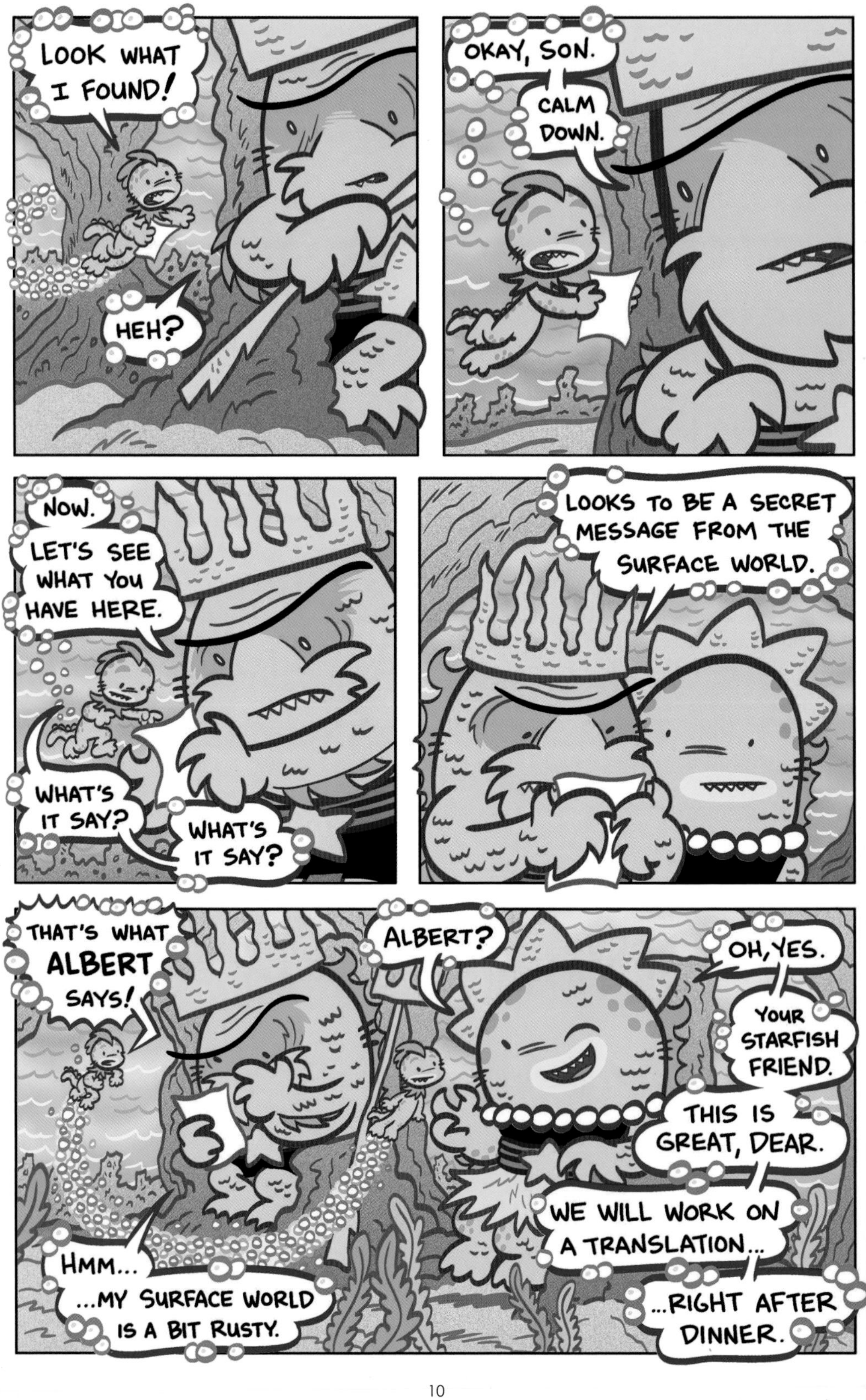
LOOK WHAT I FOUND!
HEH?
OKAY, SON.
CALM DOWN.
NOW.
LET'S SEE WHAT YOU HAVE HERE.
WHAT'S IT SAY?
WHAT'S IT SAY?
LOOKS TO BE A SECRET MESSAGE FROM THE SURFACE WORLD.
THAT'S WHAT ALBERT SAYS!
ALBERT?
OH, YES.
YOUR STARFISH FRIEND.
HMM...
...MY SURFACE WORLD IS A BIT RUSTY.
THIS IS GREAT, DEAR.
WE WILL WORK ON A TRANSLATION...
...RIGHT AFTER DINNER.

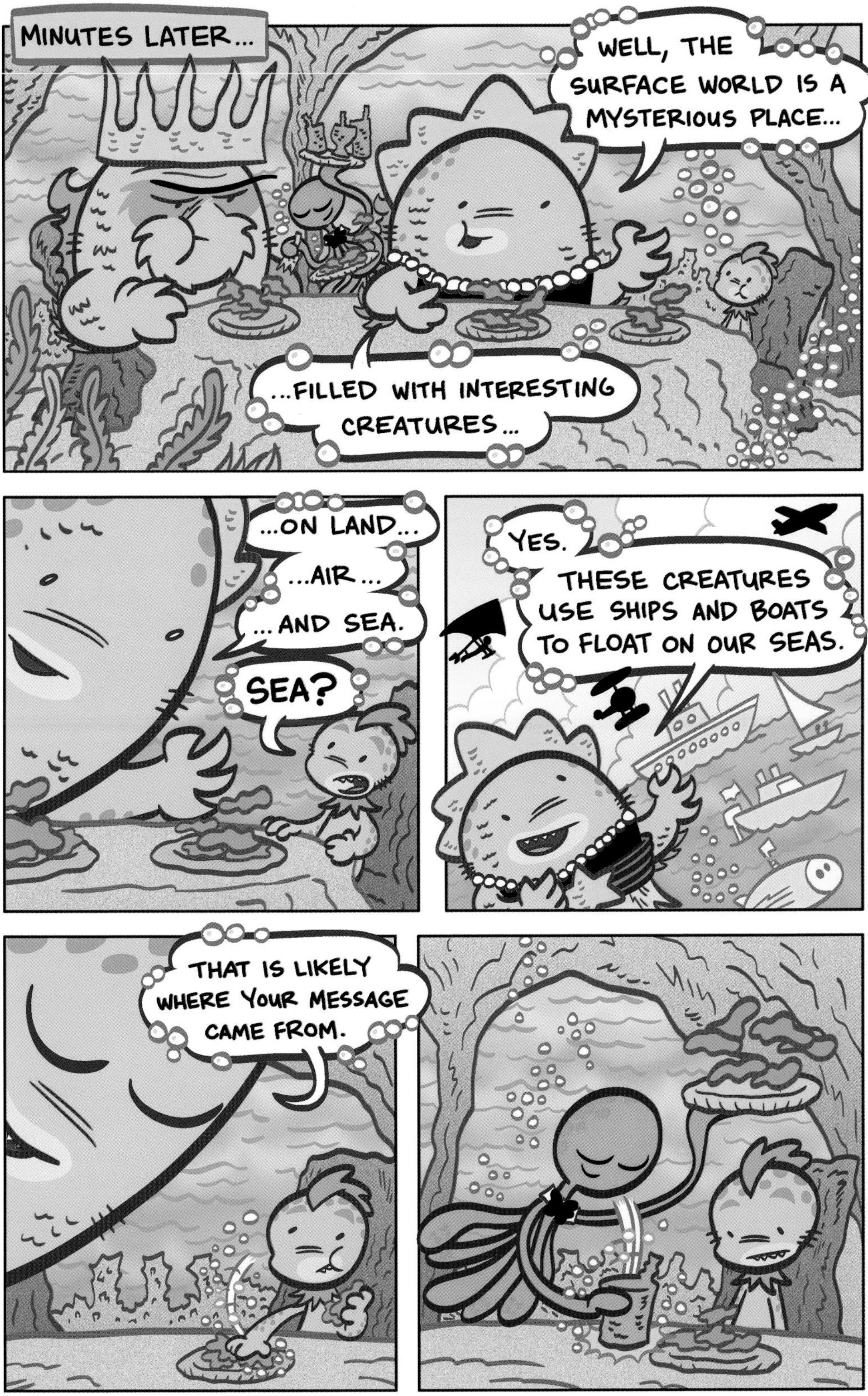
MINUTES LATER...
WELL, THE SURFACE WORLD IS A MYSTERIOUS PLACE...
...FILLED WITH INTERESTING CREATURES...
...ON LAND...
...AIR...
...AND SEA.
SEA?
YES.
THESE CREATURES USE SHIPS AND BOATS TO FLOAT ON OUR SEAS.
THAT IS LIKELY WHERE YOUR MESSAGE CAME FROM.

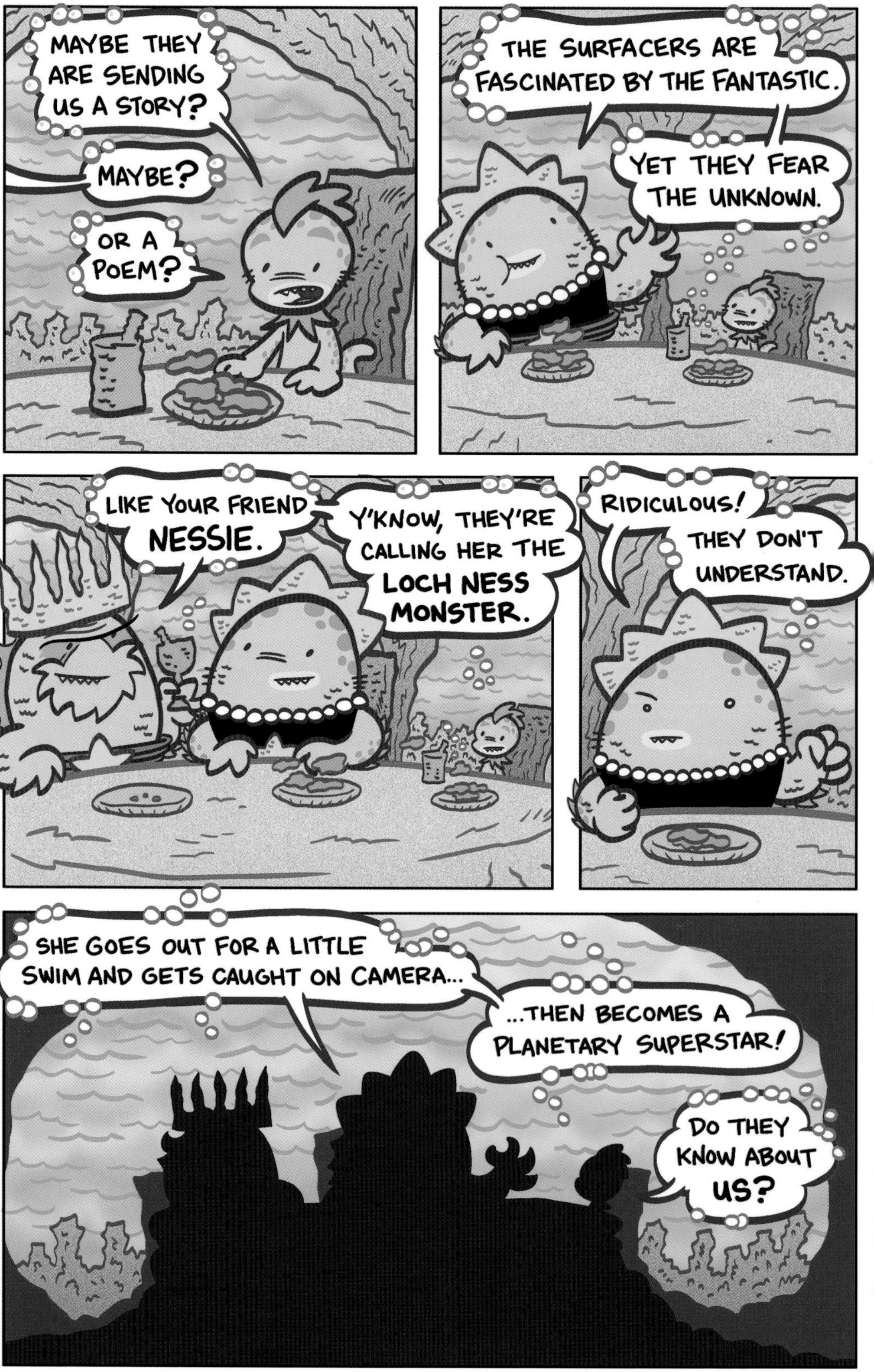
MAYBE THEY ARE SENDING US A STORY?
MAYBE?
OR A POEM?
THE SURFACERS ARE FASCINATED BY THE FANTASTIC.
YET THEY FEAR THE UNKNOWN.
LIKE YOUR FRIEND NESSIE.
Y'KNOW, THEY'RE CALLING HER THE LOCH NESS MONSTER.
RIDICULOUS!
THEY DON'T UNDERSTAND.
SHE GOES OUT FOR A LITTLE SWIM AND GETS CAUGHT ON CAMERA...
...THEN BECOMES A PLANETARY SUPERSTAR!
DO THEY KNOW ABOUT US?

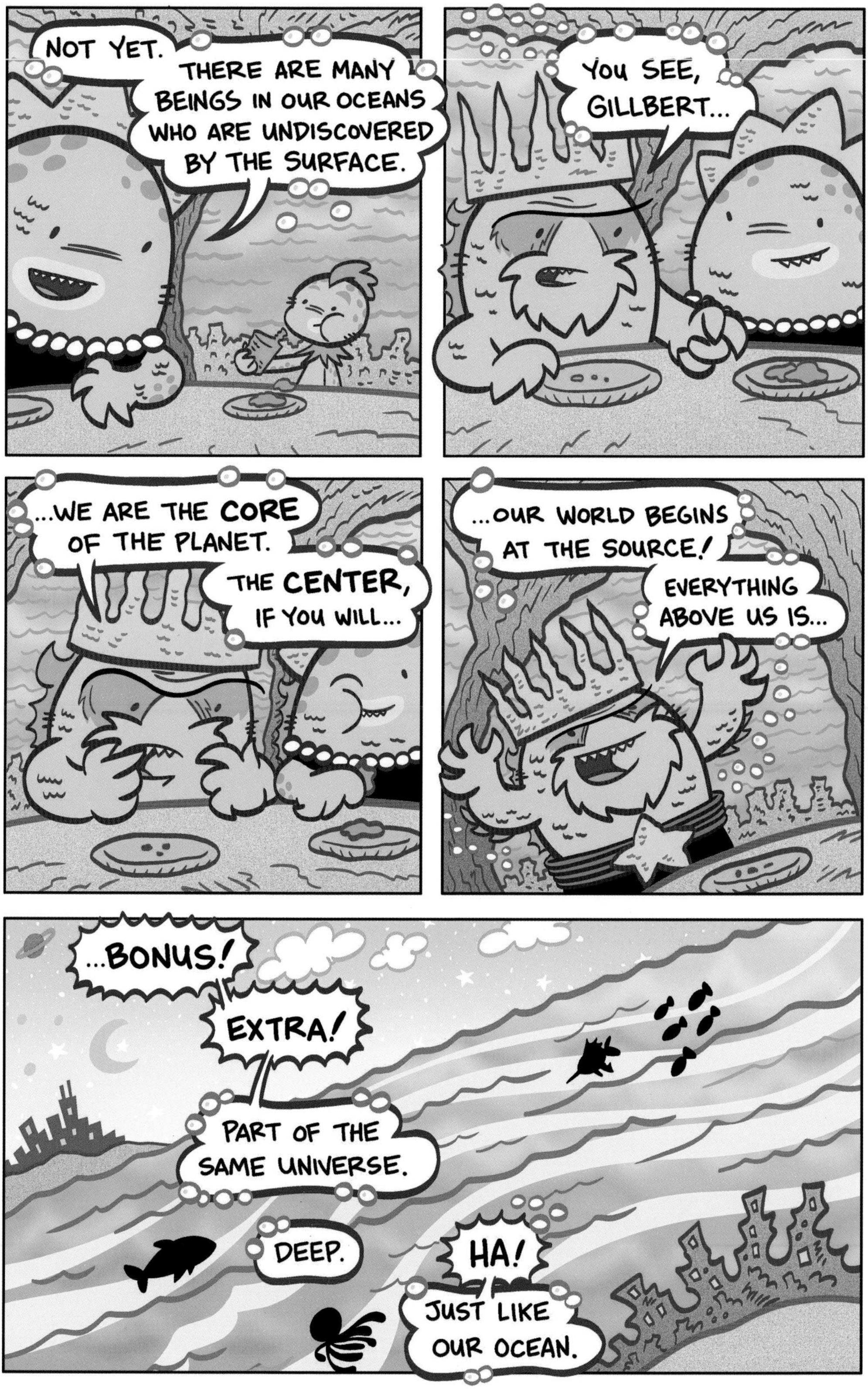
NOT YET.
THERE ARE MANY BEINGS IN OUR OCEANS WHO ARE UNDISCOVERED BY THE SURFACE.
YOU SEE, GILLBERT...
...WE ARE THE CORE OF THE PLANET.
THE CENTER, IF YOU WILL...
...OUR WORLD BEGINS AT THE SOURCE!
EVERYTHING ABOVE US IS...
...BONUS!
EXTRA!
PART OF THE SAME UNIVERSE.
DEEP.
HA!
JUST LIKE OUR OCEAN.

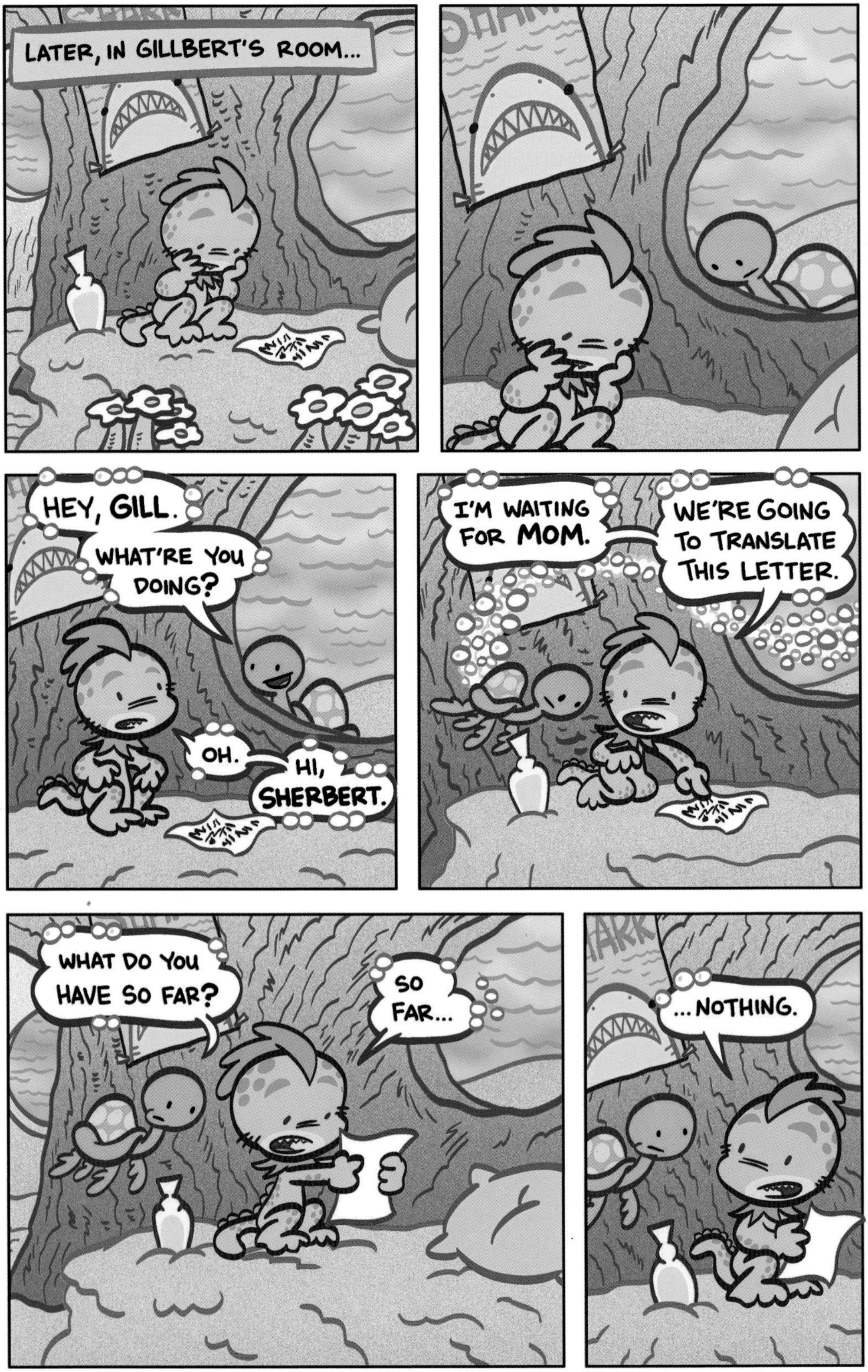
LATER, IN GILLBERT'S ROOM...
HEY, GILL.
WHAT'RE YOU DOING?
OH.
HI, SHERBERT.
I'M WAITING FOR MOM.
WE'RE GOING TO TRANSLATE THIS LETTER.
WHAT DO YOU HAVE SO FAR?
SO FAR...
...NOTHING.

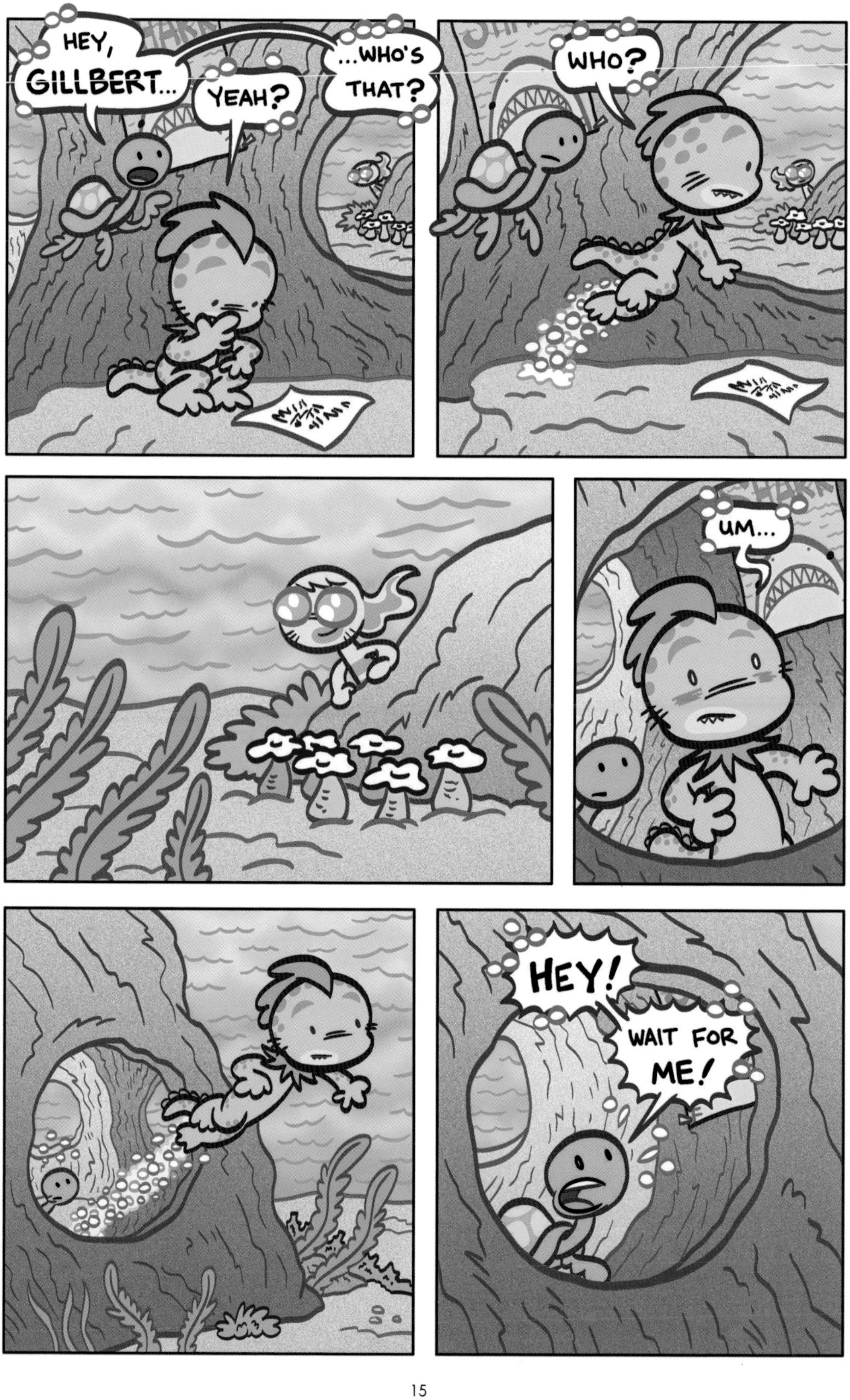
HEY, GILLBERT...
YEAH?
...WHO'S THAT?
WHO?
UM...
HEY!
WAIT FOR ME!

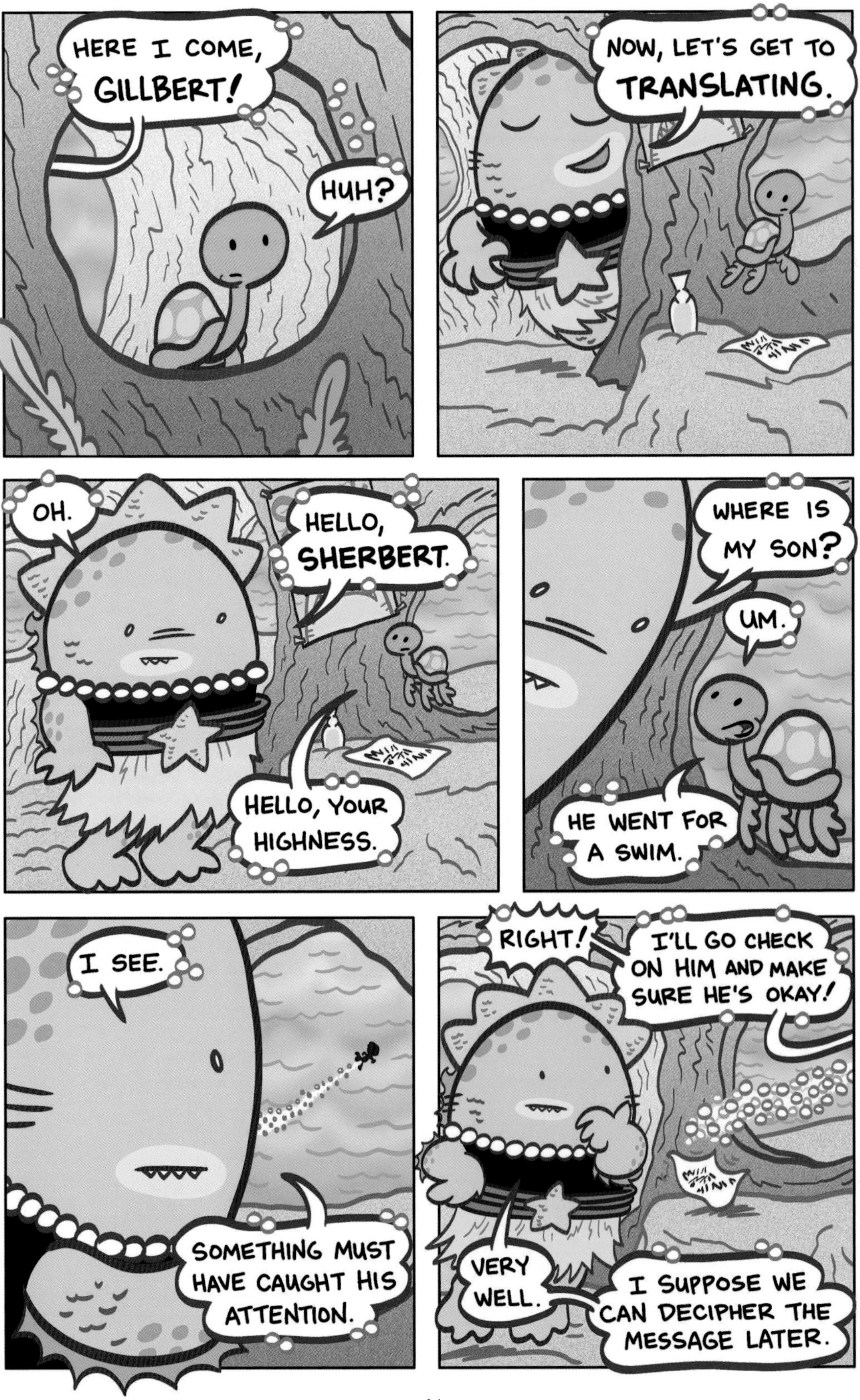
HERE I COME, GILLBERT!
HUH?
NOW, LET'S GET TO TRANSLATING.
OH.
HELLO, SHERBERT.
HELLO, YOUR HIGHNESS.
WHERE IS MY SON?
UM.
HE WENT FOR A SWIM.
I SEE.
SOMETHING MUST HAVE CAUGHT HIS ATTENTION.
RIGHT!
I'LL GO CHECK ON HIM AND MAKE SURE HE'S OKAY!
VERY WELL.
I SUPPOSE WE CAN DECIPHER THE MESSAGE LATER.

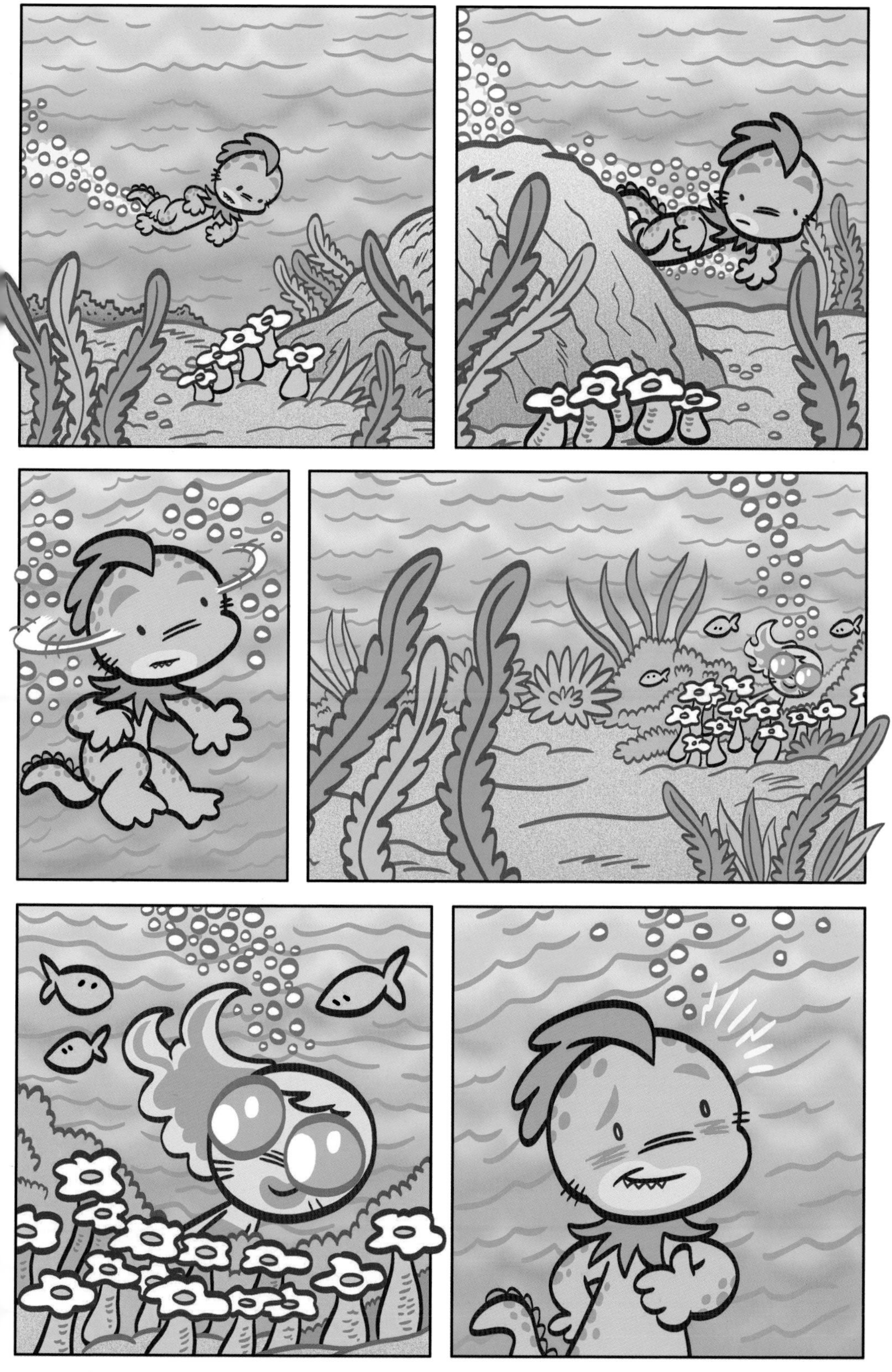

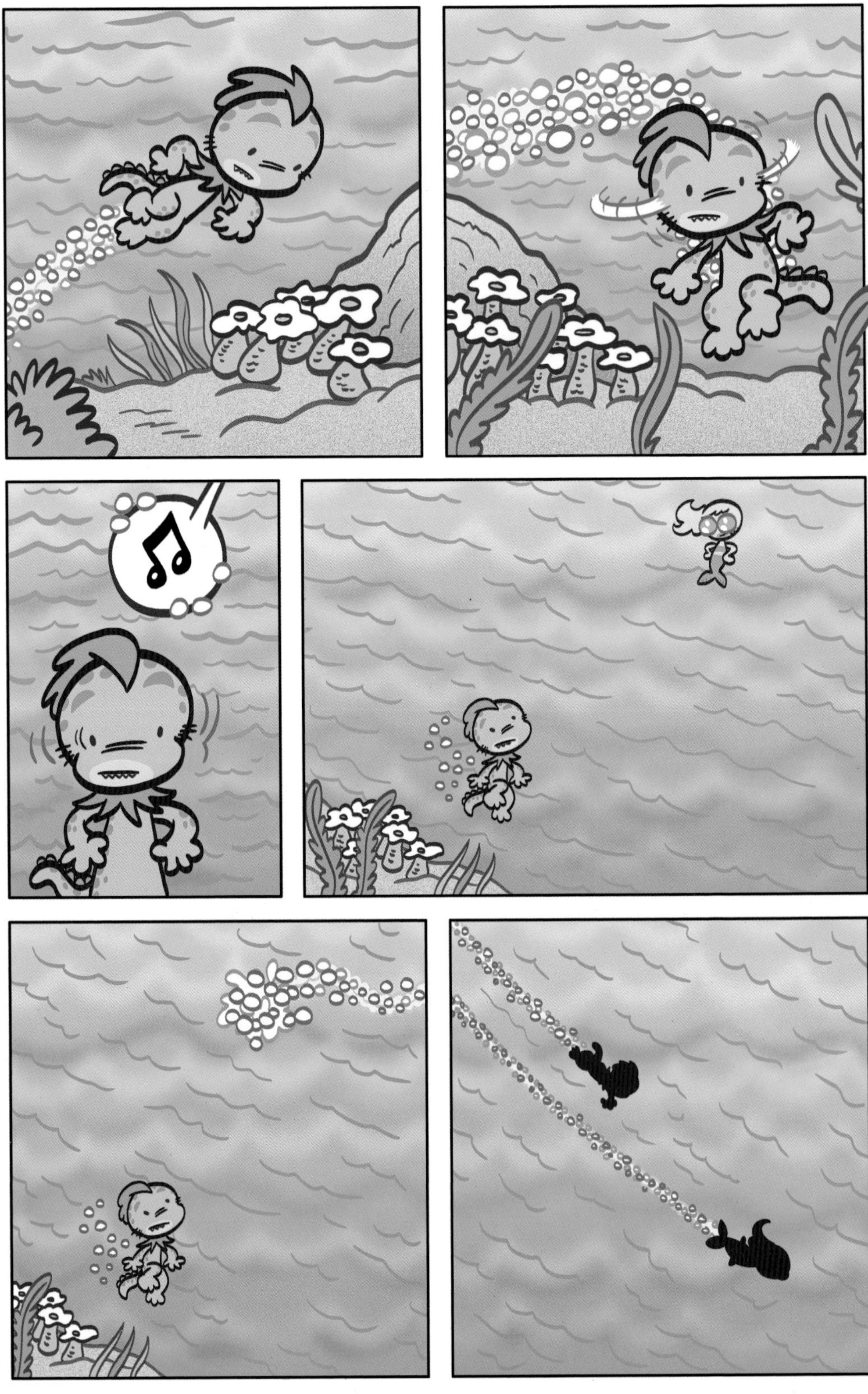

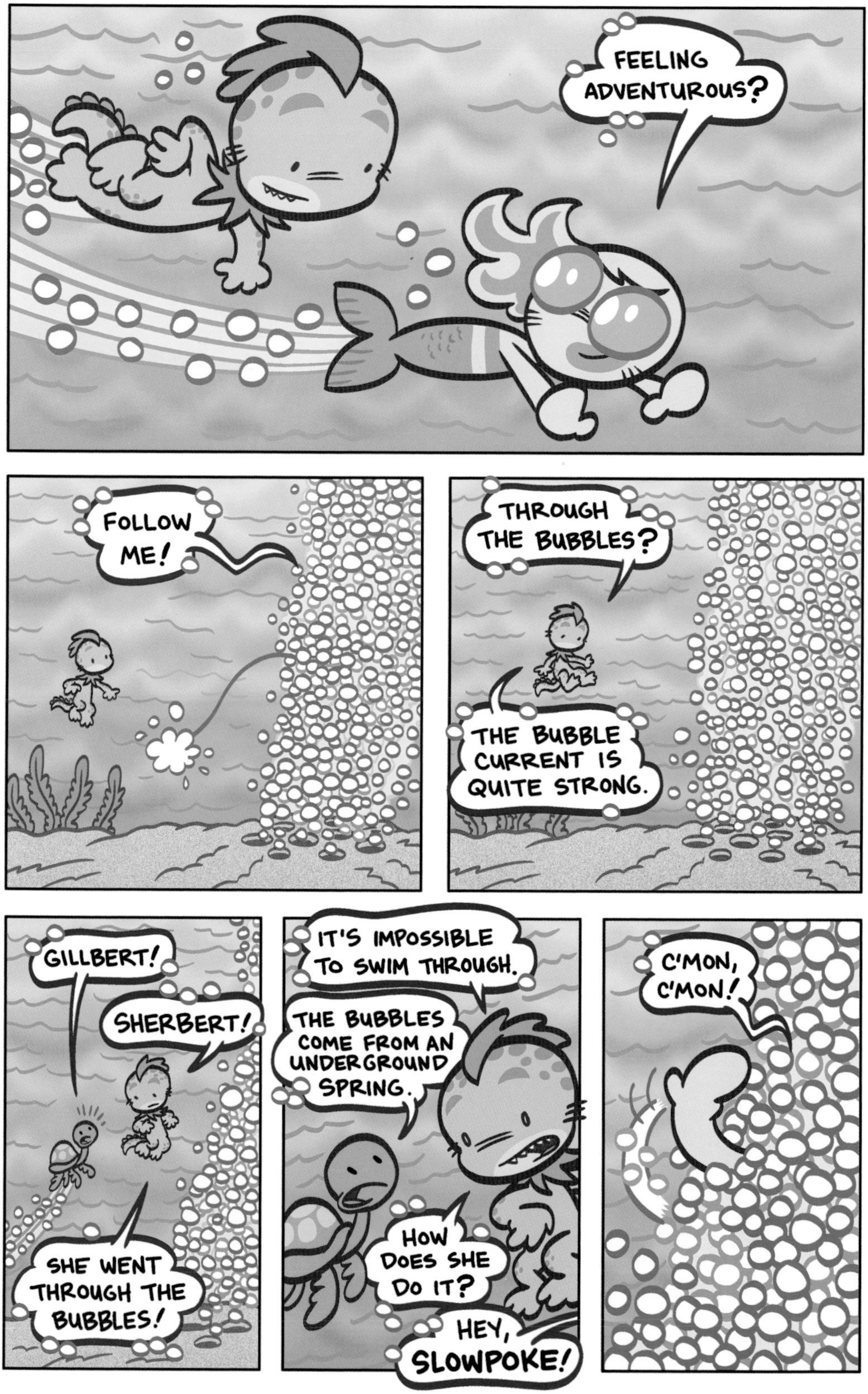
FEELING ADVENTUROUS?
FOLLOW ME!
THROUGH THE BUBBLES?
THE BUBBLE CURRENT IS QUITE STRONG.
GILLBERT!
SHERBERT!
SHE WENT THROUGH THE BUBBLES!
IT'S IMPOSSIBLE TO SWIM THROUGH.
THE BUBBLES COME FROM AN UNDERGROUND SPRING.
HOW DOES SHE DO IT?
HEY, SLOWPOKE!
C'MON, C'MON!

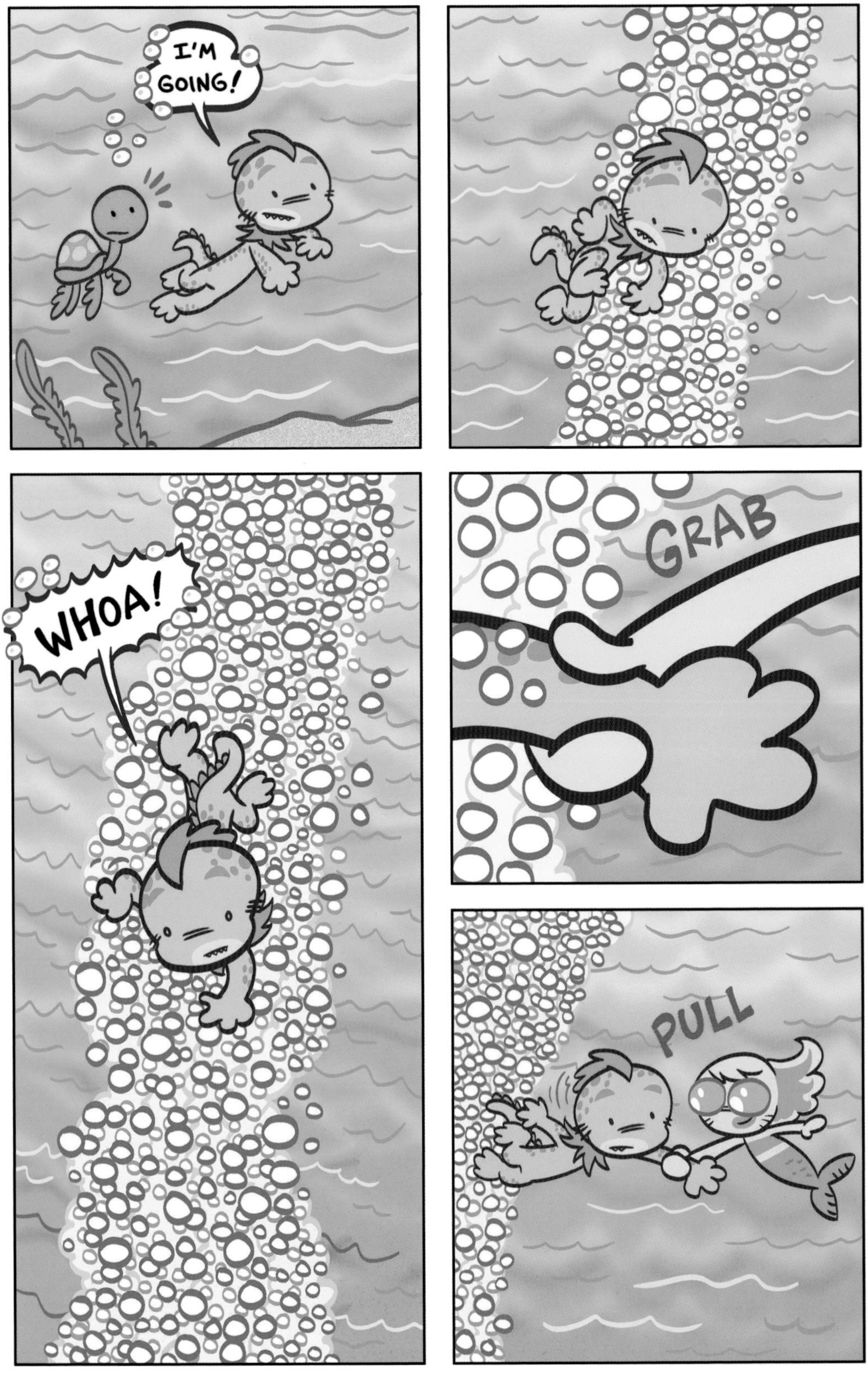
I'M GOING!
WHOA!
GRAB
PULL

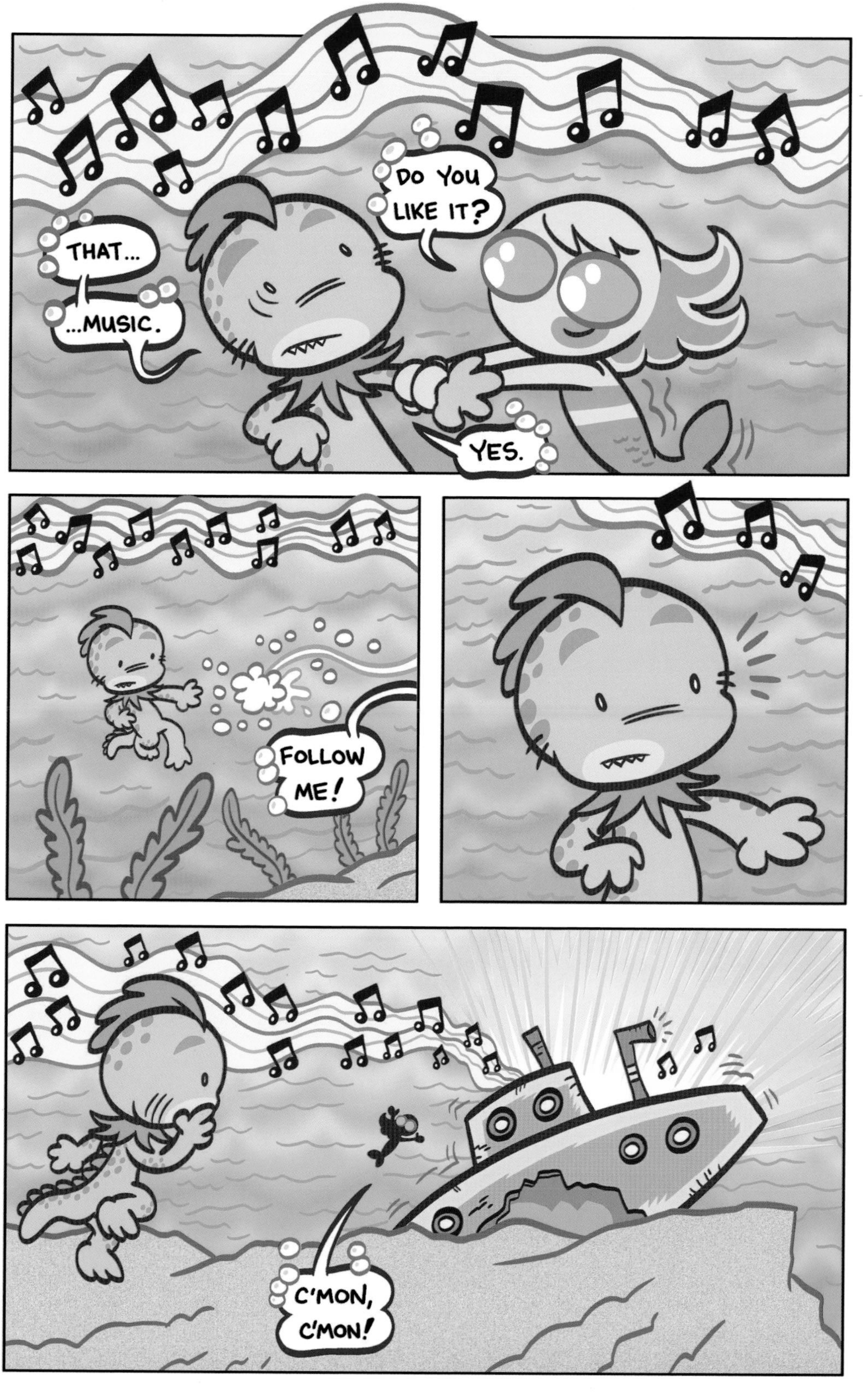
DO YOU LIKE IT?
THAT...
...MUSIC.
YES.
FOLLOW ME!
C'MON, C'MON!

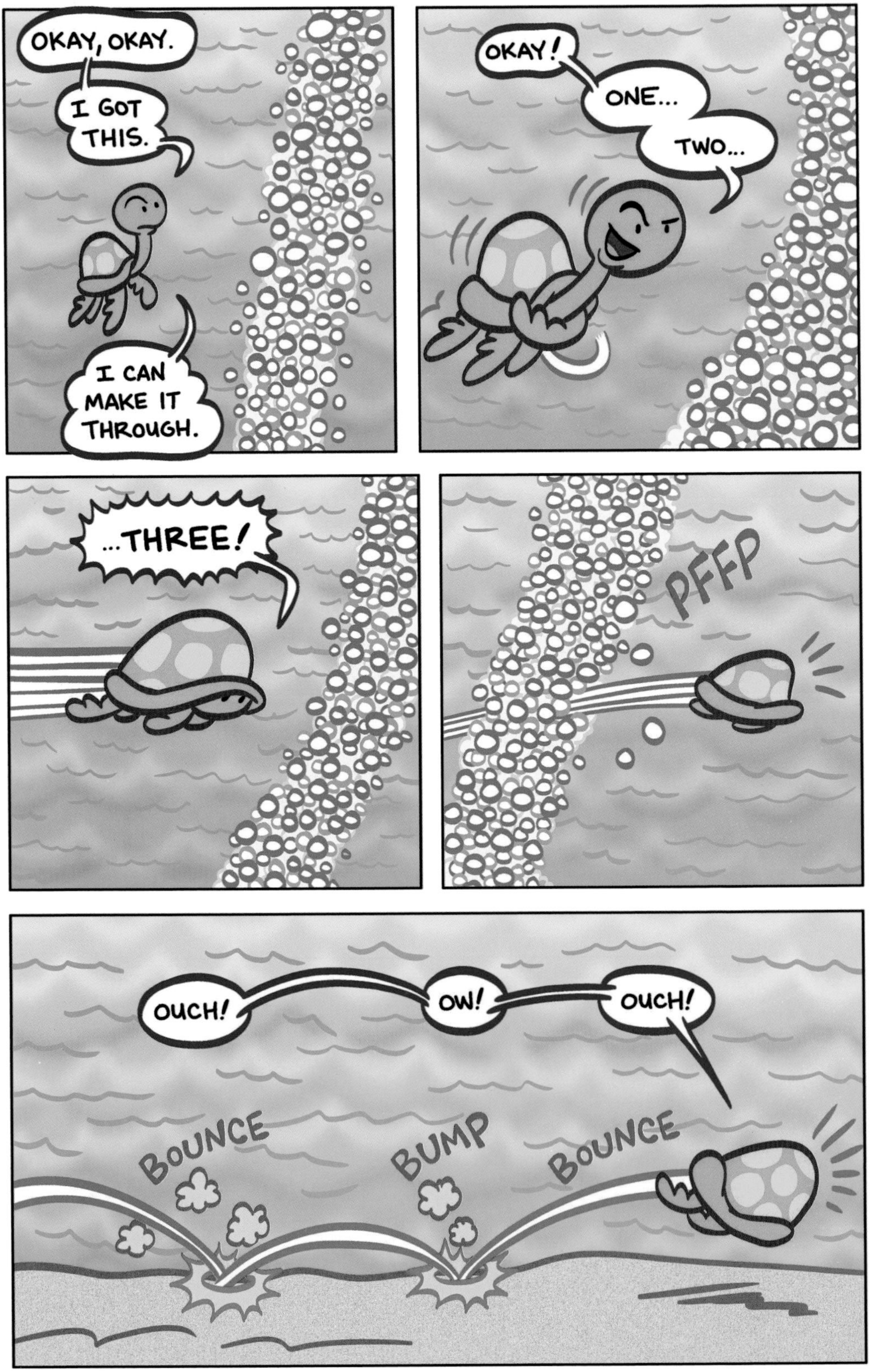
OKAY, OKAY.
I GOT THIS.
I CAN MAKE IT THROUGH.
OKAY!
ONE...
TWO...
...THREE!
PFFP
OUCH!
OW!
OUCH!
BOUNCE
BUMP
BOUNCE

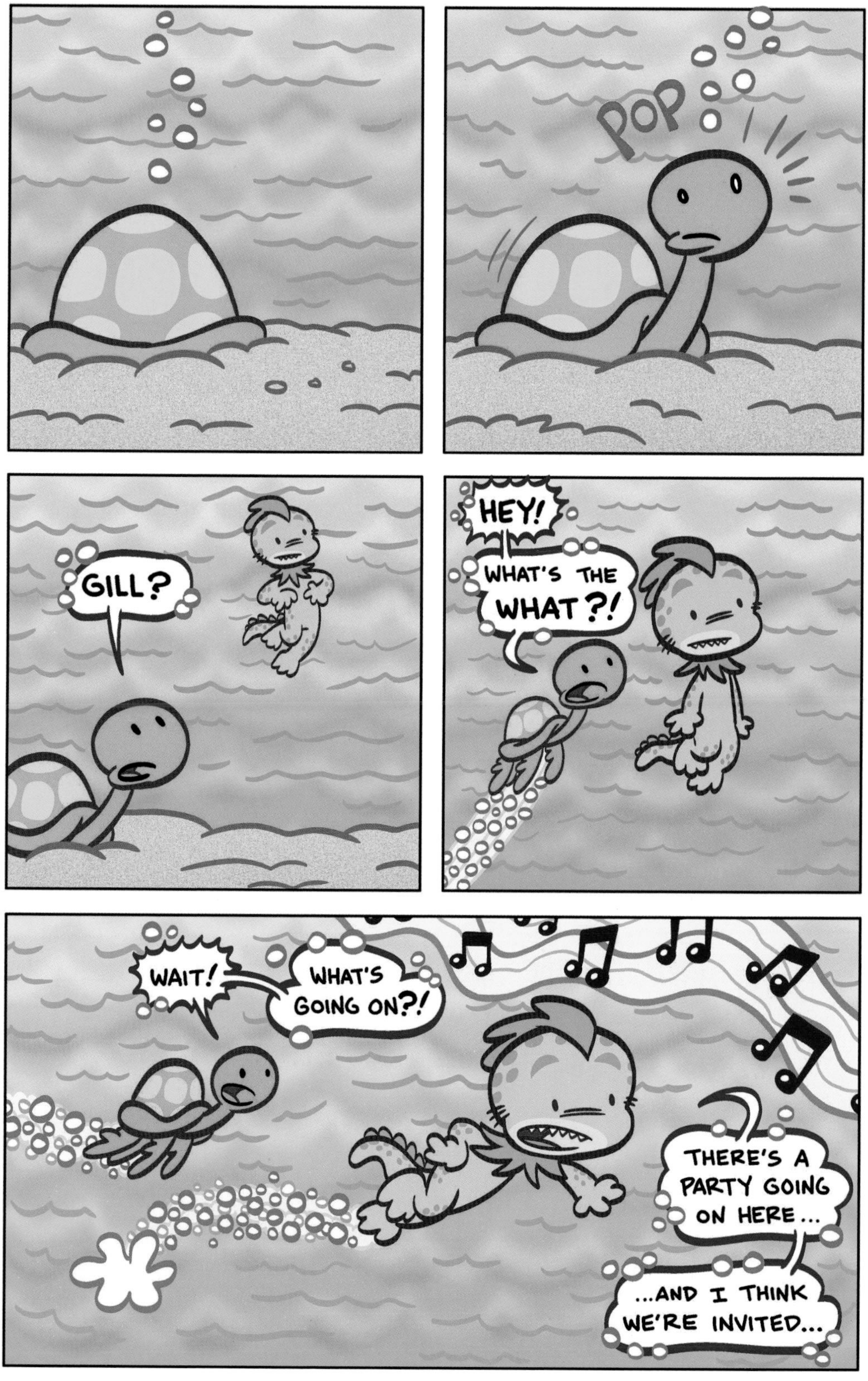
POP
GILL?
HEY!
WHAT'S THE WHAT?!
WAIT!
WHAT'S GOING ON?!
THERE'S A PARTY GOING ON HERE...
...AND I THINK WE'RE INVITED...

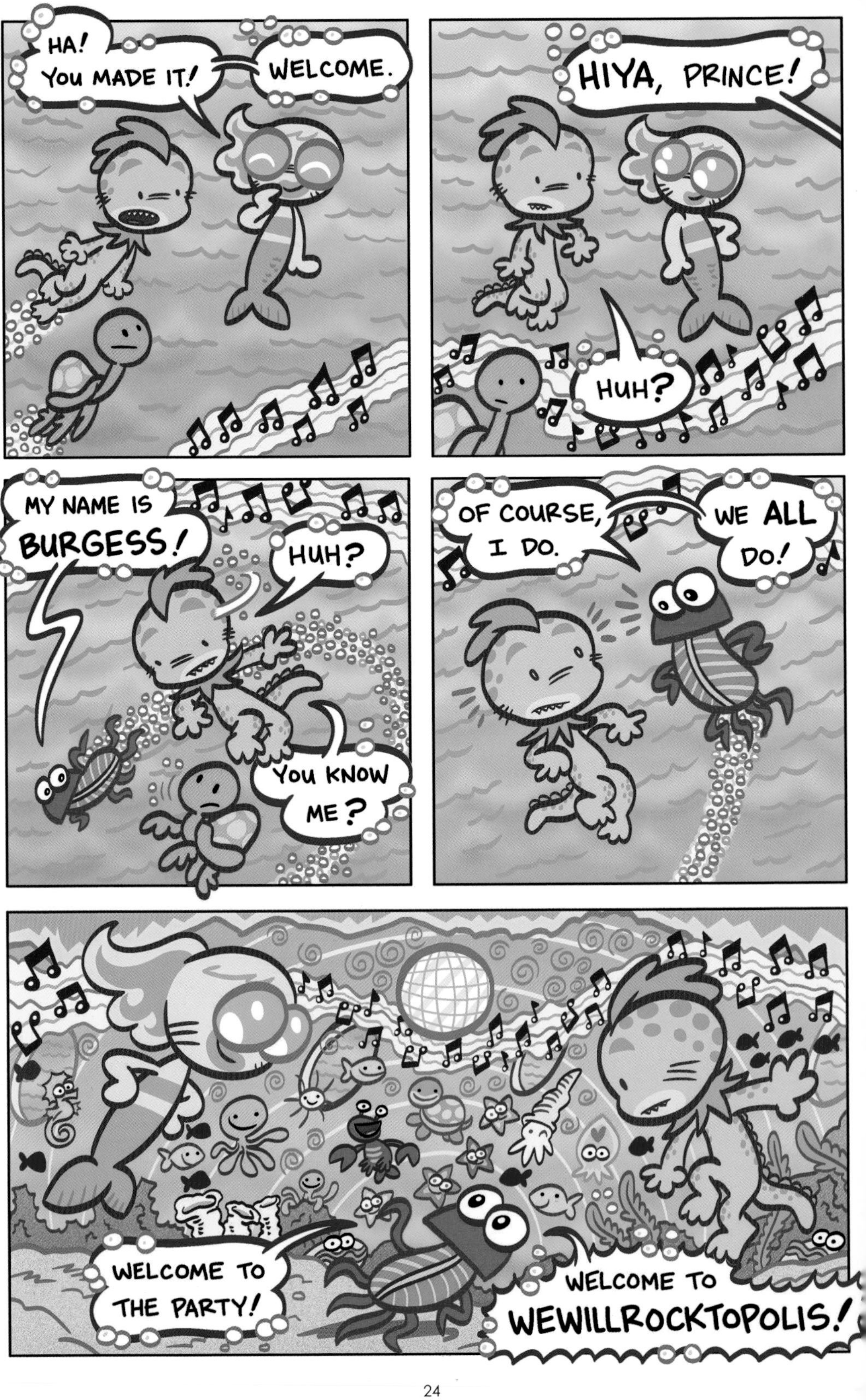
HA! YOU MADE IT!
WELCOME.
HIYA, PRINCE!
HUH?
MY NAME IS BURGESS!
HUH?
YOU KNOW ME?
OF COURSE, I DO.
WE ALL DO!
WELCOME TO THE PARTY!
WELCOME TO WEWILLROCKTOPOLIS!

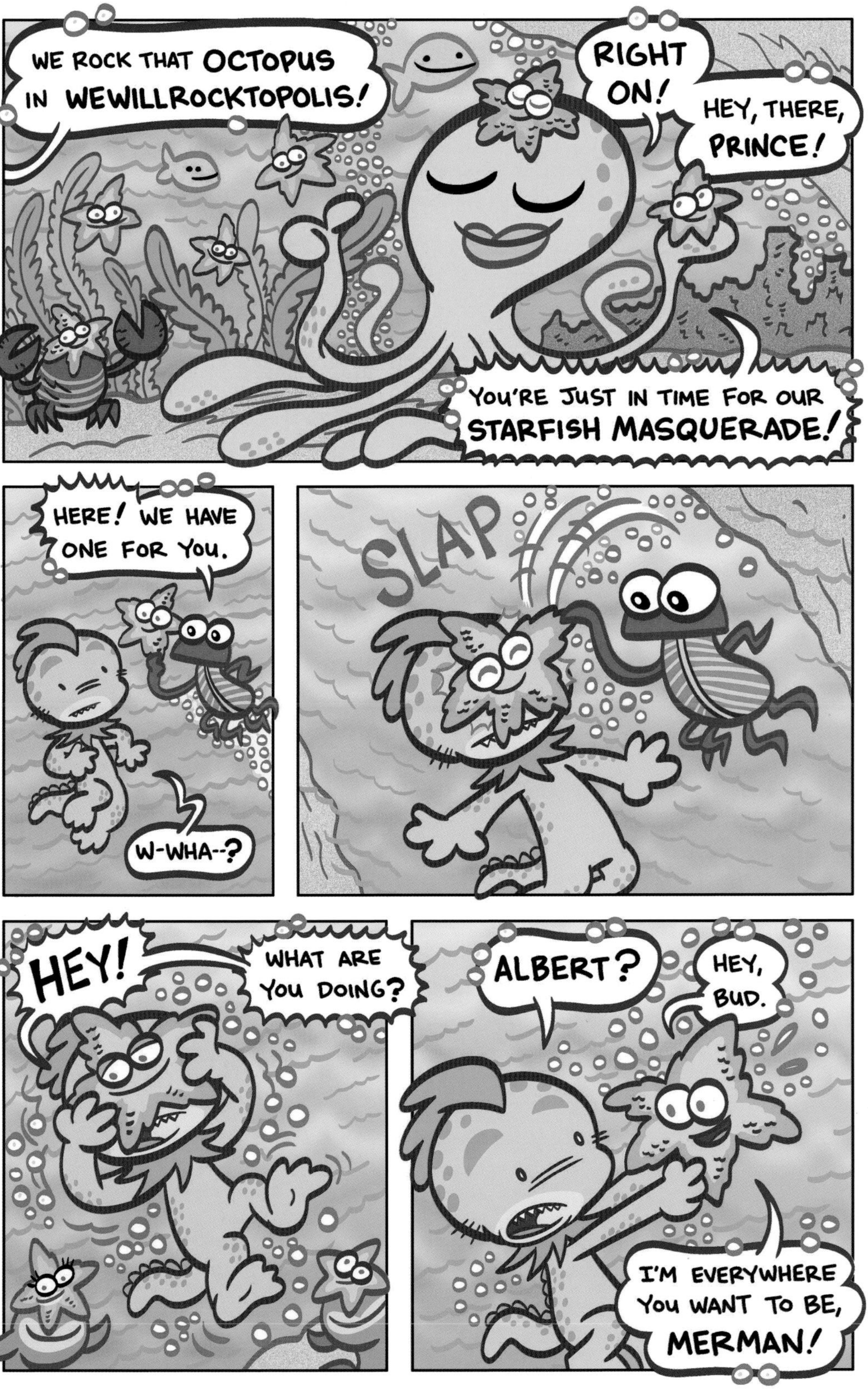

WE ROCK THAT OCTOPUS IN WEWILLROCKTOPOLIS!
RIGHT ON!
HEY, THERE, PRINCE!
YOU'RE JUST IN TIME FOR OUR STARFISH MASQUERADE!
HERE! WE HAVE ONE FOR YOU.
W-WHA--?
SLAP
HEY!
WHAT ARE YOU DOING?
ALBERT?
HEY, BUD.
I'M EVERYWHERE YOU WANT TO BE, MERMAN!

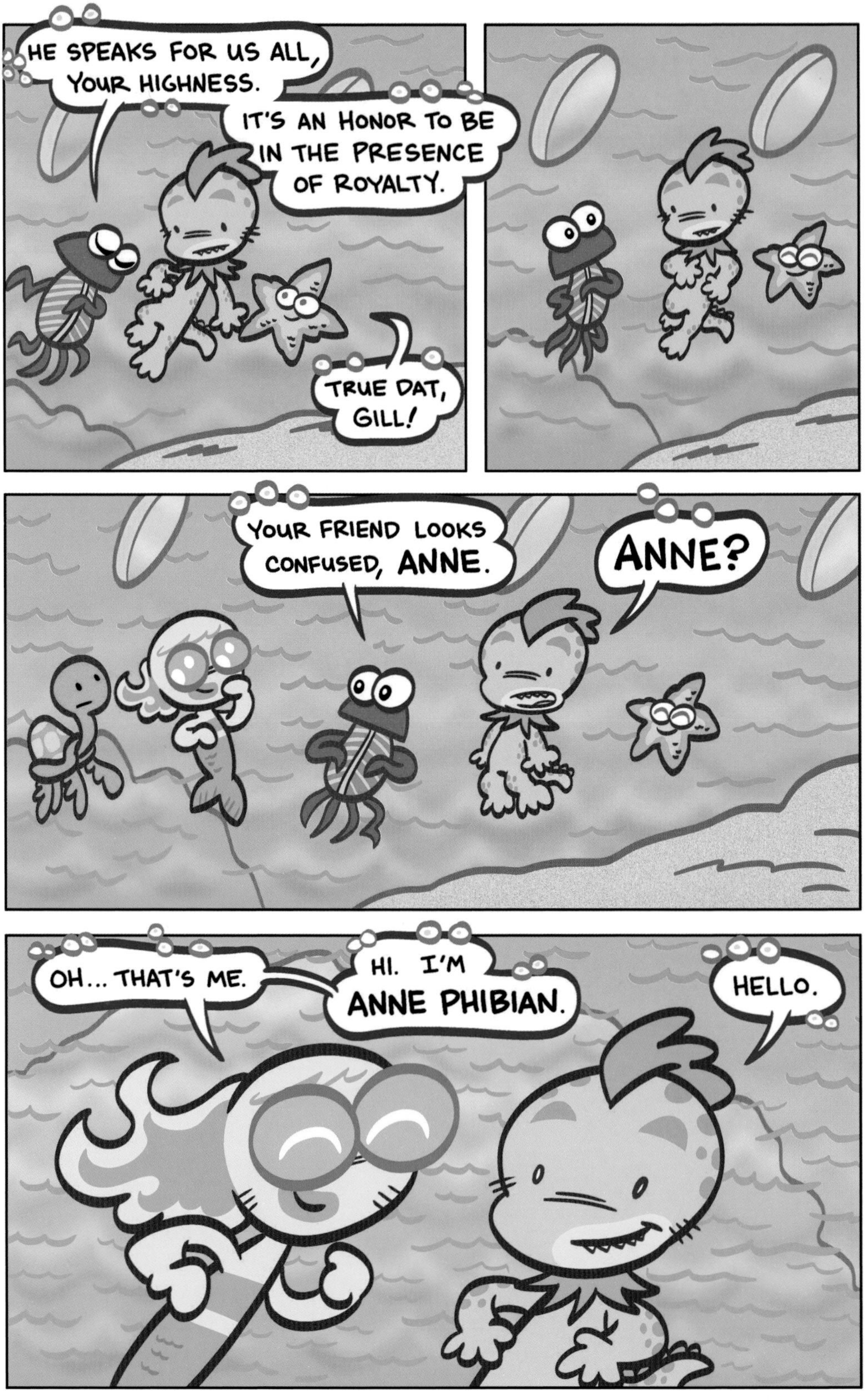
HE SPEAKS FOR US ALL, YOUR HIGHNESS.
IT'S AN HONOR TO BE IN THE PRESENCE OF ROYALTY.
TRUE DAT, GILL!
YOUR FRIEND LOOKS CONFUSED, ANNE.
ANNE?
OH... THAT'S ME.
HI. I'M ANNE PHIBIAN.
HELLO.

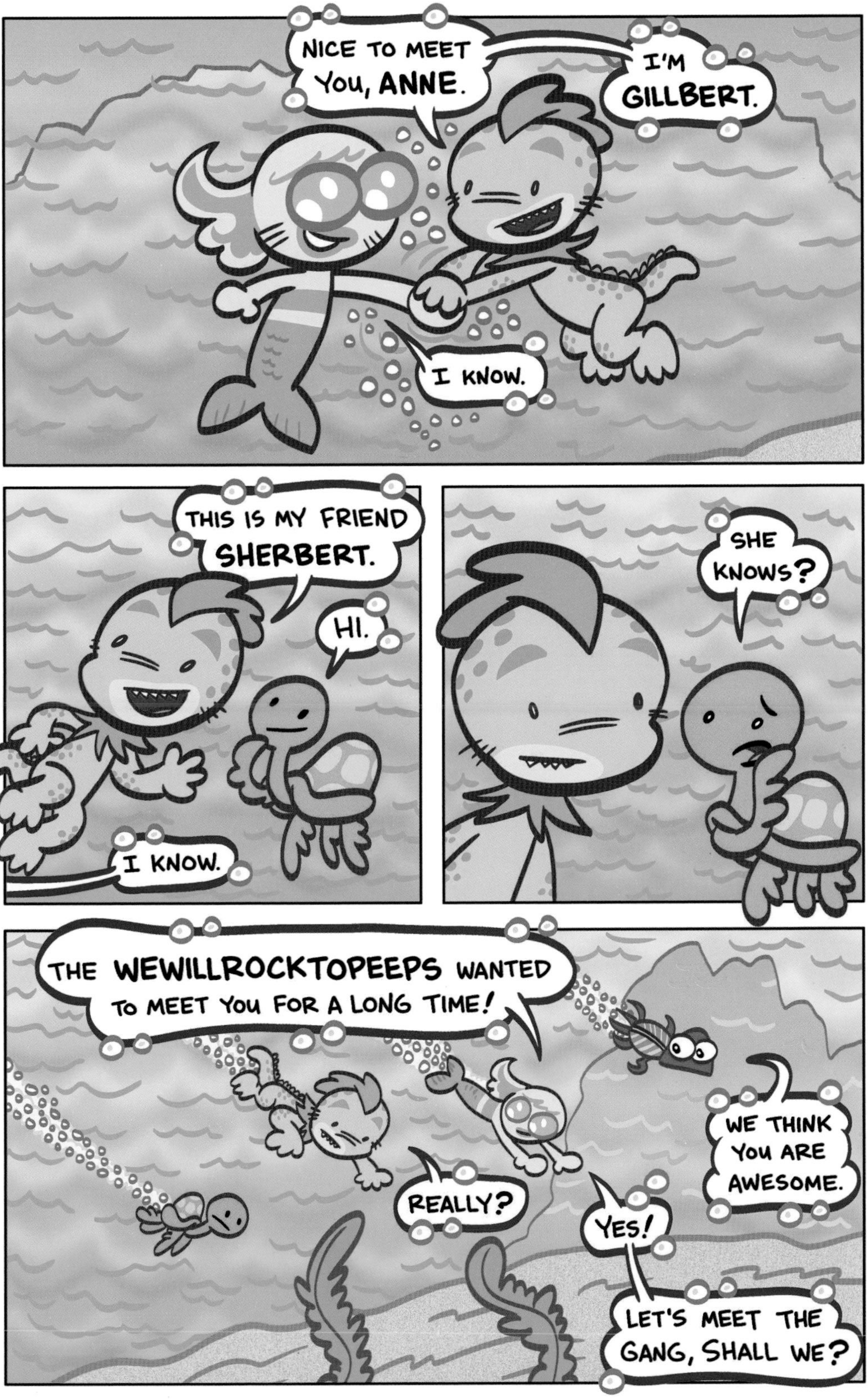
NICE TO MEET YOU, ANNE.
I'M GILLBERT.
I KNOW.
THIS IS MY FRIEND SHERBERT.
HI.
I KNOW.
SHE KNOWS?
THE WEWILLROCKTOPEEPS WANTED TO MEET YOU FOR A LONG TIME!
WE THINK YOU ARE AWESOME.
REALLY?
YES!
LET'S MEET THE GANG, SHALL WE?

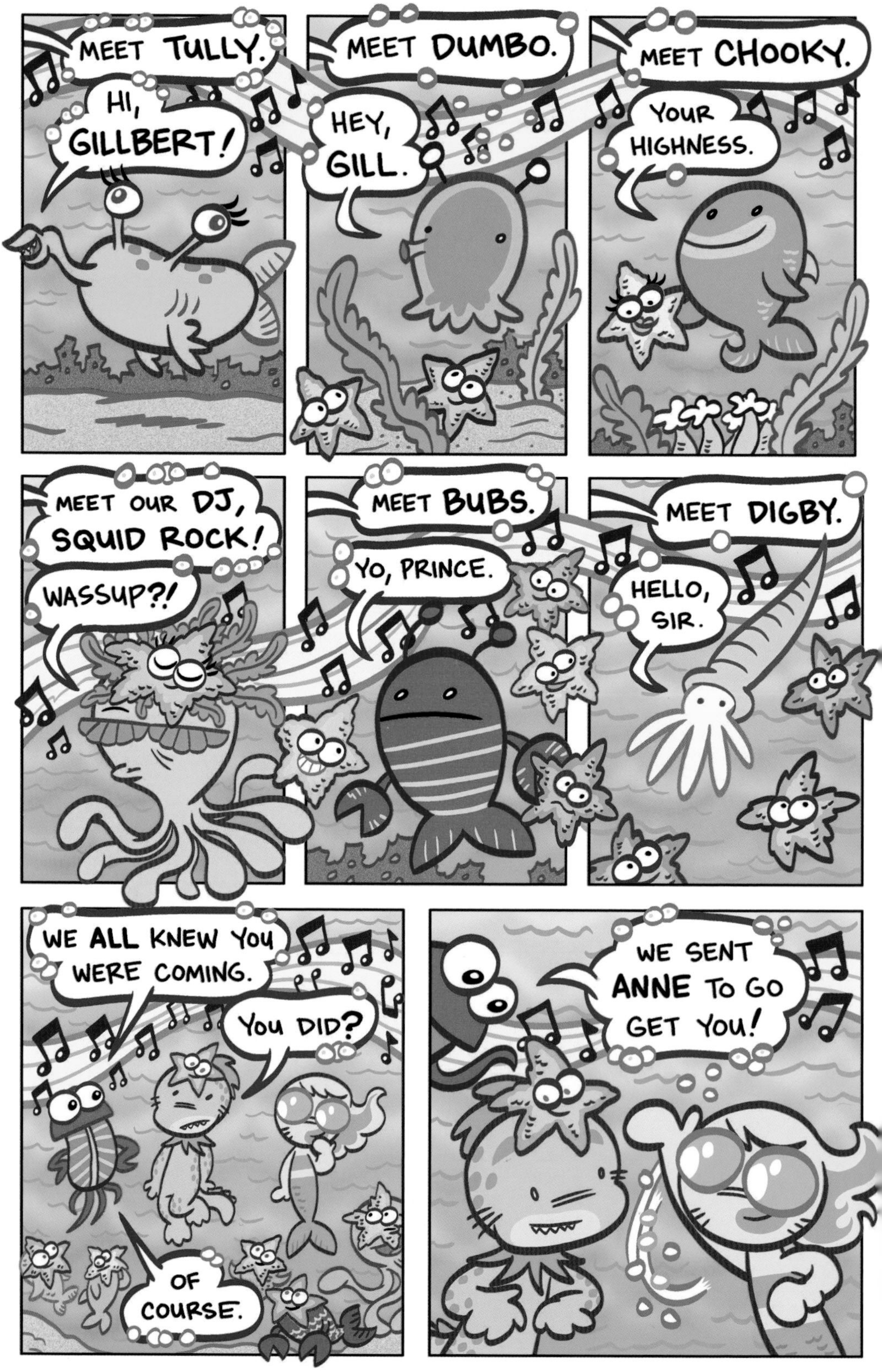
MEET TULLY.
HI, GILLBERT!
MEET DUMBO.
HEY, GILL.
MEET CHOOKY.
YOUR HIGHNESS.
MEET OUR DJ, SQUID ROCK!
WASSUP?!
MEET BUBS.
YO, PRINCE.
MEET DIGBY.
HELLO, SIR.
WE ALL KNEW YOU WERE COMING.
YOU DID?
OF COURSE.
WE SENT ANNE TO GO GET YOU!

MEANWHILE, IN DEEP SPACE...

...A FIERY ASTEROID IS ON A COLLISION COURSE WITH **EARTH!**

SPLASH

SSSSSS

THUMP

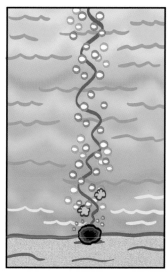

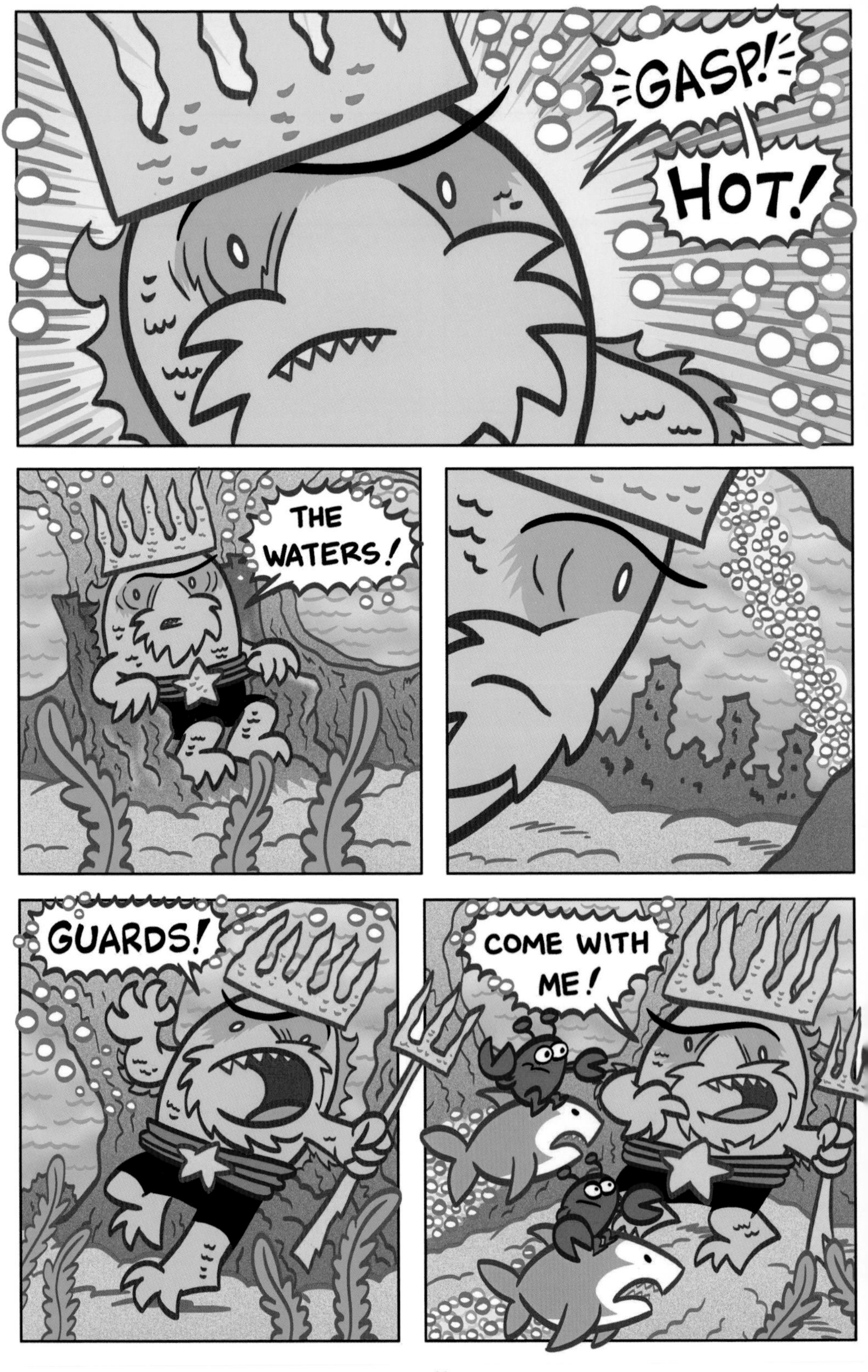
GASP!
HOT!
THE WATERS!
GUARDS!
COME WITH ME!

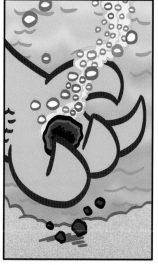

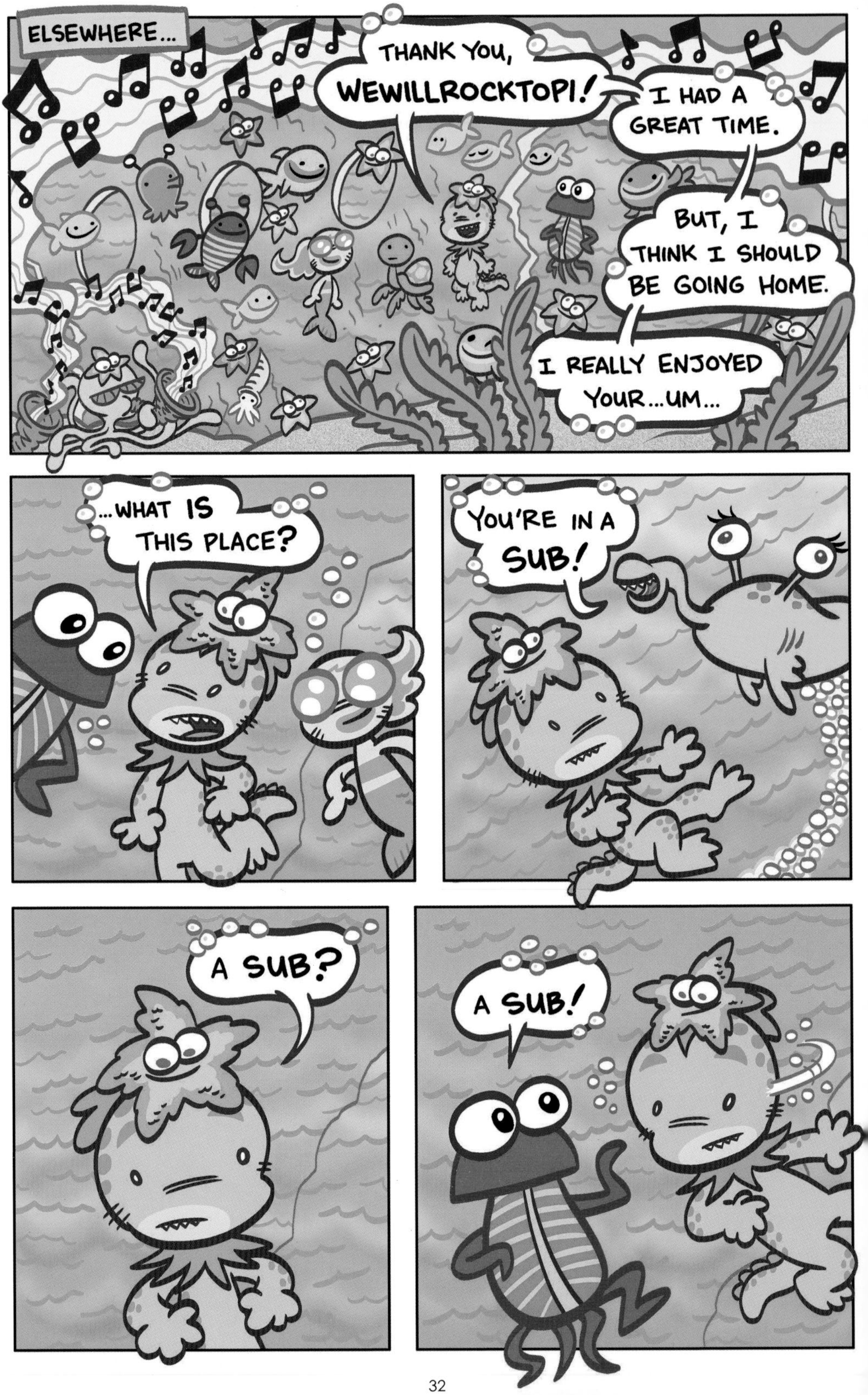
ELSEWHERE...
THANK YOU, WEWILLROCKTOPI!
I HAD A GREAT TIME.
BUT, I THINK I SHOULD BE GOING HOME.
I REALLY ENJOYED YOUR...UM...
...WHAT IS THIS PLACE?
YOU'RE IN A SUB!
A SUB?
A SUB!

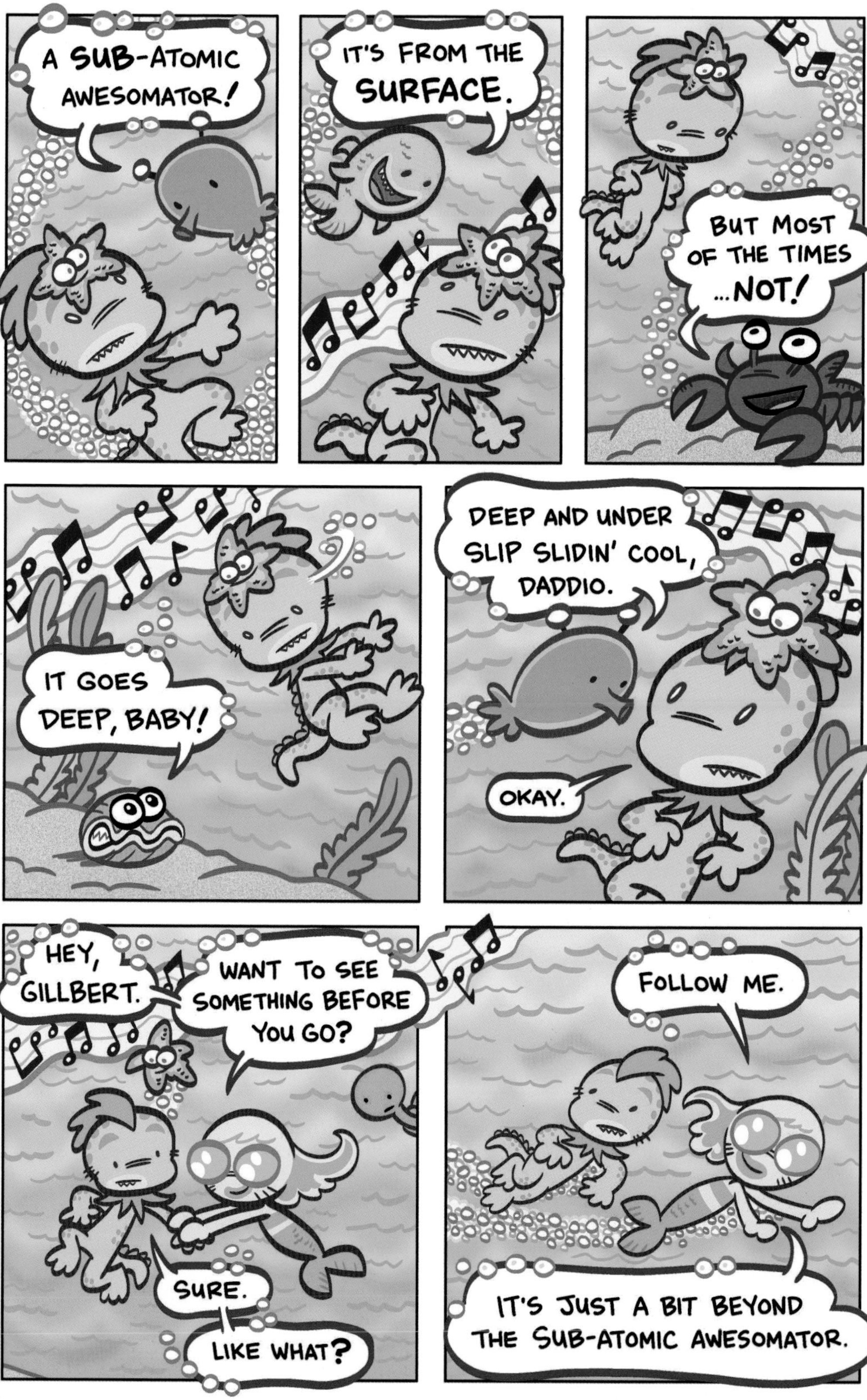
A SUB-ATOMIC AWESOMATOR!
IT'S FROM THE SURFACE.
BUT MOST OF THE TIMES ...NOT!
IT GOES DEEP, BABY!
DEEP AND UNDER SLIP SLIDIN' COOL, DADDIO.
OKAY.
HEY, GILLBERT.
WANT TO SEE SOMETHING BEFORE YOU GO?
SURE.
LIKE WHAT?
FOLLOW ME.
IT'S JUST A BIT BEYOND THE SUB-ATOMIC AWESOMATOR.

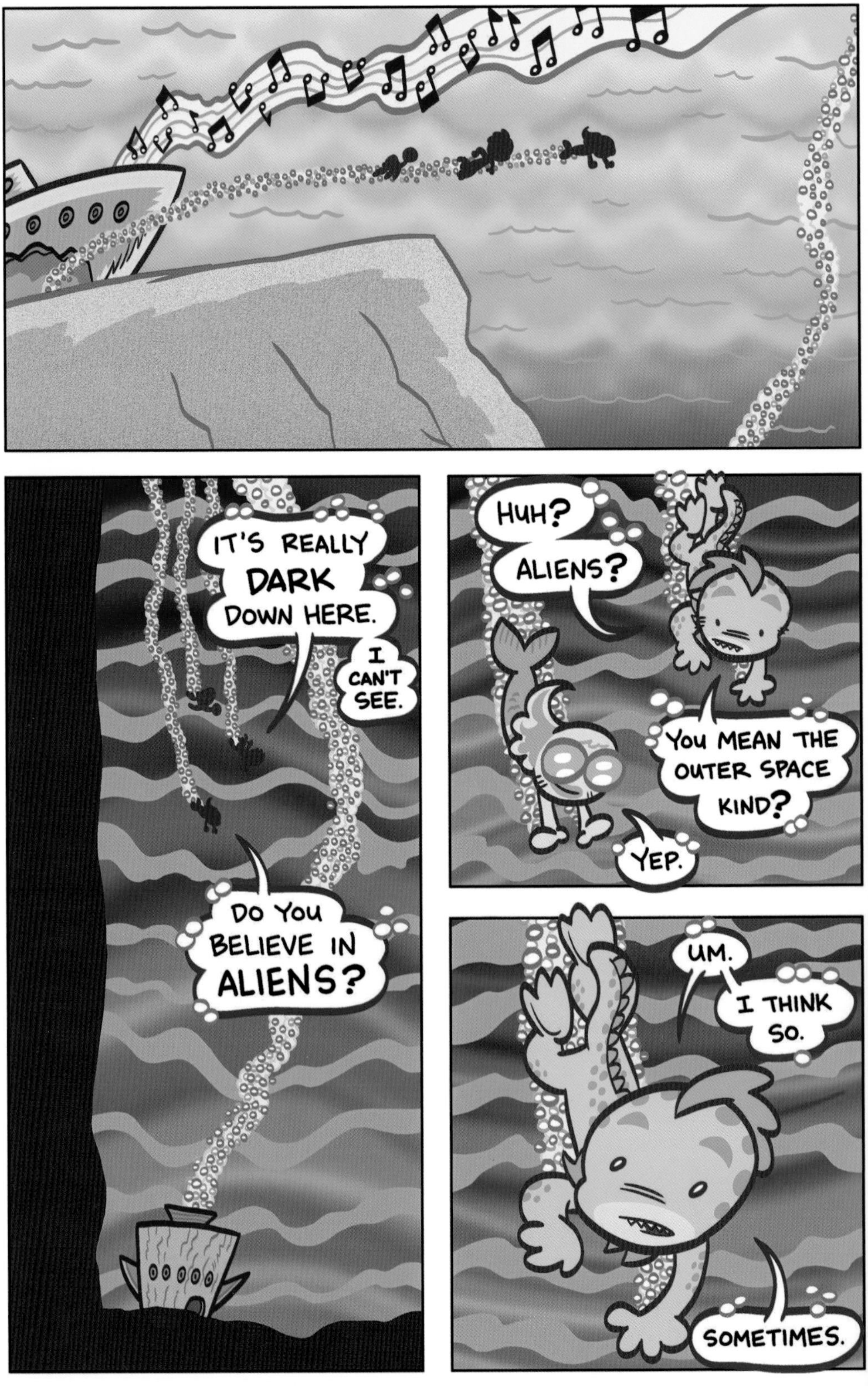
IT'S REALLY DARK DOWN HERE.
I CAN'T SEE.
DO YOU BELIEVE IN ALIENS?
HUH?
ALIENS?
YOU MEAN THE OUTER SPACE KIND?
YEP.
UM.
I THINK SO.
SOMETIMES.

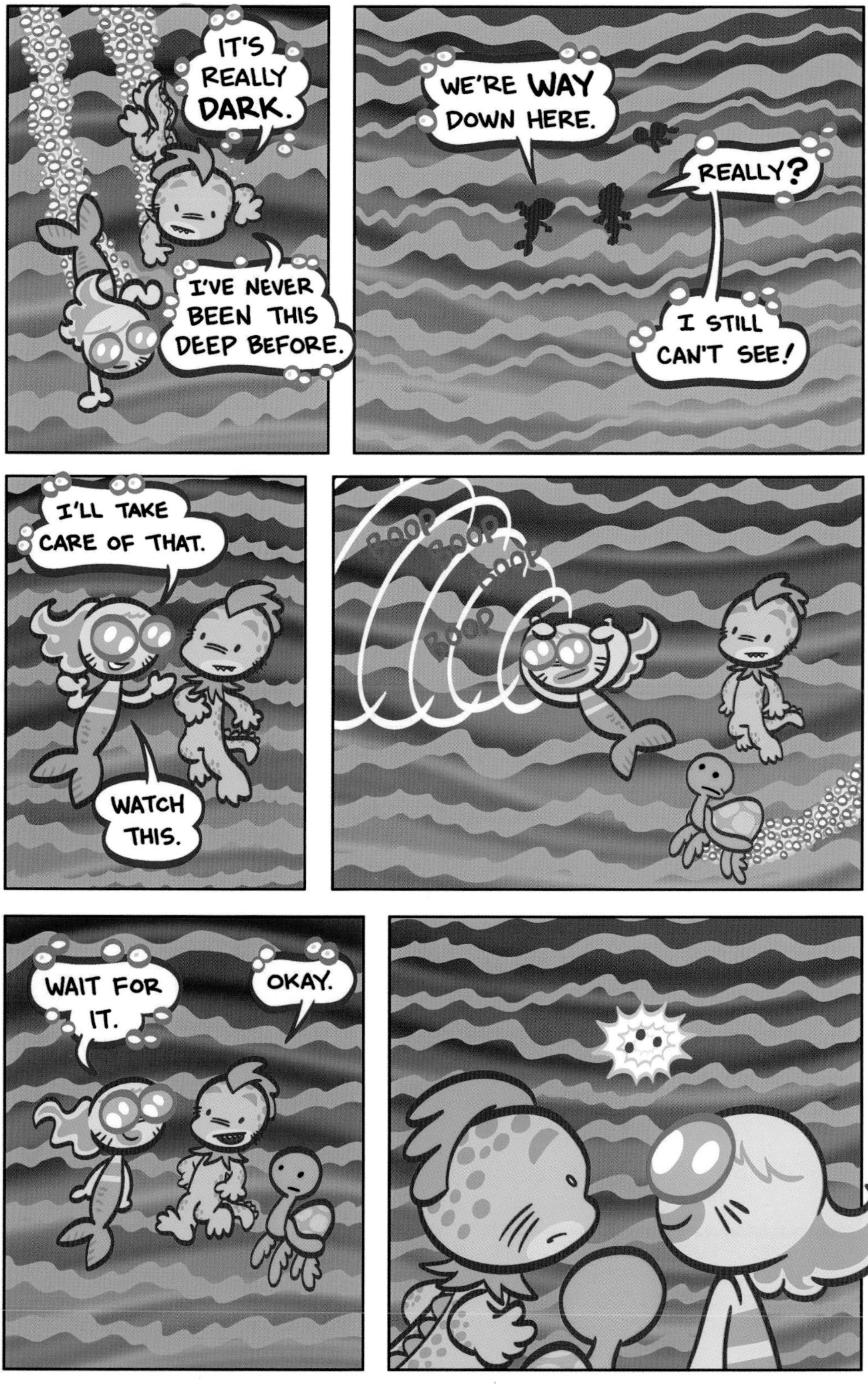
IT'S REALLY DARK.
I'VE NEVER BEEN THIS DEEP BEFORE.
WE'RE WAY DOWN HERE.
REALLY?
I STILL CAN'T SEE!
I'LL TAKE CARE OF THAT.
WATCH THIS.
BOOP BOOP BOOP BOOP
WAIT FOR IT.
OKAY.

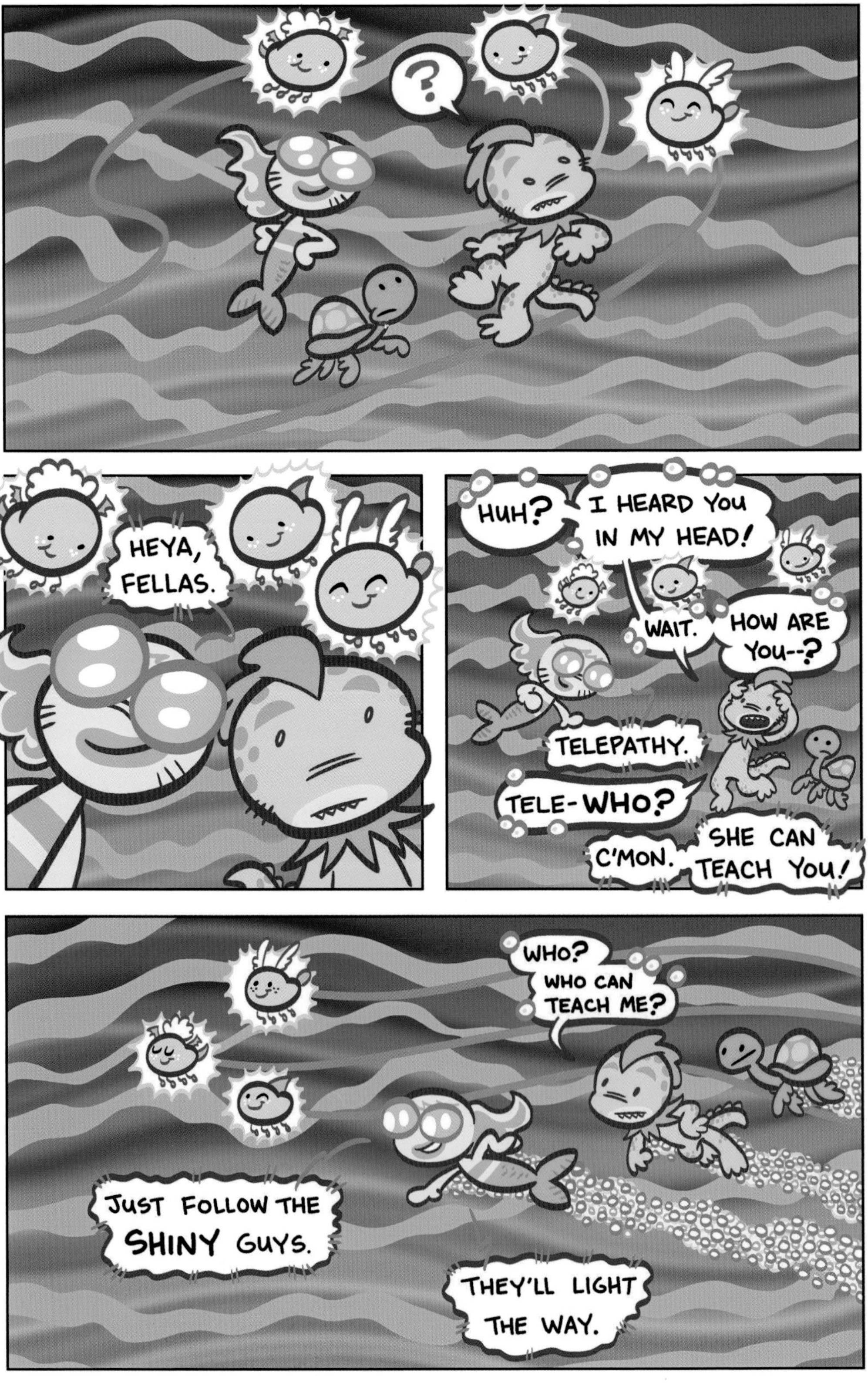
?
HEYA, FELLAS.
HUH?
I HEARD YOU IN MY HEAD!
WAIT.
HOW ARE YOU--?
TELEPATHY.
TELE-WHO?
C'MON.
SHE CAN TEACH YOU!
WHO? WHO CAN TEACH ME?
JUST FOLLOW THE SHINY GUYS.
THEY'LL LIGHT THE WAY.

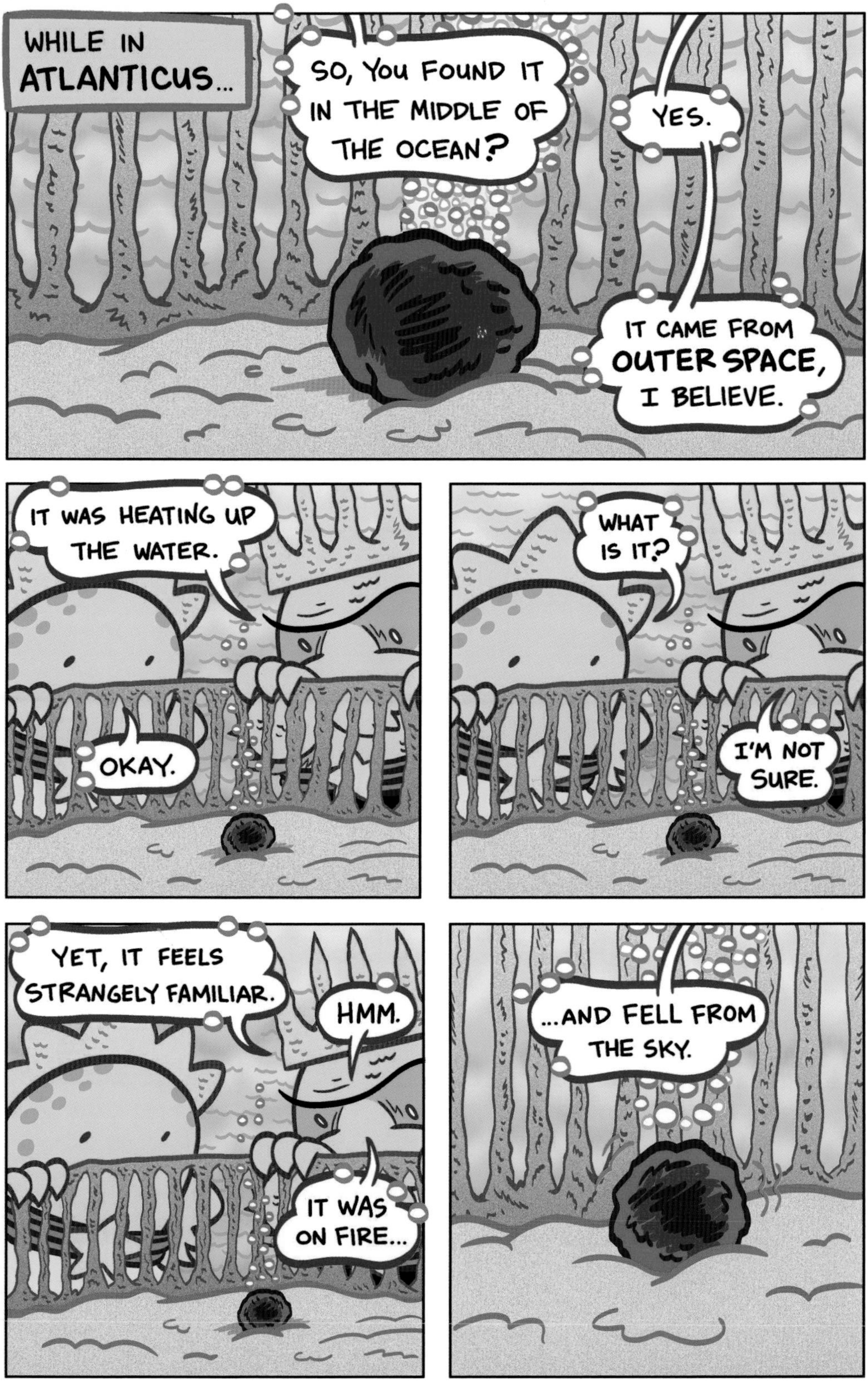
WHILE IN ATLANTICUS...
SO, YOU FOUND IT IN THE MIDDLE OF THE OCEAN?
YES.
IT CAME FROM OUTER SPACE, I BELIEVE.
IT WAS HEATING UP THE WATER.
OKAY.
WHAT IS IT?
I'M NOT SURE.
YET, IT FEELS STRANGELY FAMILIAR.
HMM.
IT WAS ON FIRE...
...AND FELL FROM THE SKY.

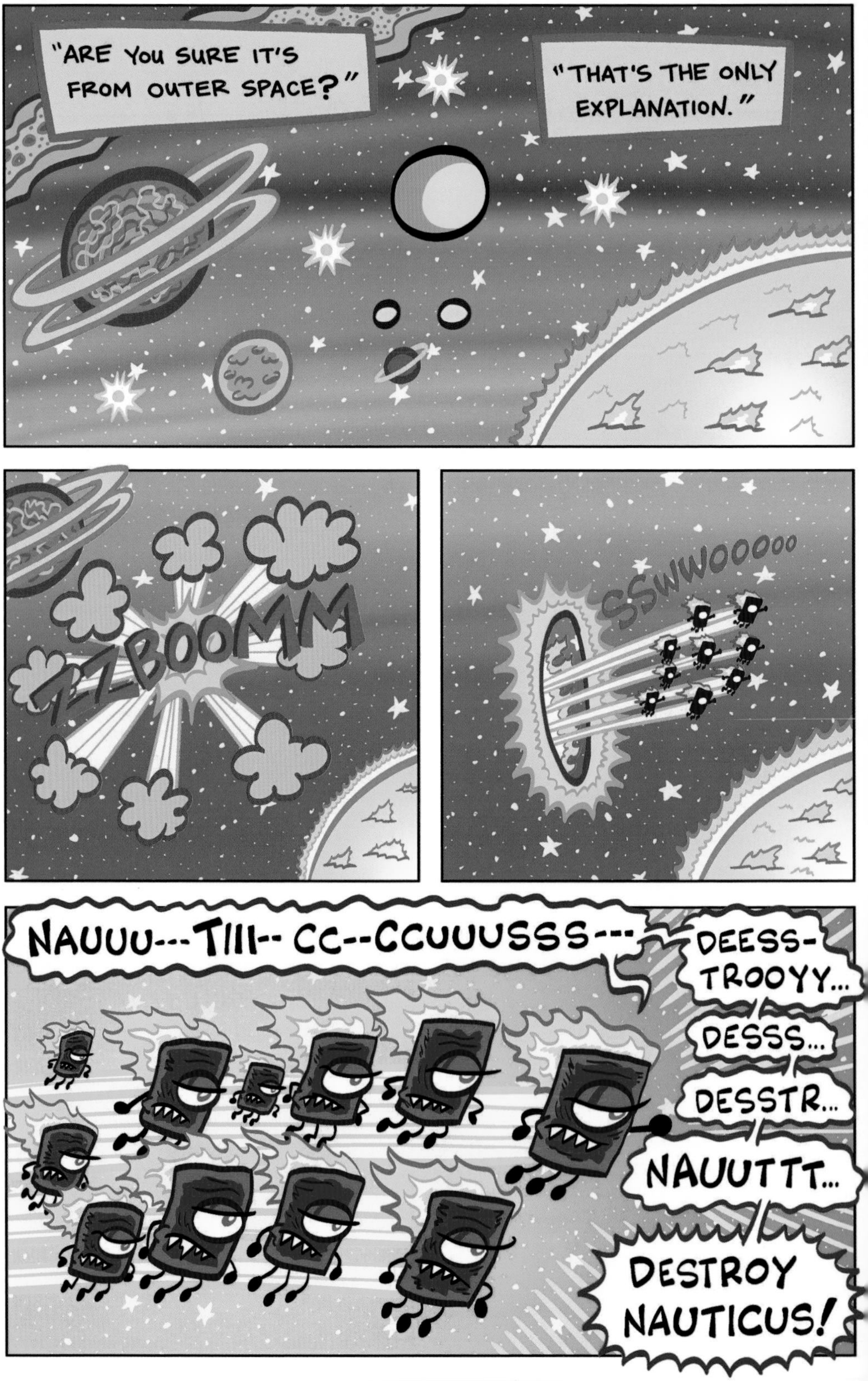
"ARE YOU SURE IT'S FROM OUTER SPACE?"
"THAT'S THE ONLY EXPLANATION."
ZZBOOMM
SSWWOOOOO
NAUUU---TIII-- CC--CCUUUSSS---
DEESS-TROOYY...
DESSS...
DESSTR...
NAUUTTT...
DESTROY NAUTICUS!

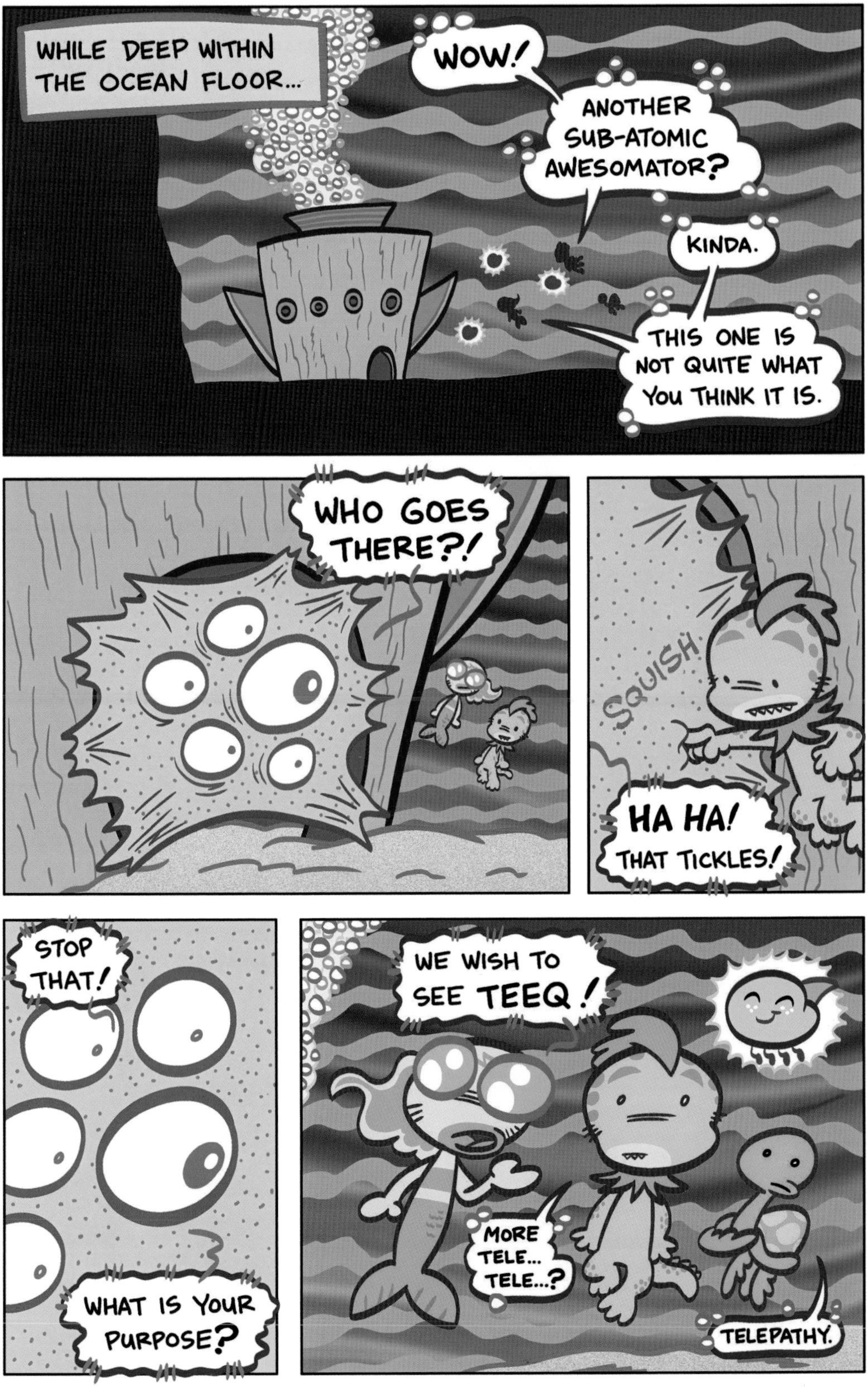
WHILE DEEP WITHIN THE OCEAN FLOOR...
WOW!
ANOTHER SUB-ATOMIC AWESOMATOR?
KINDA.
THIS ONE IS NOT QUITE WHAT YOU THINK IT IS.
WHO GOES THERE?!
SQUISH
HA HA! THAT TICKLES!
STOP THAT!
WHAT IS YOUR PURPOSE?
WE WISH TO SEE TEEQ!
MORE TELE... TELE...?
TELEPATHY.

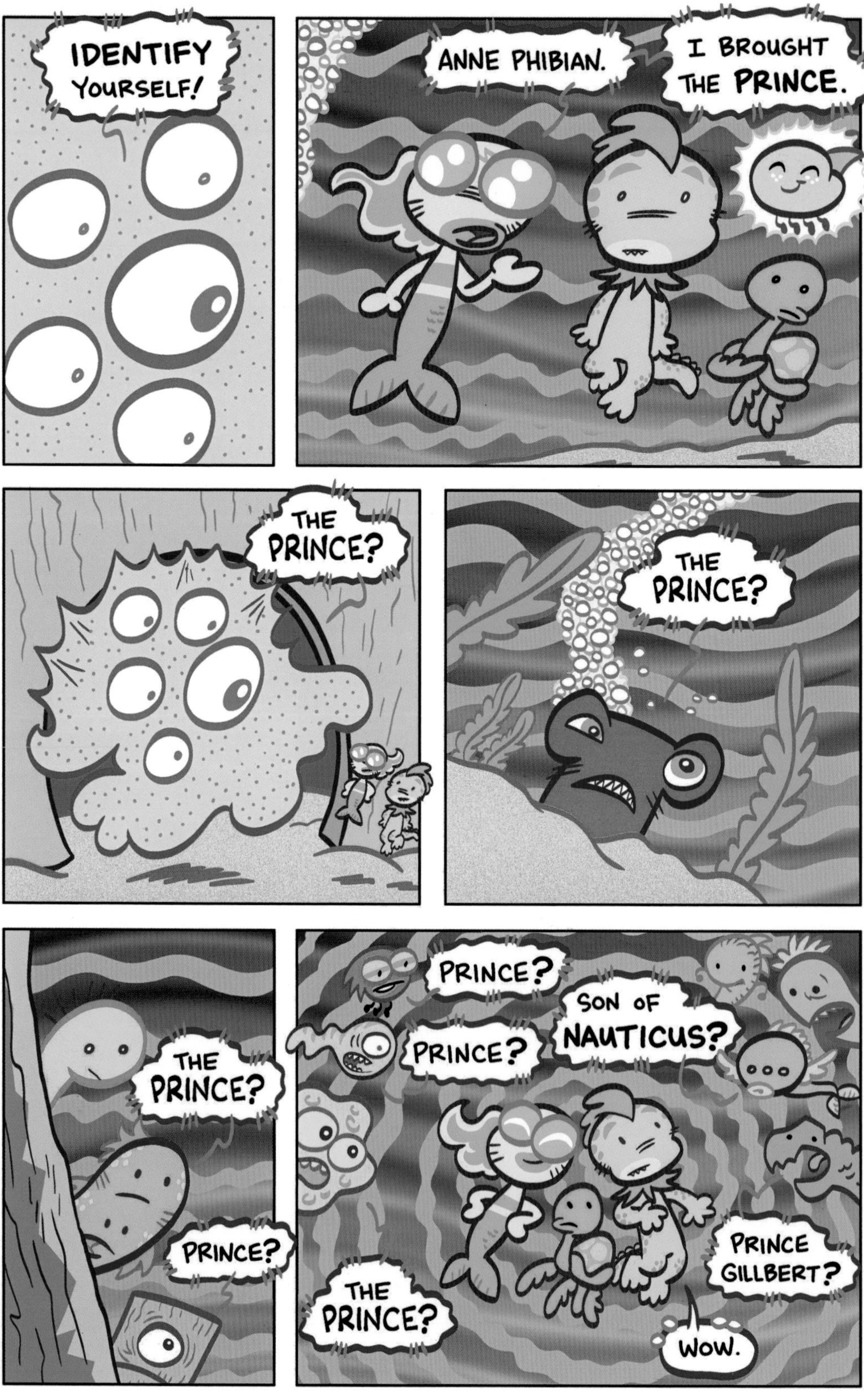
IDENTIFY YOURSELF!
ANNE PHIBIAN.
I BROUGHT THE PRINCE.
THE PRINCE?
THE PRINCE?
THE PRINCE?
PRINCE?
PRINCE?
PRINCE?
SON OF NAUTICUS?
THE PRINCE?
PRINCE GILLBERT?
WOW.

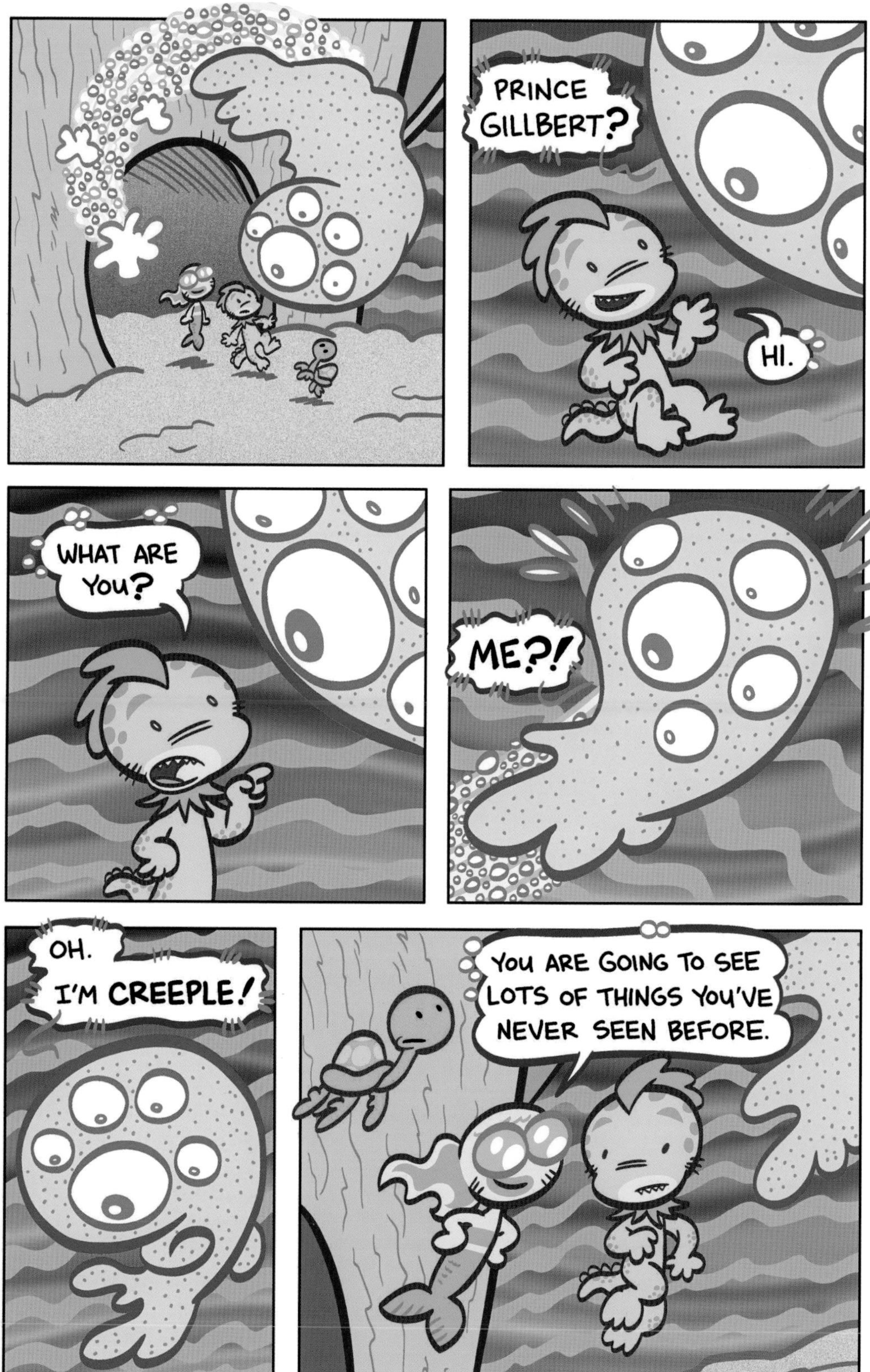
PRINCE GILLBERT?
HI.
WHAT ARE YOU?
ME?!
OH. I'M CREEPLE!
YOU ARE GOING TO SEE LOTS OF THINGS YOU'VE NEVER SEEN BEFORE.

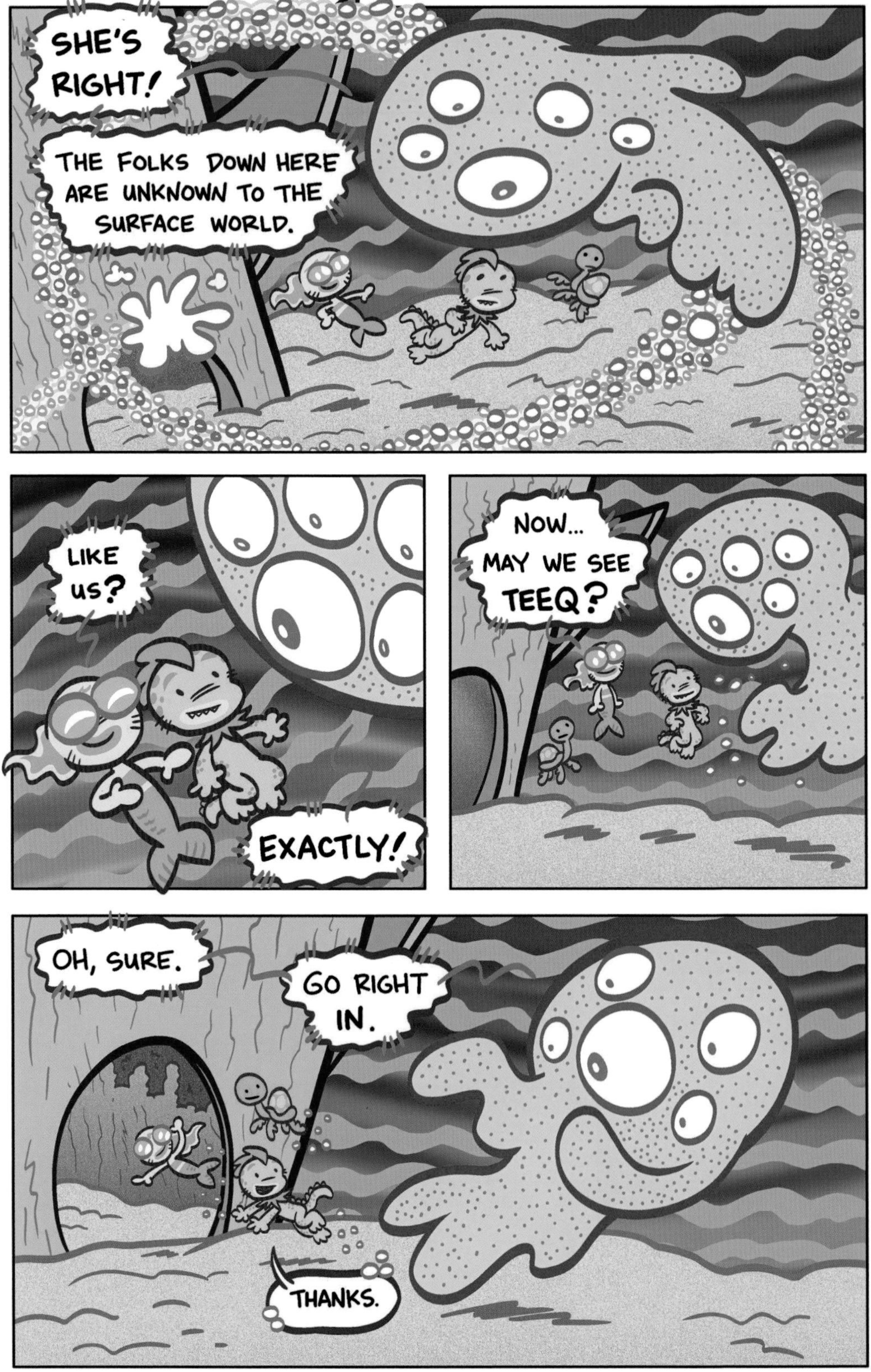
SHE'S RIGHT!
THE FOLKS DOWN HERE ARE UNKNOWN TO THE SURFACE WORLD.
LIKE US?
EXACTLY!
NOW... MAY WE SEE TEEQ?
OH, SURE.
GO RIGHT IN.
THANKS.

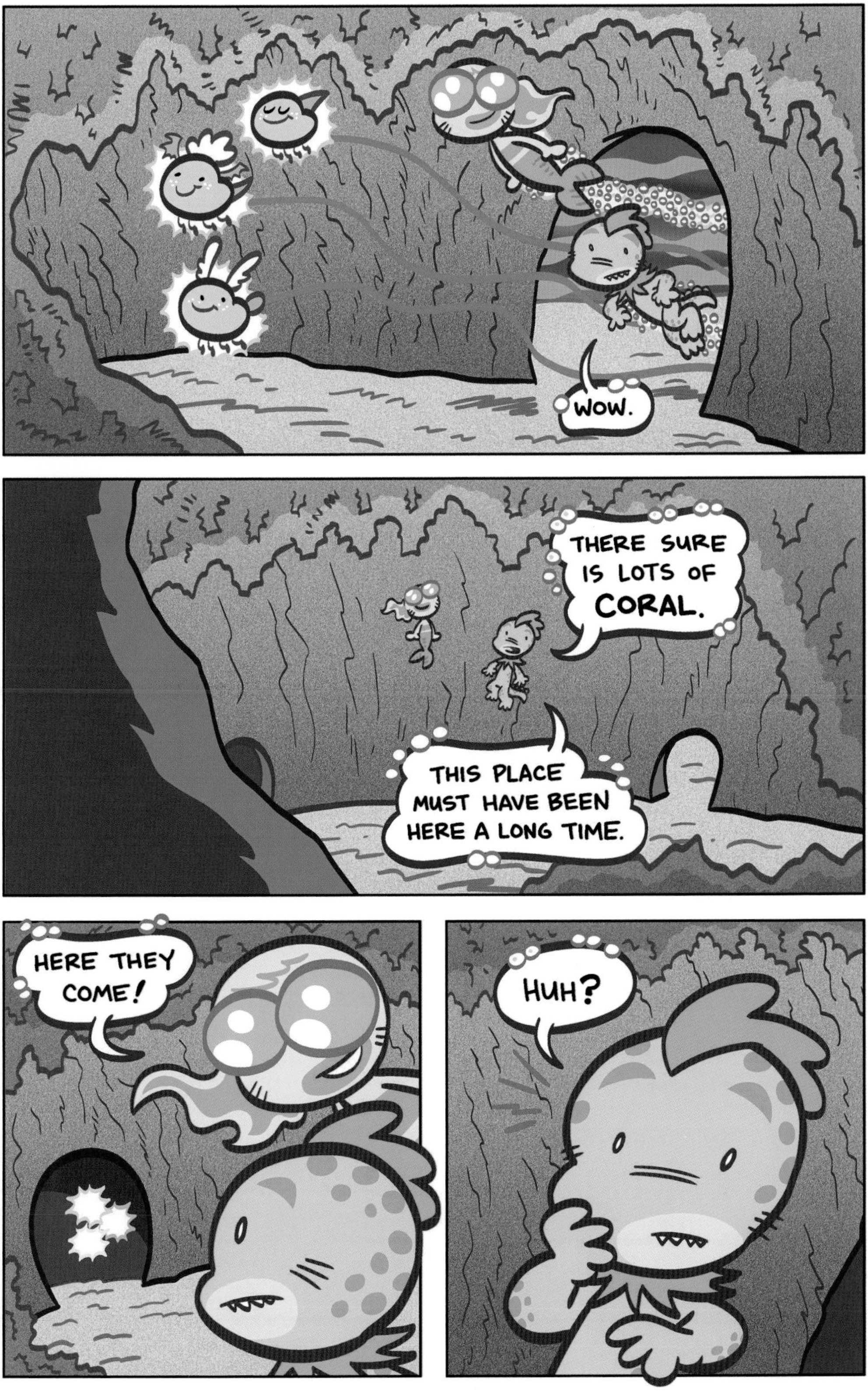
WOW.
THERE SURE IS LOTS OF CORAL.
THIS PLACE MUST HAVE BEEN HERE A LONG TIME.
HERE THEY COME!
HUH?

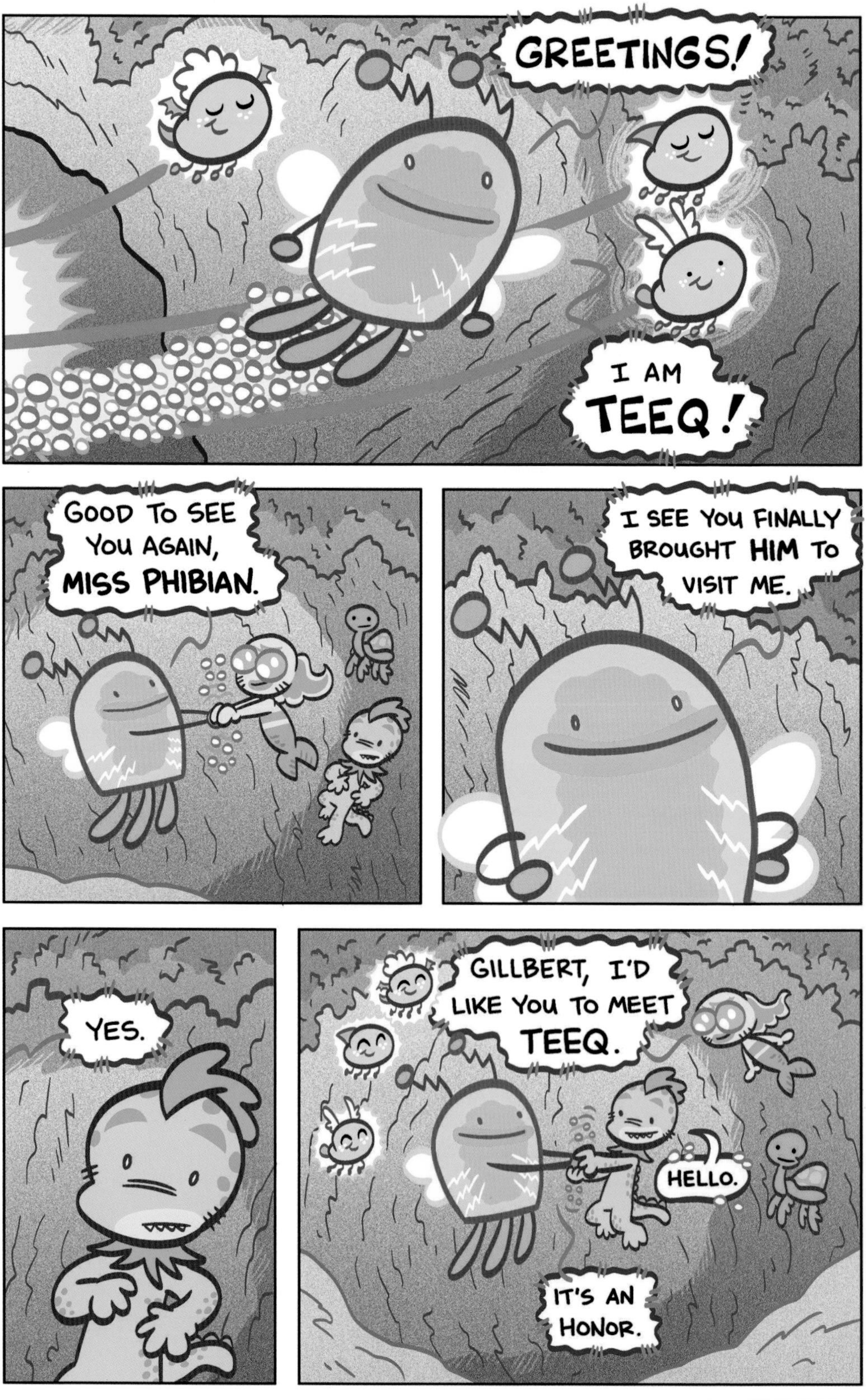
GREETINGS!
I AM TEEQ!
GOOD TO SEE YOU AGAIN, MISS PHIBIAN.
I SEE YOU FINALLY BROUGHT HIM TO VISIT ME.
YES.
GILLBERT, I'D LIKE YOU TO MEET TEEQ.
HELLO.
IT'S AN HONOR.

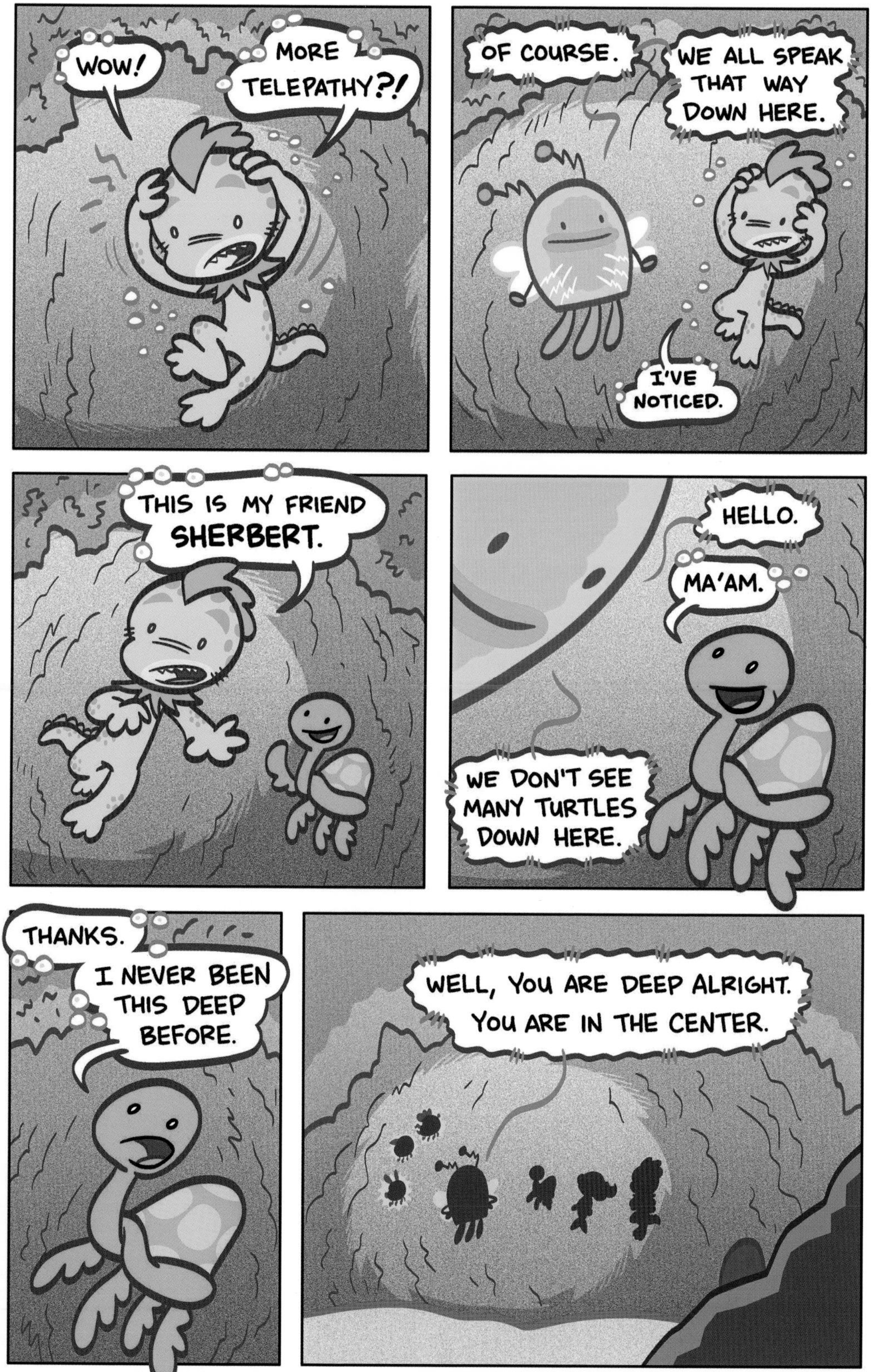
WOW!
MORE TELEPATHY?!
OF COURSE.
WE ALL SPEAK THAT WAY DOWN HERE.
I'VE NOTICED.
THIS IS MY FRIEND SHERBERT.
HELLO.
MA'AM.
WE DON'T SEE MANY TURTLES DOWN HERE.
THANKS.
I NEVER BEEN THIS DEEP BEFORE.
WELL, YOU ARE DEEP ALRIGHT. YOU ARE IN THE CENTER.

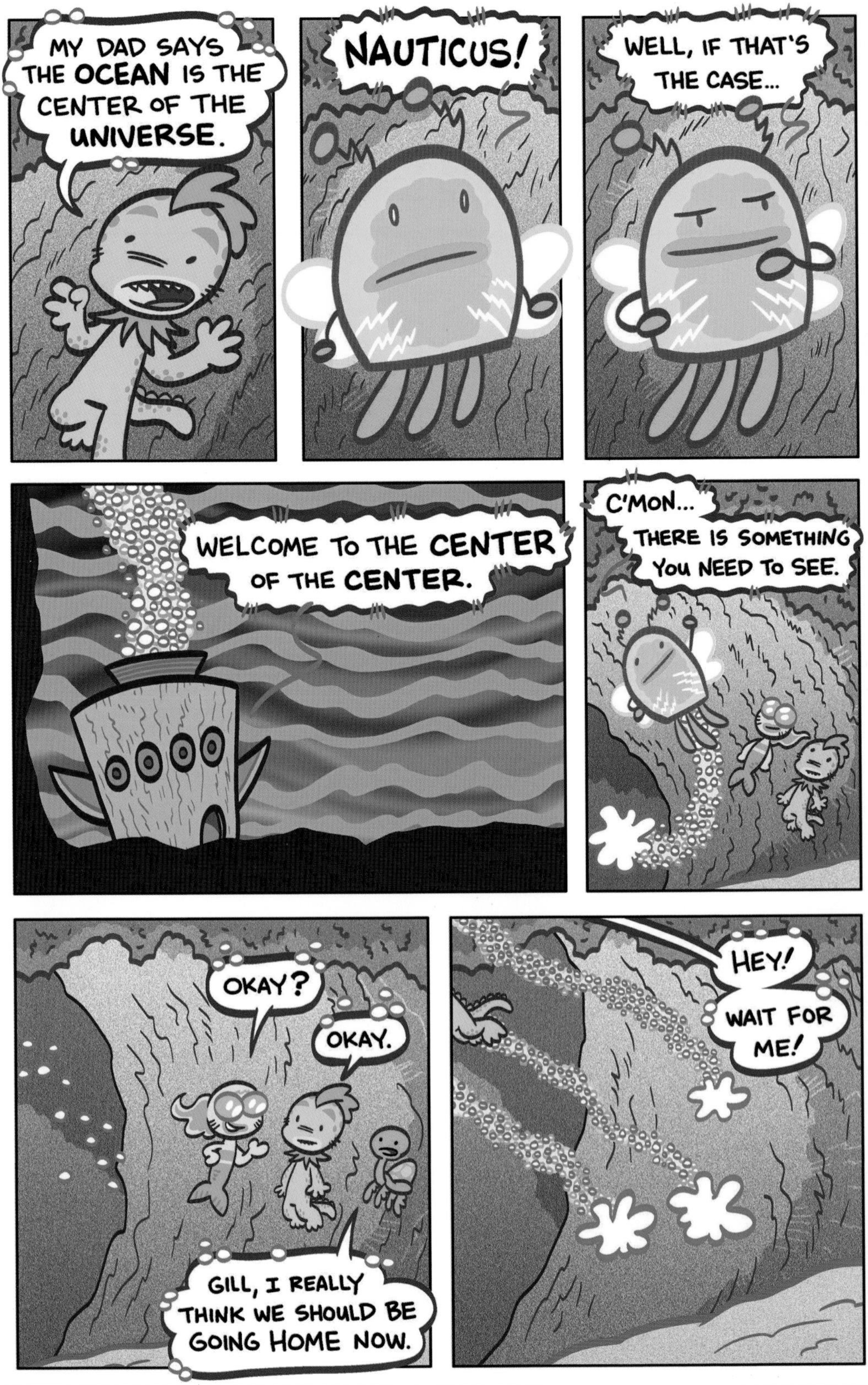
MY DAD SAYS THE OCEAN IS THE CENTER OF THE UNIVERSE.
NAUTICUS!
WELL, IF THAT'S THE CASE...
WELCOME TO THE CENTER OF THE CENTER.
C'MON...
THERE IS SOMETHING YOU NEED TO SEE.
OKAY?
OKAY.
GILL, I REALLY THINK WE SHOULD BE GOING HOME NOW.
HEY!
WAIT FOR ME!

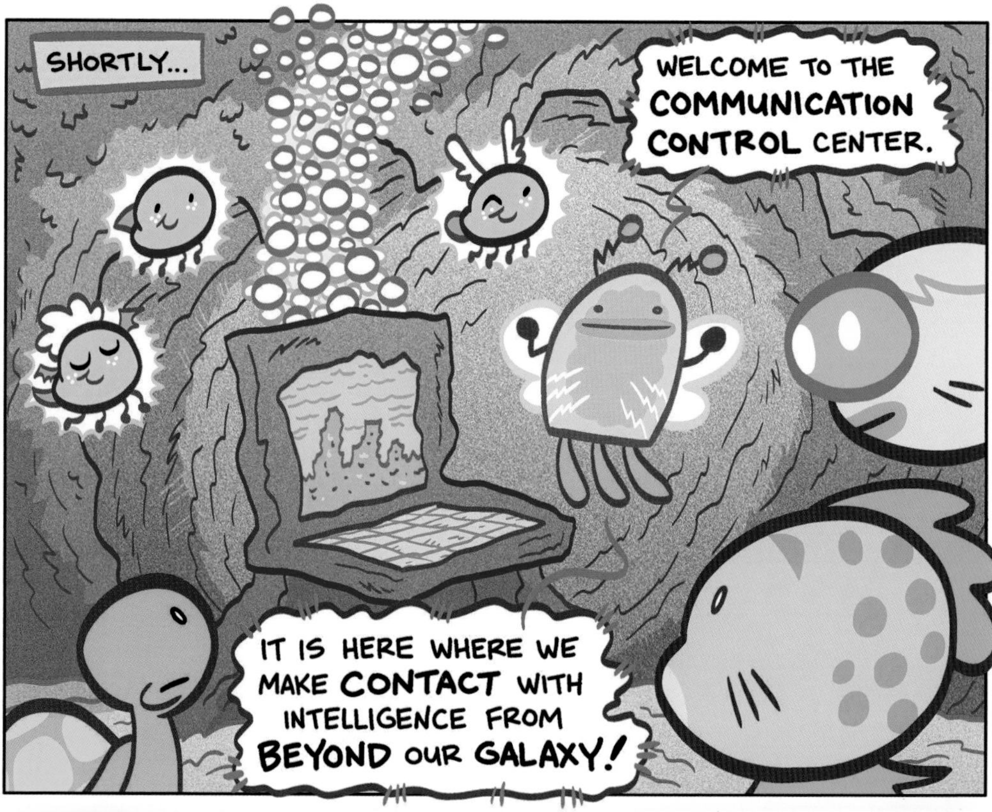
SHORTLY...
WELCOME TO THE COMMUNICATION CONTROL CENTER.
IT IS HERE WHERE WE MAKE CONTACT WITH INTELLIGENCE FROM BEYOND OUR GALAXY!

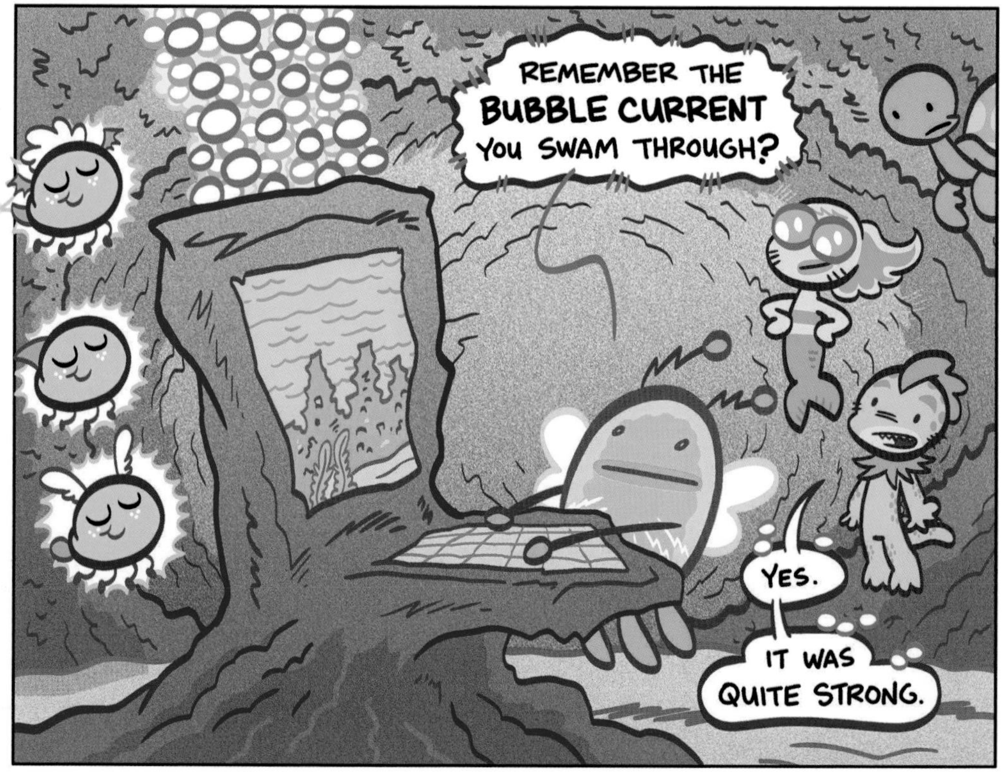
REMEMBER THE BUBBLE CURRENT YOU SWAM THROUGH?
YES.
IT WAS QUITE STRONG.

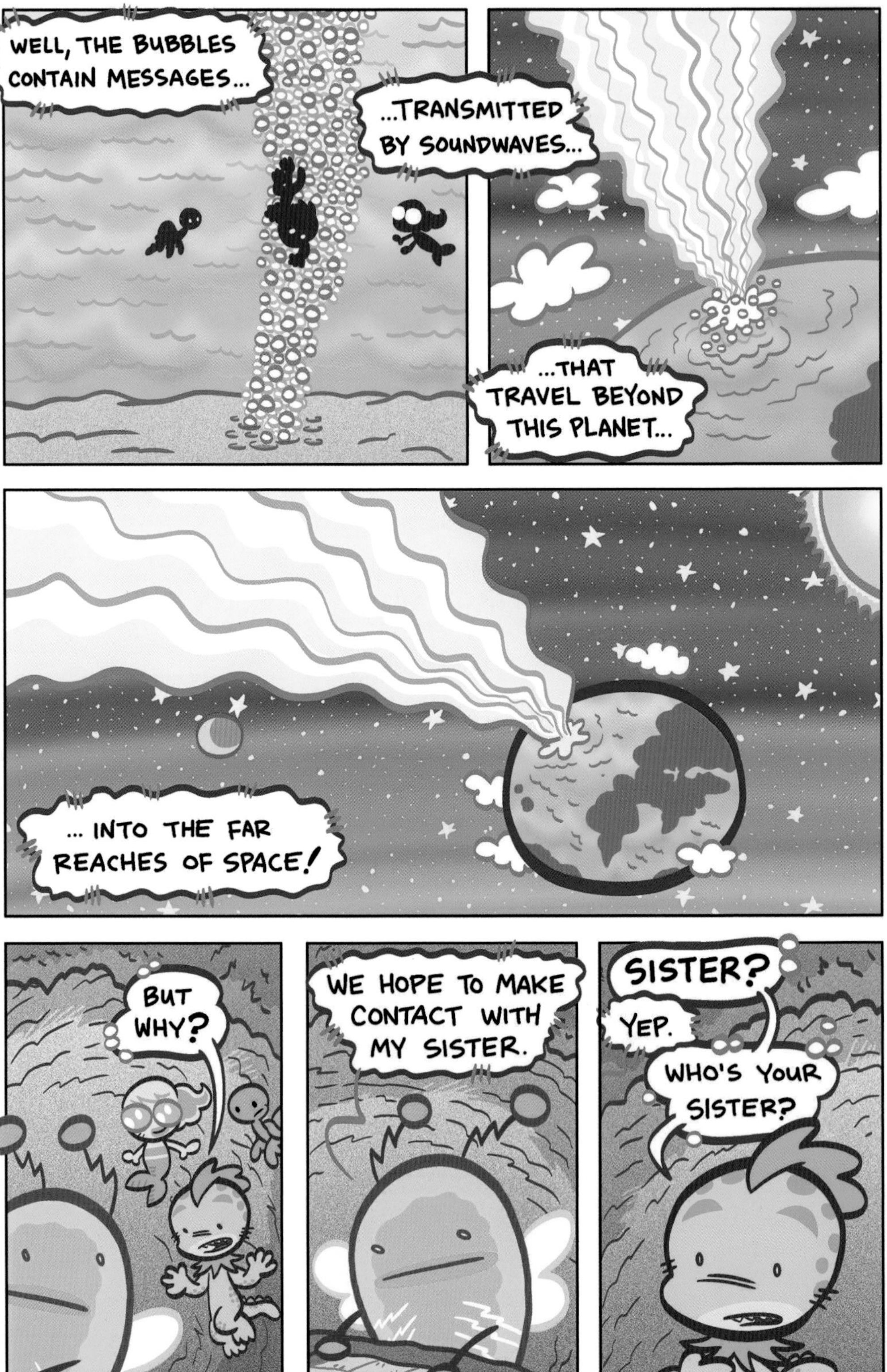
WELL, THE BUBBLES CONTAIN MESSAGES...
...TRANSMITTED BY SOUNDWAVES...
...THAT TRAVEL BEYOND THIS PLANET...
... INTO THE FAR REACHES OF SPACE!
BUT WHY?
WE HOPE TO MAKE CONTACT WITH MY SISTER.
SISTER?
YEP.
WHO'S YOUR SISTER?

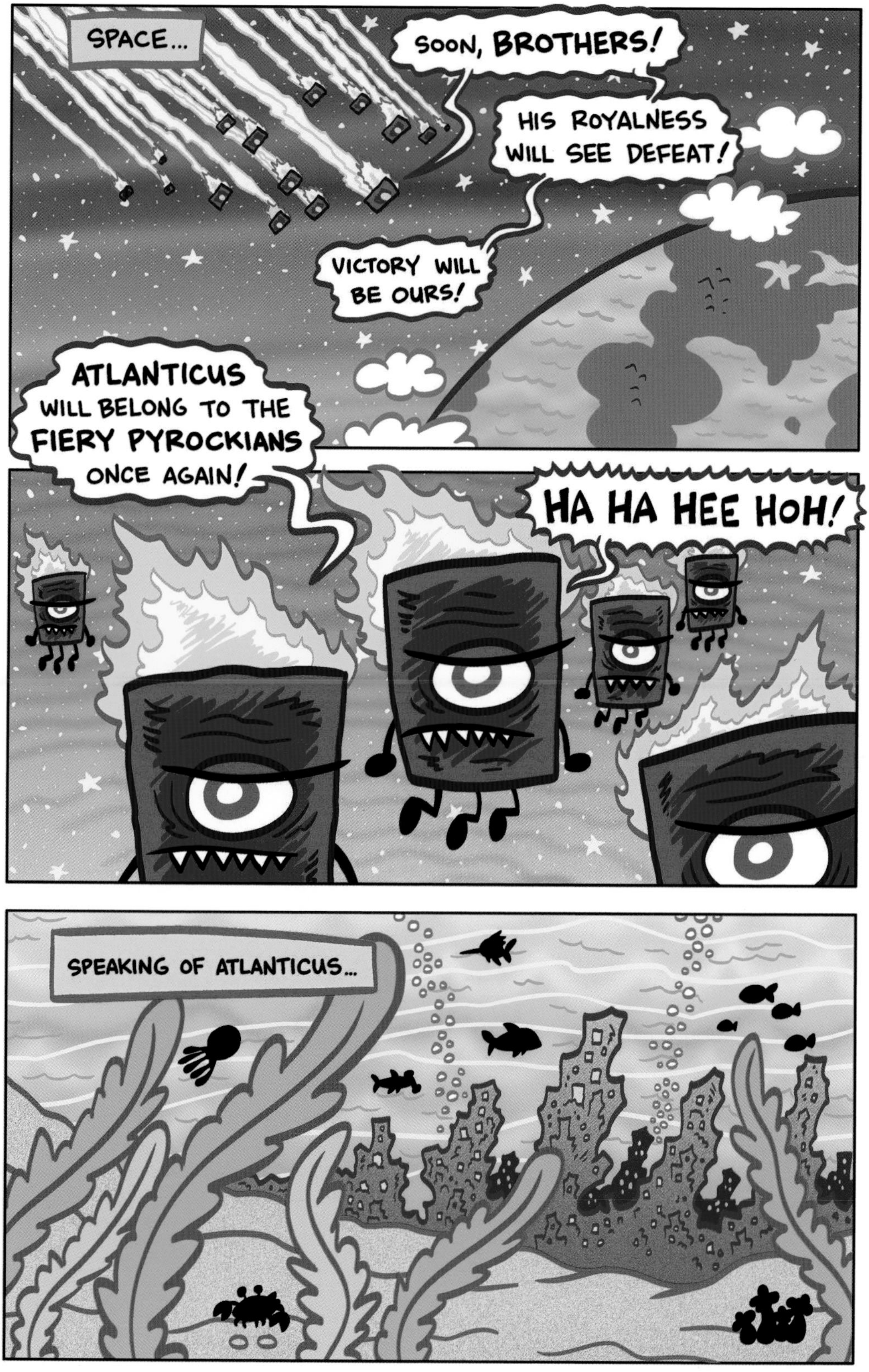
SPACE...
SOON, BROTHERS!
HIS ROYALNESS WILL SEE DEFEAT!
VICTORY WILL BE OURS!
ATLANTICUS WILL BELONG TO THE FIERY PYROCKIANS ONCE AGAIN!
HA HA HEE HOH!
SPEAKING OF ATLANTICUS...

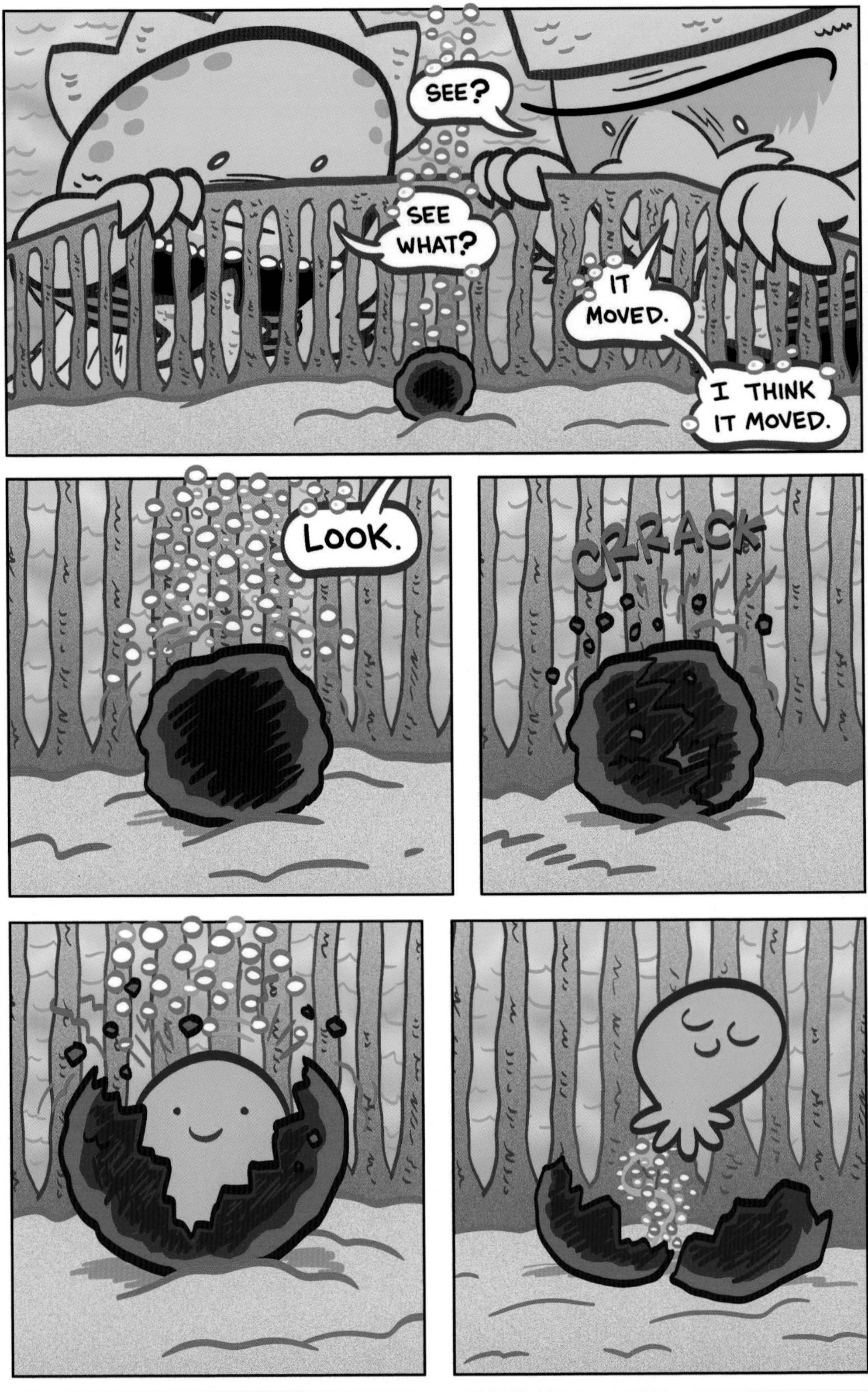
SEE?
SEE WHAT?
IT MOVED.
I THINK IT MOVED.
LOOK.
CRRACK

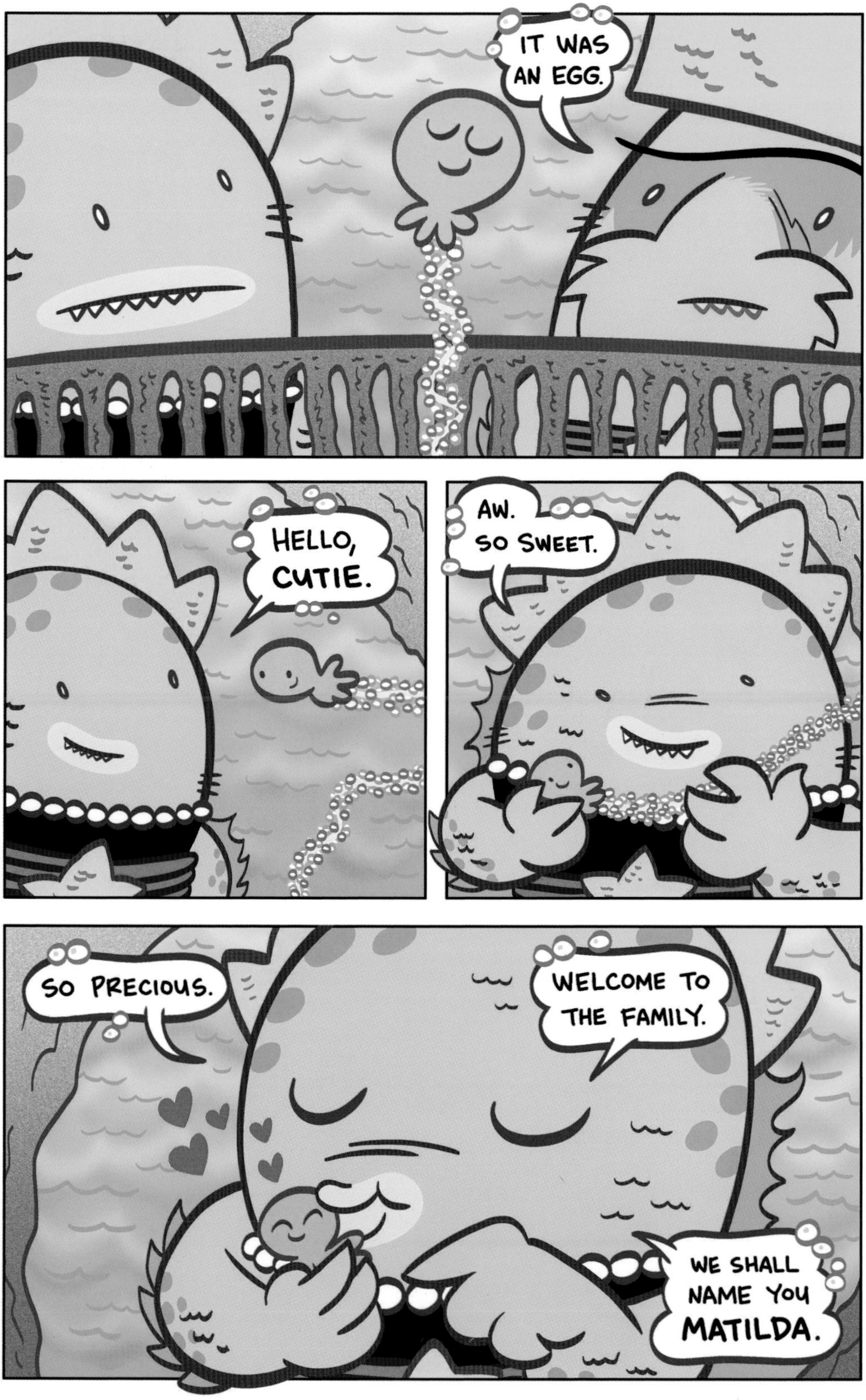
IT WAS AN EGG.
HELLO, CUTIE.
AW. SO SWEET.
SO PRECIOUS.
WELCOME TO THE FAMILY.
WE SHALL NAME YOU MATILDA.

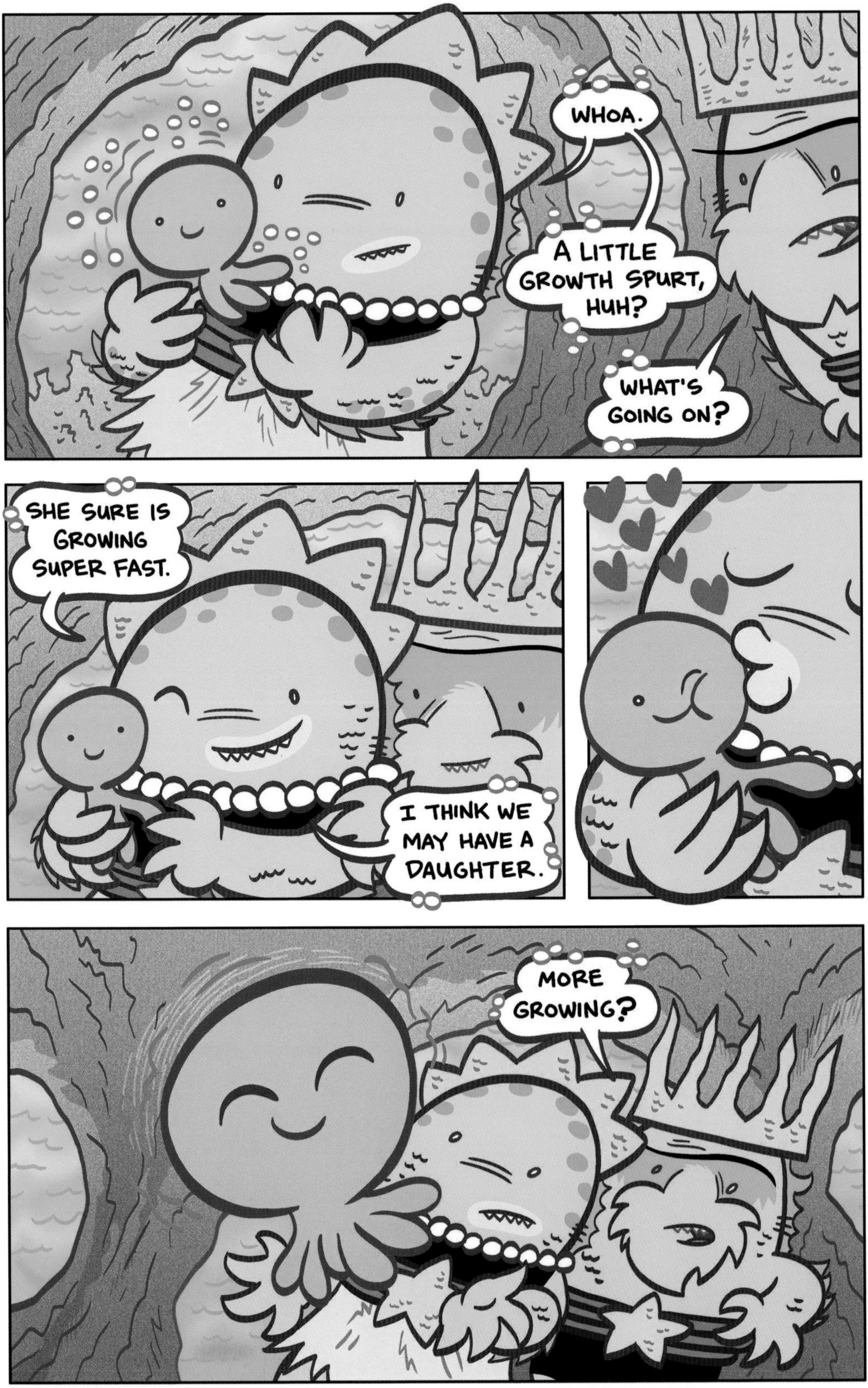
WHOA.
A LITTLE GROWTH SPURT, HUH?
WHAT'S GOING ON?
SHE SURE IS GROWING SUPER FAST.
I THINK WE MAY HAVE A DAUGHTER.
MORE GROWING?

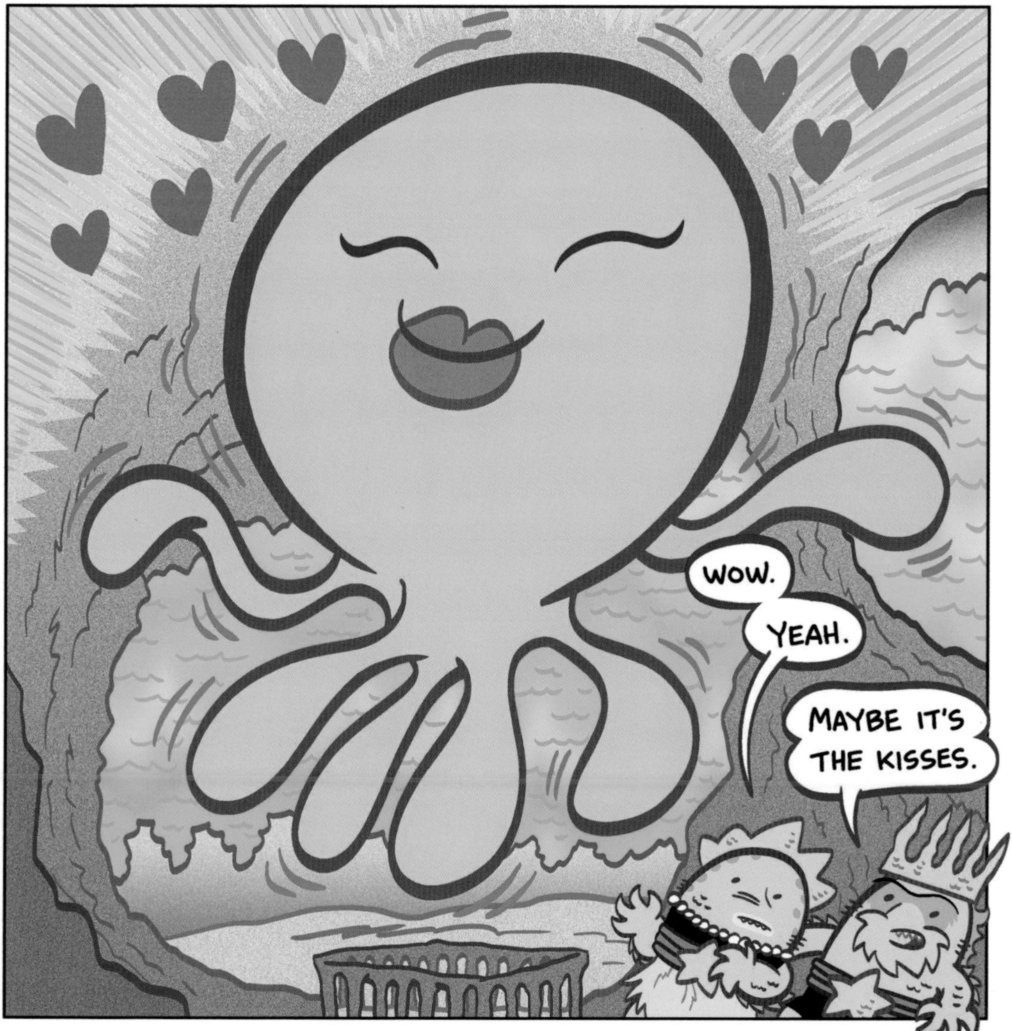
WOW.
YEAH.
MAYBE IT'S THE KISSES.

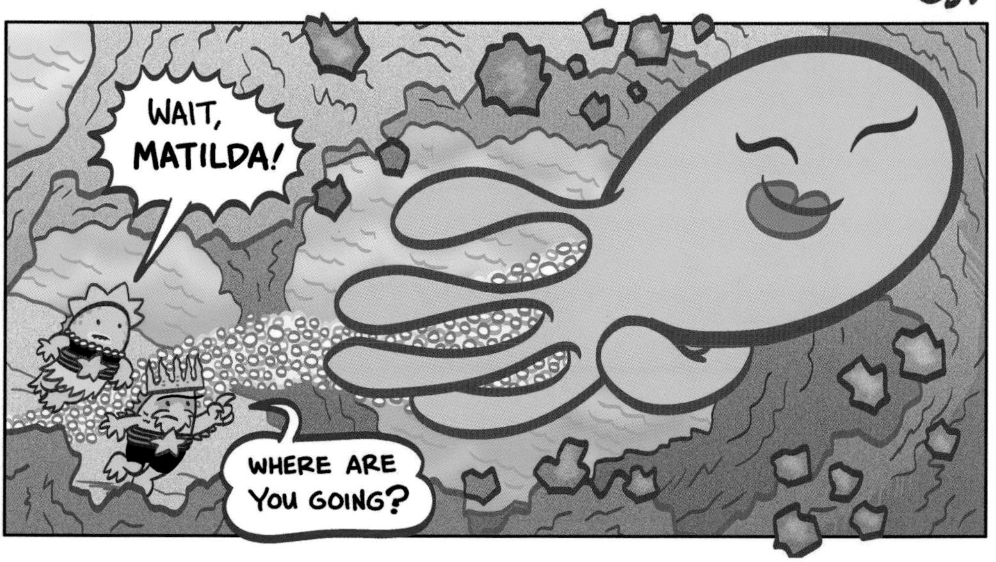
WAIT, MATILDA!
WHERE ARE YOU GOING?

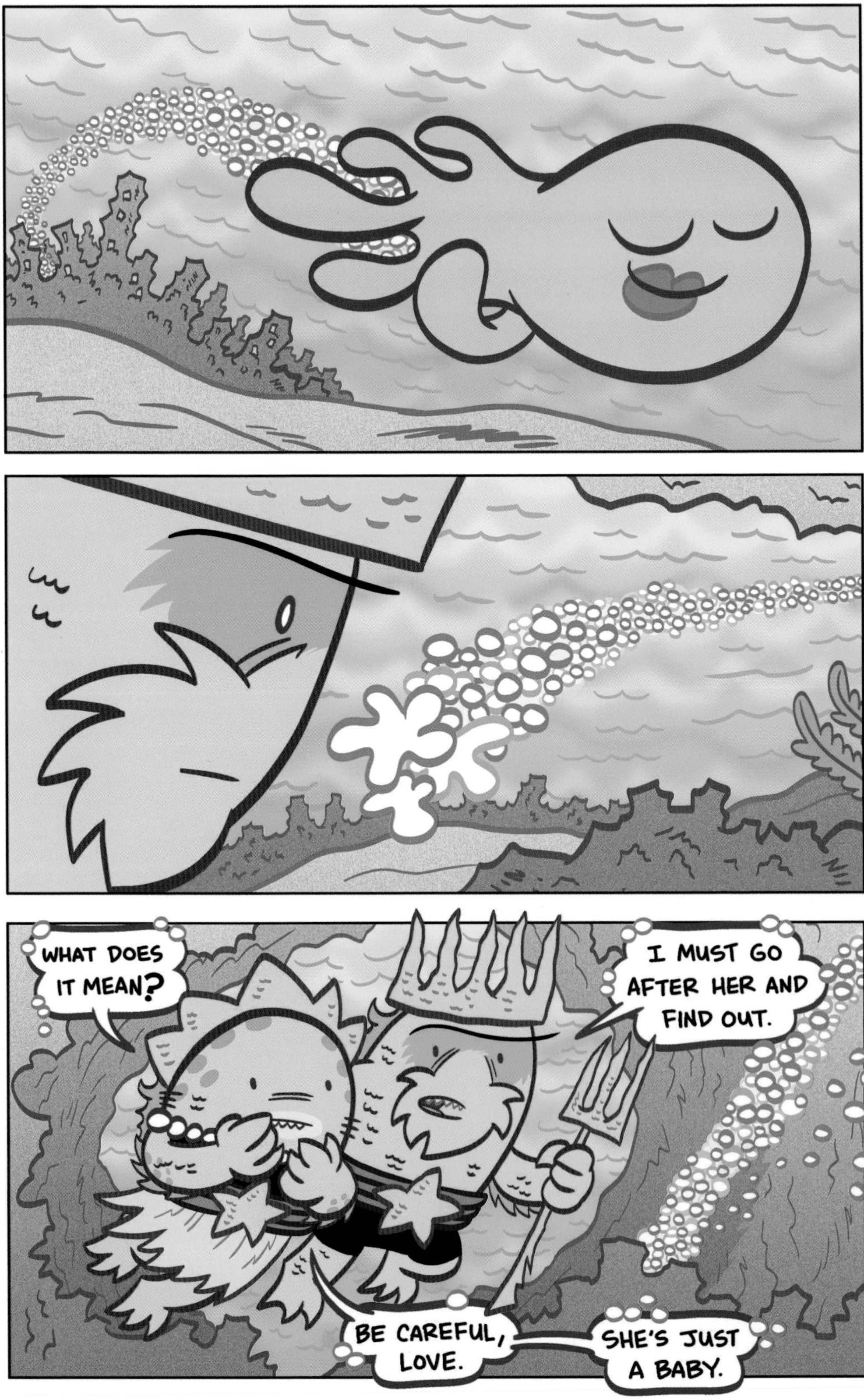
WHAT DOES IT MEAN?
I MUST GO AFTER HER AND FIND OUT.
BE CAREFUL, LOVE.
SHE'S JUST A BABY.

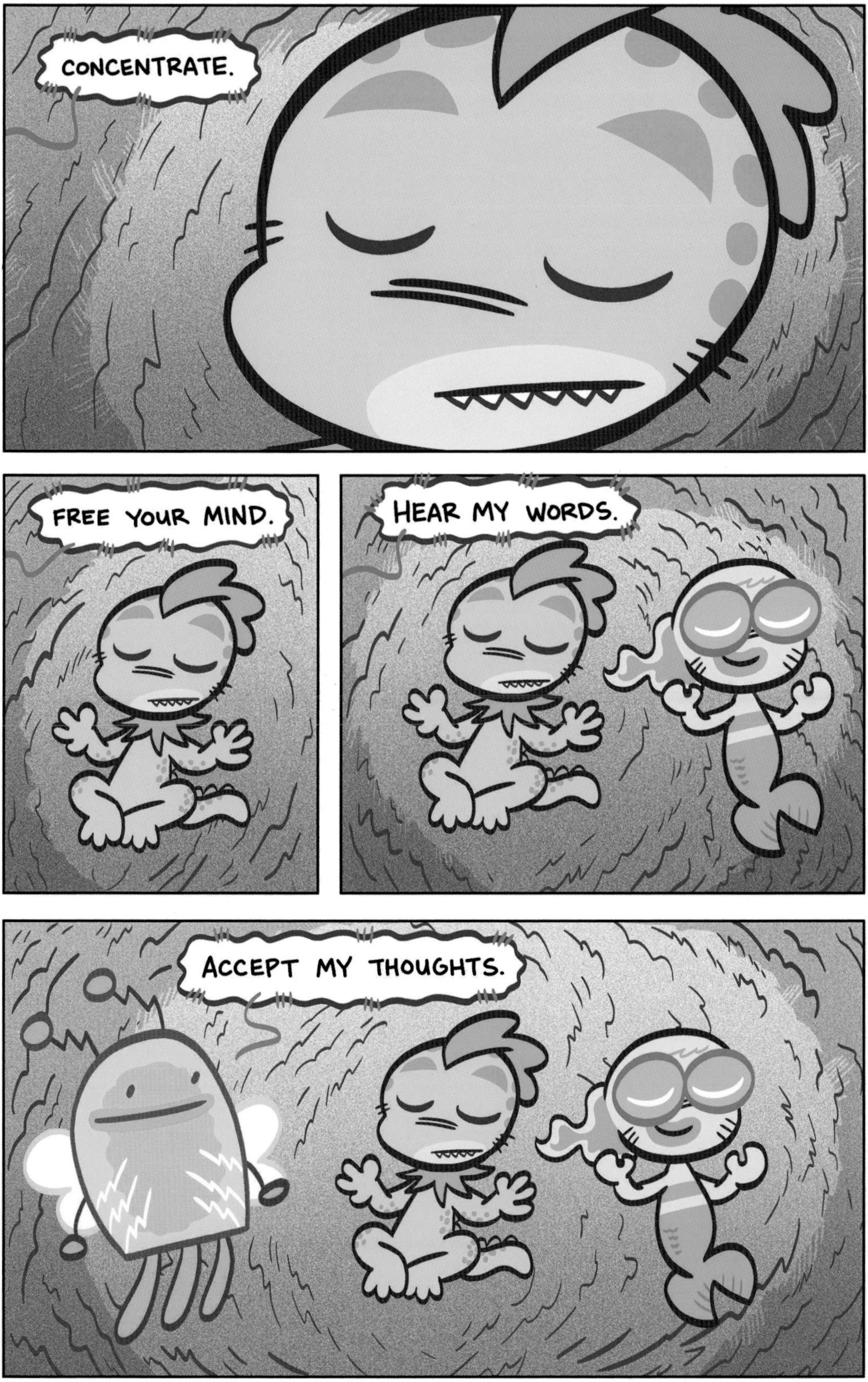
CONCENTRATE.
FREE YOUR MIND.
HEAR MY WORDS.
ACCEPT MY THOUGHTS.

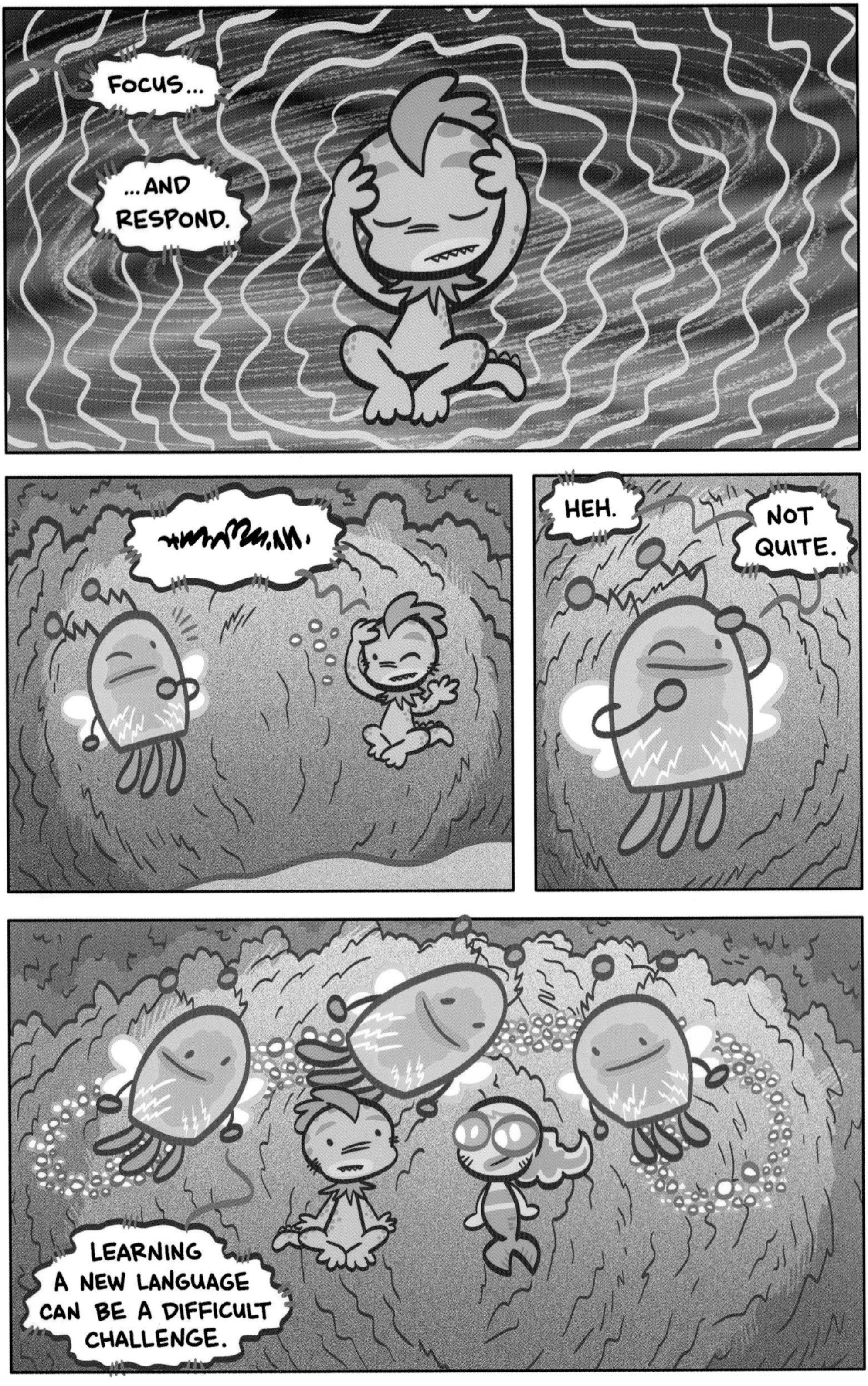
FOCUS...
...AND RESPOND.
HEH.
NOT QUITE.
LEARNING A NEW LANGUAGE CAN BE A DIFFICULT CHALLENGE.

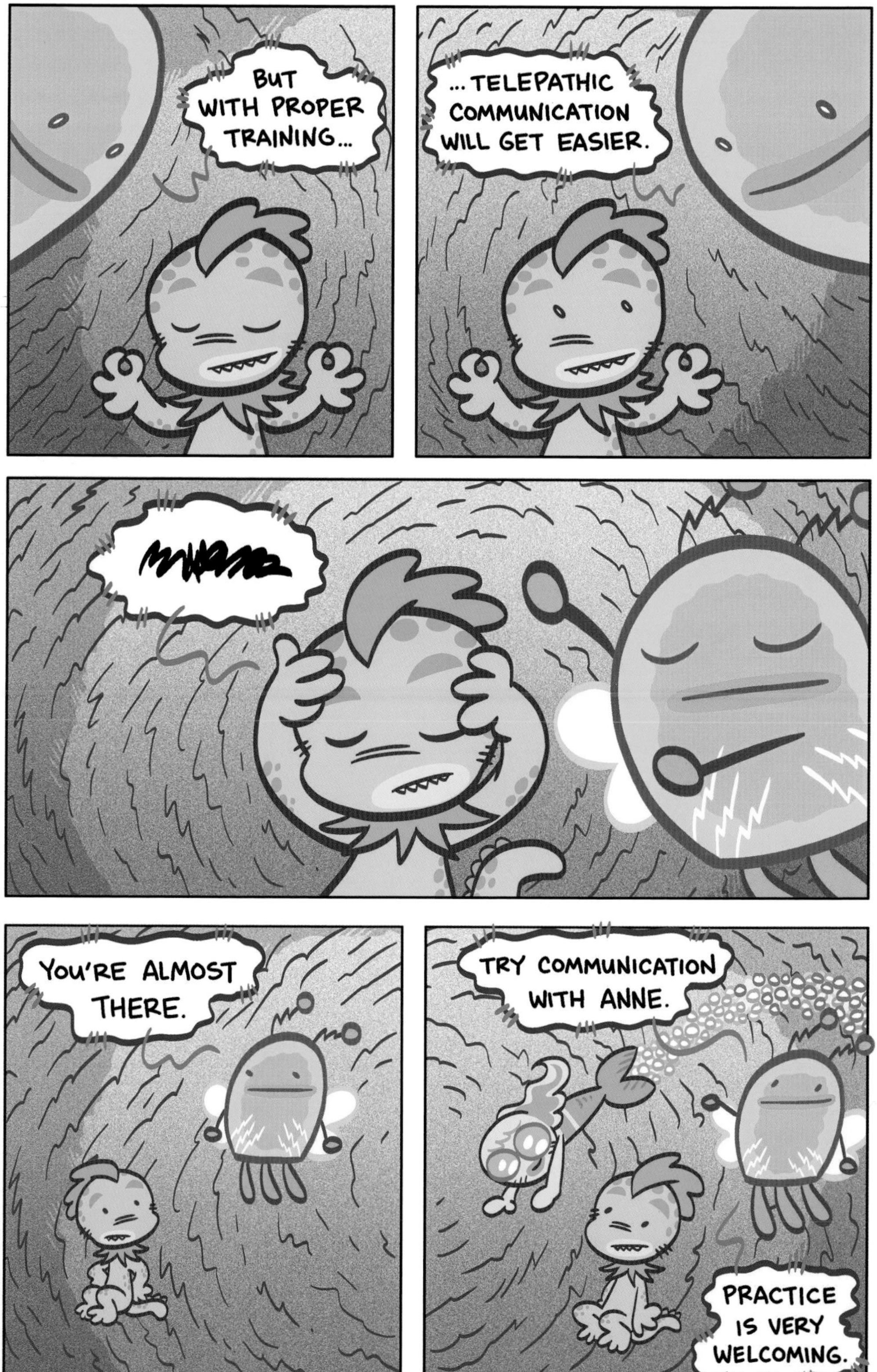
BUT WITH PROPER TRAINING...
...TELEPATHIC COMMUNICATION WILL GET EASIER.
YOU'RE ALMOST THERE.
TRY COMMUNICATION WITH ANNE.
PRACTICE IS VERY WELCOMING.

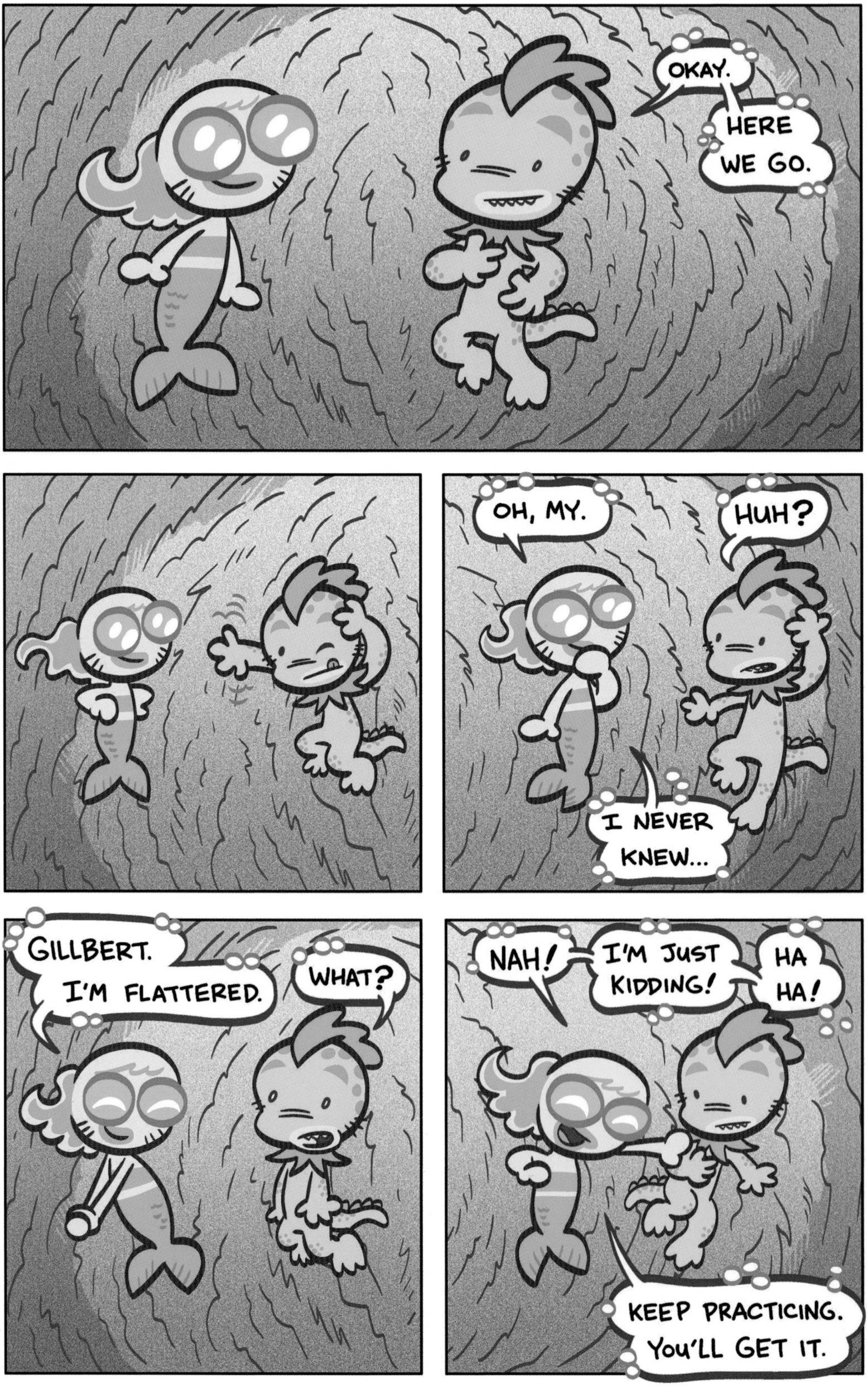
OKAY.
HERE WE GO.
OH, MY.
HUH?
I NEVER KNEW...
GILLBERT. I'M FLATTERED.
WHAT?
NAH!
I'M JUST KIDDING!
HA HA!
KEEP PRACTICING. YOU'LL GET IT.

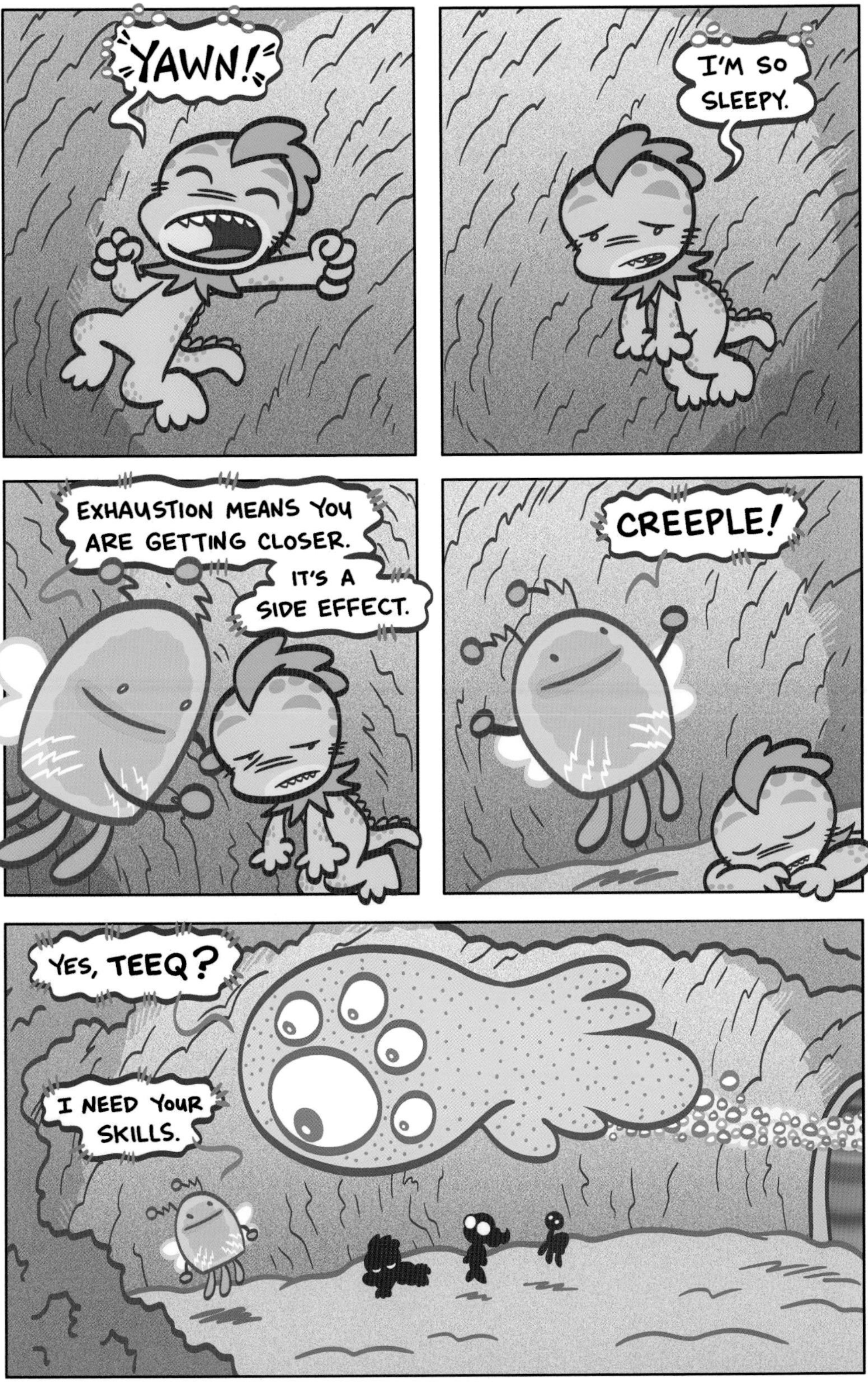
YAWN!
I'M SO SLEEPY.
EXHAUSTION MEANS YOU ARE GETTING CLOSER.
IT'S A SIDE EFFECT.
CREEPLE!
YES, TEEQ?
I NEED YOUR SKILLS.

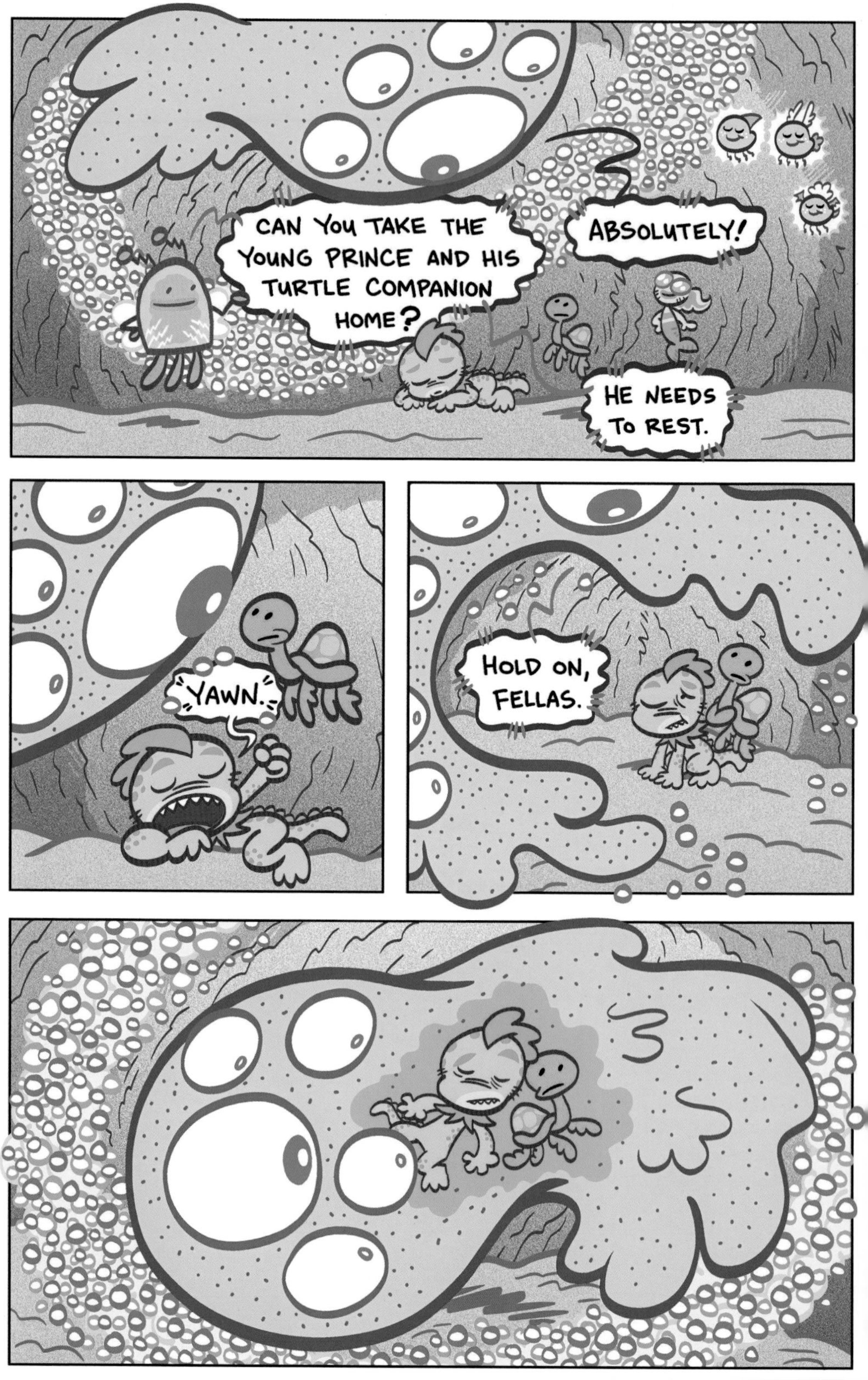
CAN YOU TAKE THE YOUNG PRINCE AND HIS TURTLE COMPANION HOME?
ABSOLUTELY!
HE NEEDS TO REST.
YAWN.
HOLD ON, FELLAS.

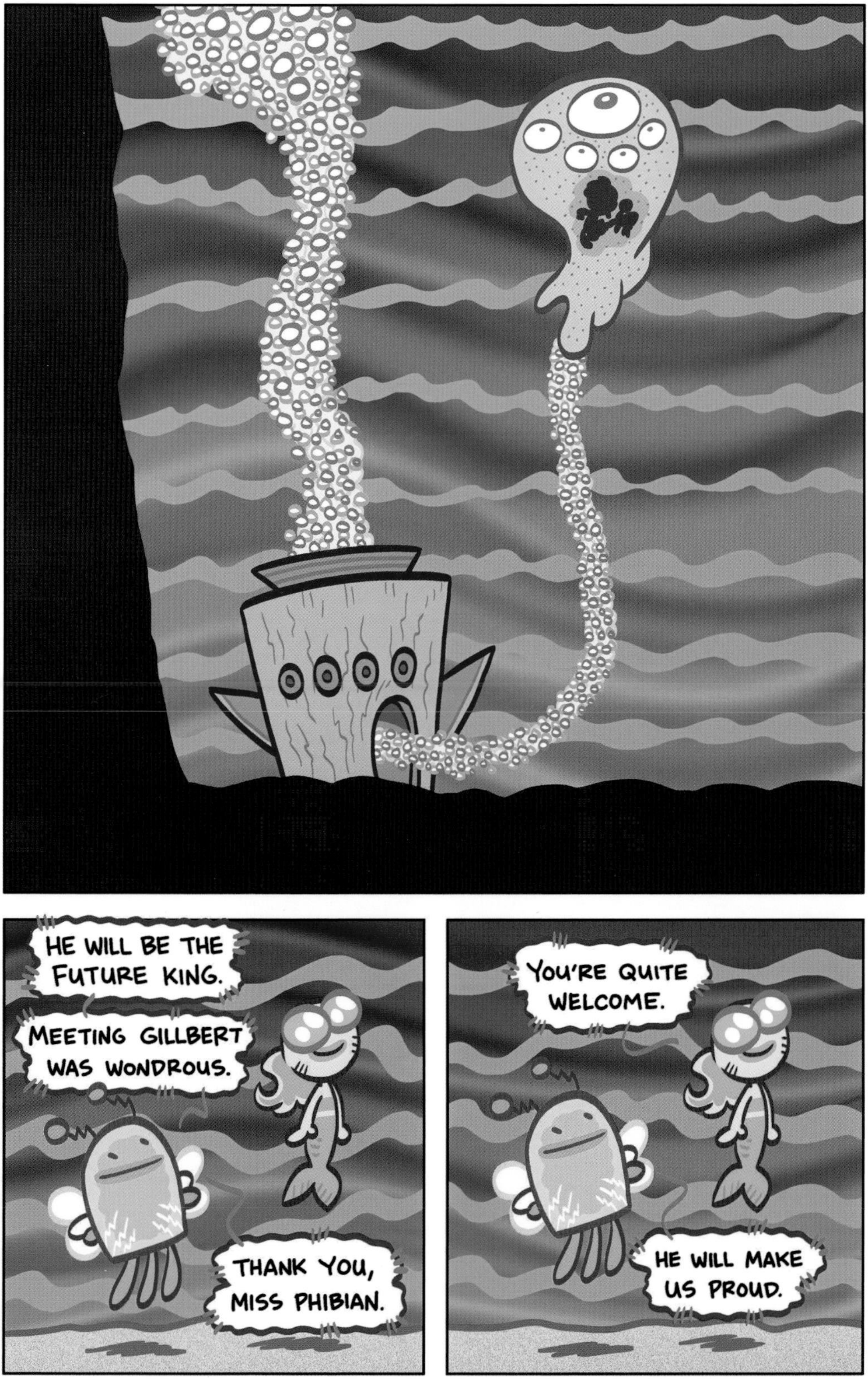
HE WILL BE THE FUTURE KING.
MEETING GILLBERT WAS WONDROUS.
THANK YOU, MISS PHIBIAN.
YOU'RE QUITE WELCOME.
HE WILL MAKE US PROUD.

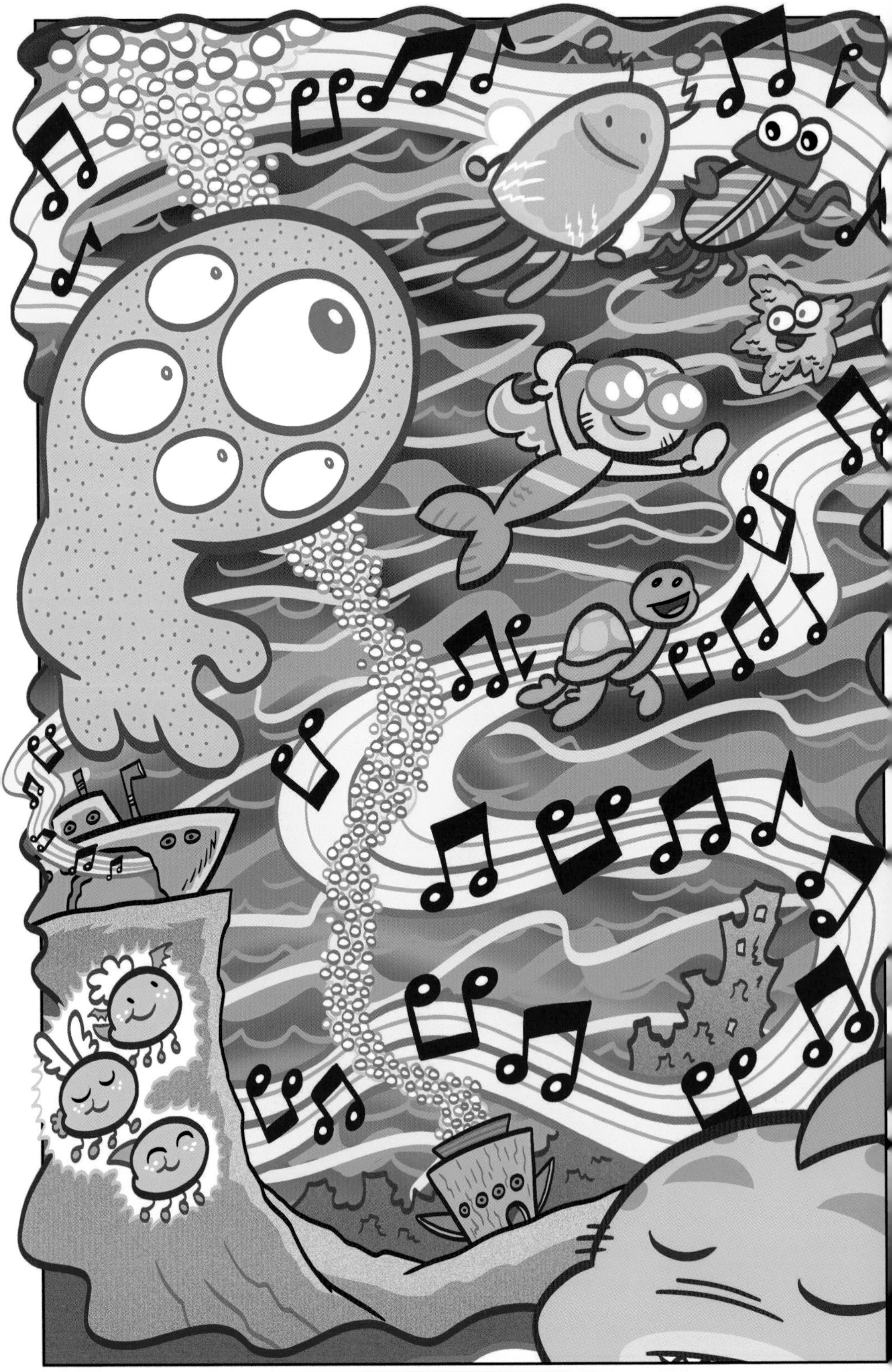

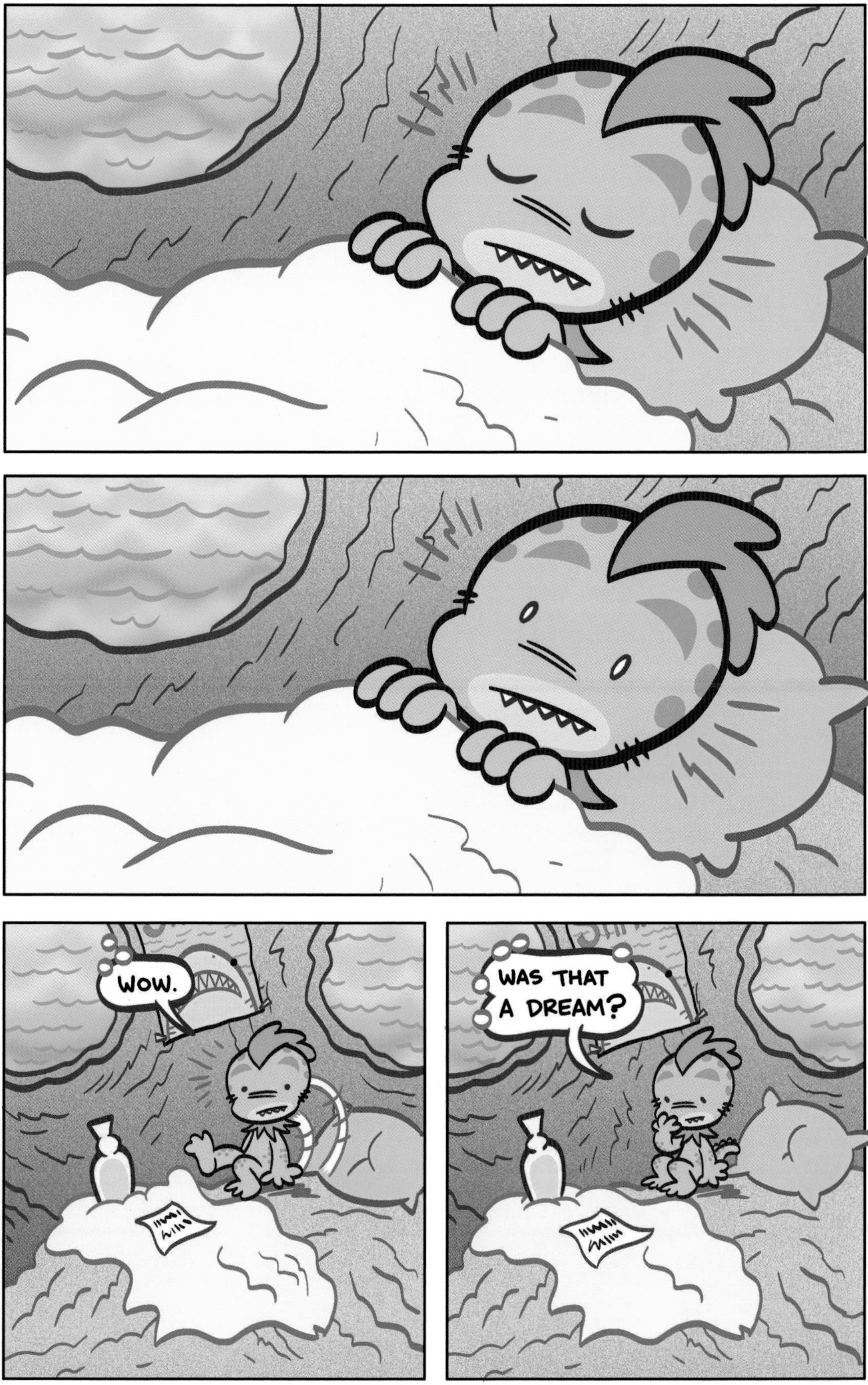
WOW.
WAS THAT A DREAM?

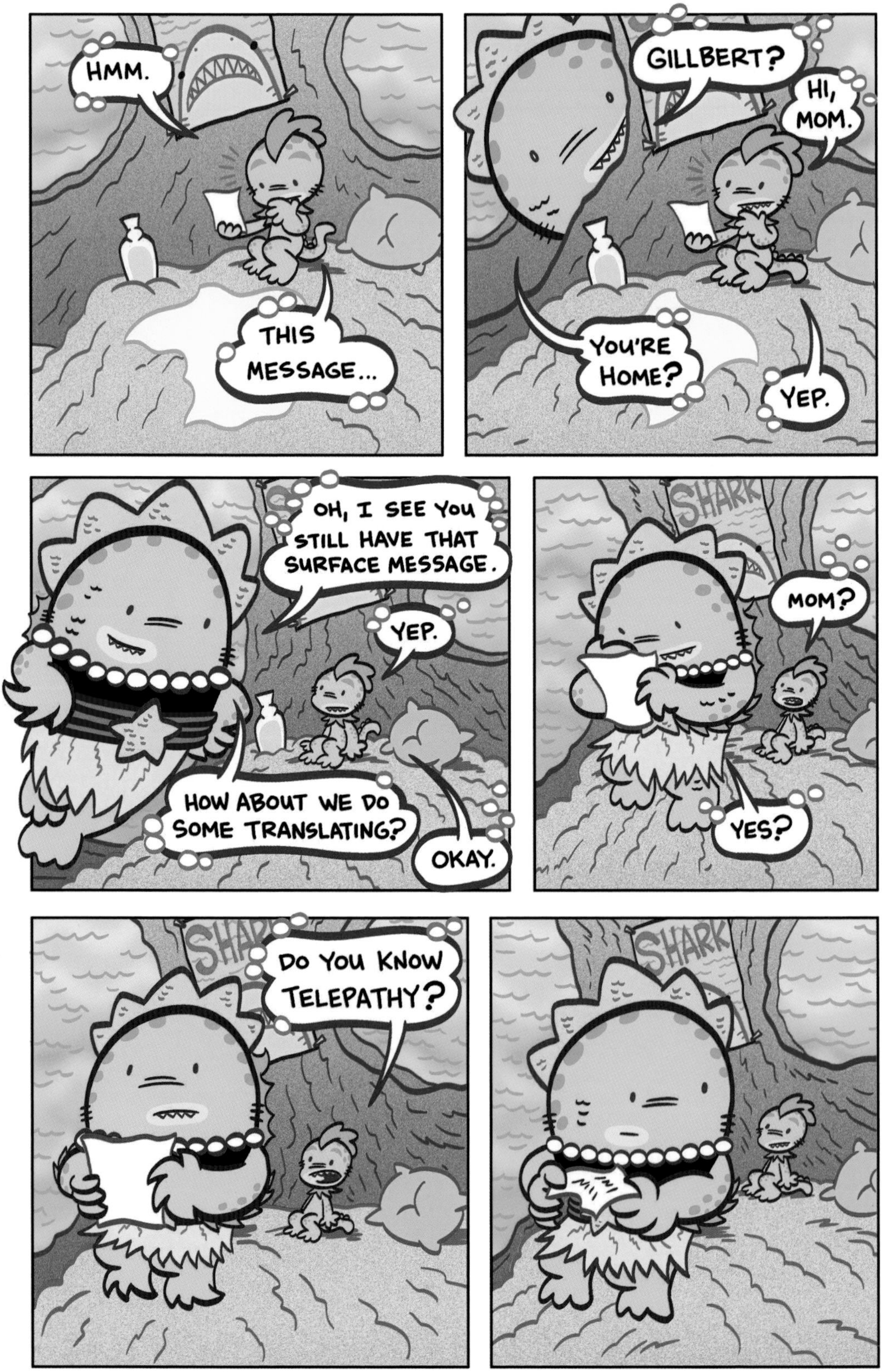
HMM.
THIS MESSAGE...
GILLBERT?
HI, MOM.
YOU'RE HOME?
YEP.
OH, I SEE YOU STILL HAVE THAT SURFACE MESSAGE.
YEP.
HOW ABOUT WE DO SOME TRANSLATING?
OKAY.
SHARK
MOM?
YES?
SHARK
DO YOU KNOW TELEPATHY?
SHARK

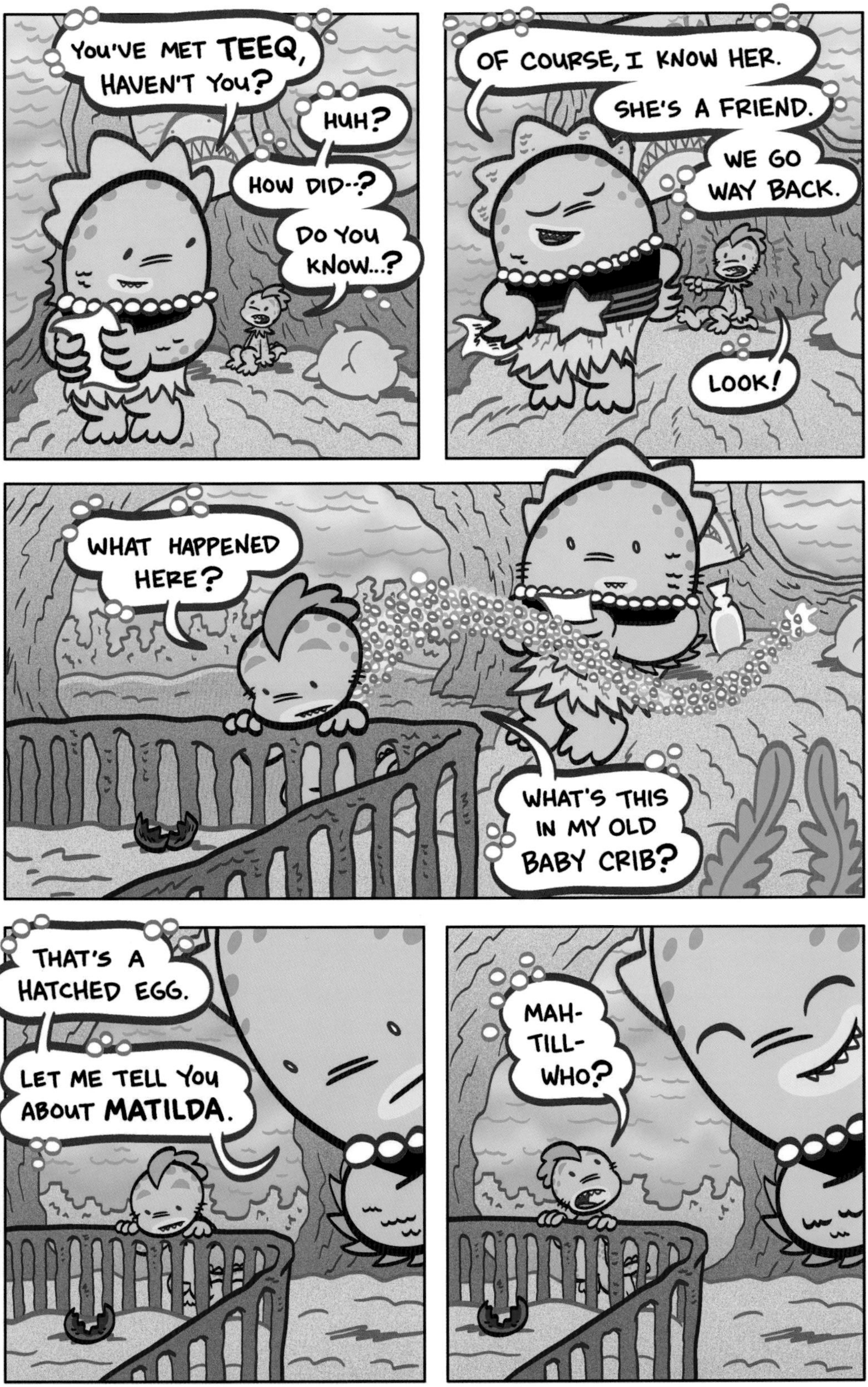

YOU'VE MET TEEQ, HAVEN'T YOU?
HUH?
HOW DID--?
DO YOU KNOW...?
OF COURSE, I KNOW HER.
SHE'S A FRIEND.
WE GO WAY BACK.
LOOK!
WHAT HAPPENED HERE?
WHAT'S THIS IN MY OLD BABY CRIB?
THAT'S A HATCHED EGG.
LET ME TELL YOU ABOUT MATILDA.
MAH-TILL-WHO?

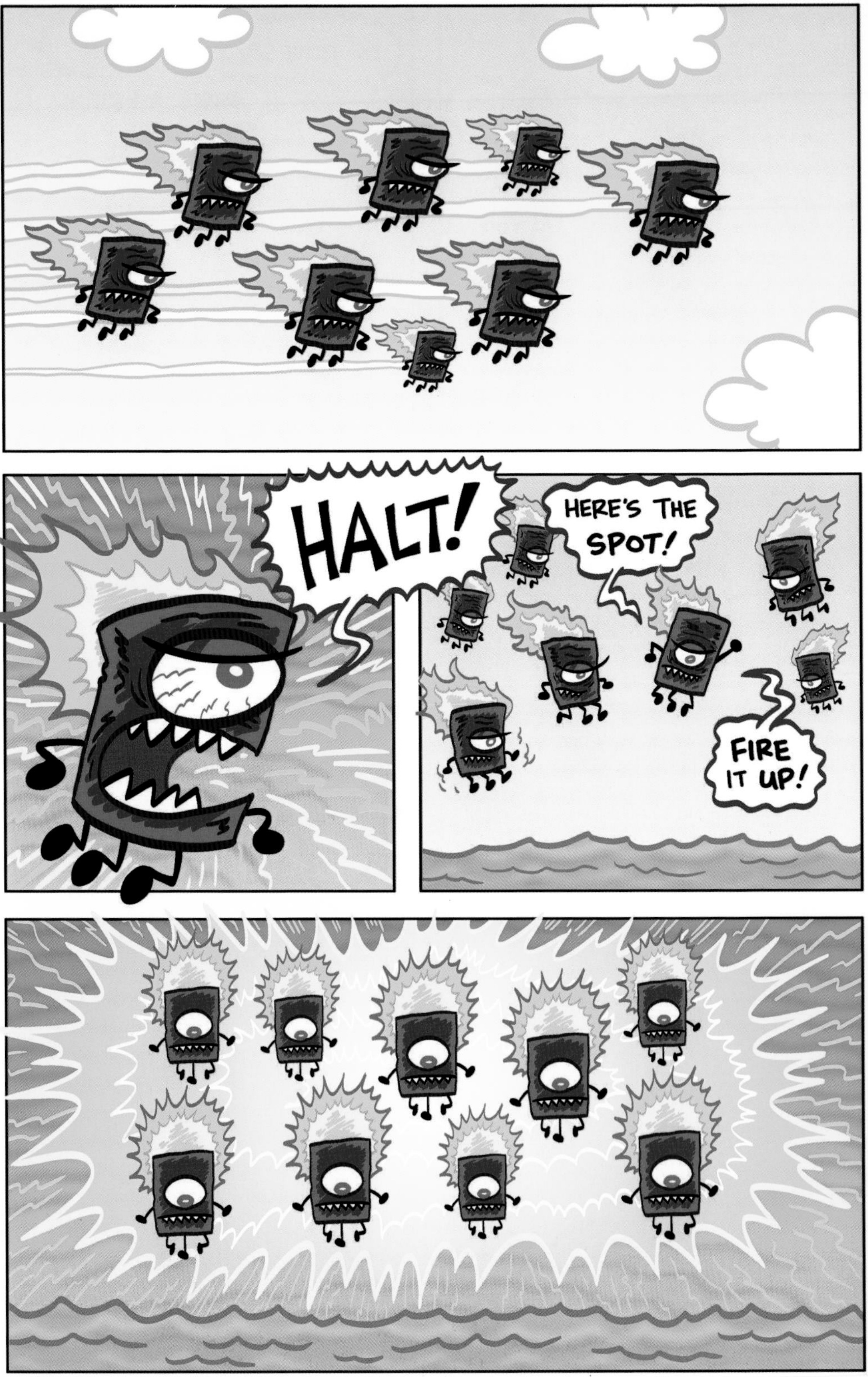
HALT!
HERE'S THE SPOT!
FIRE IT UP!

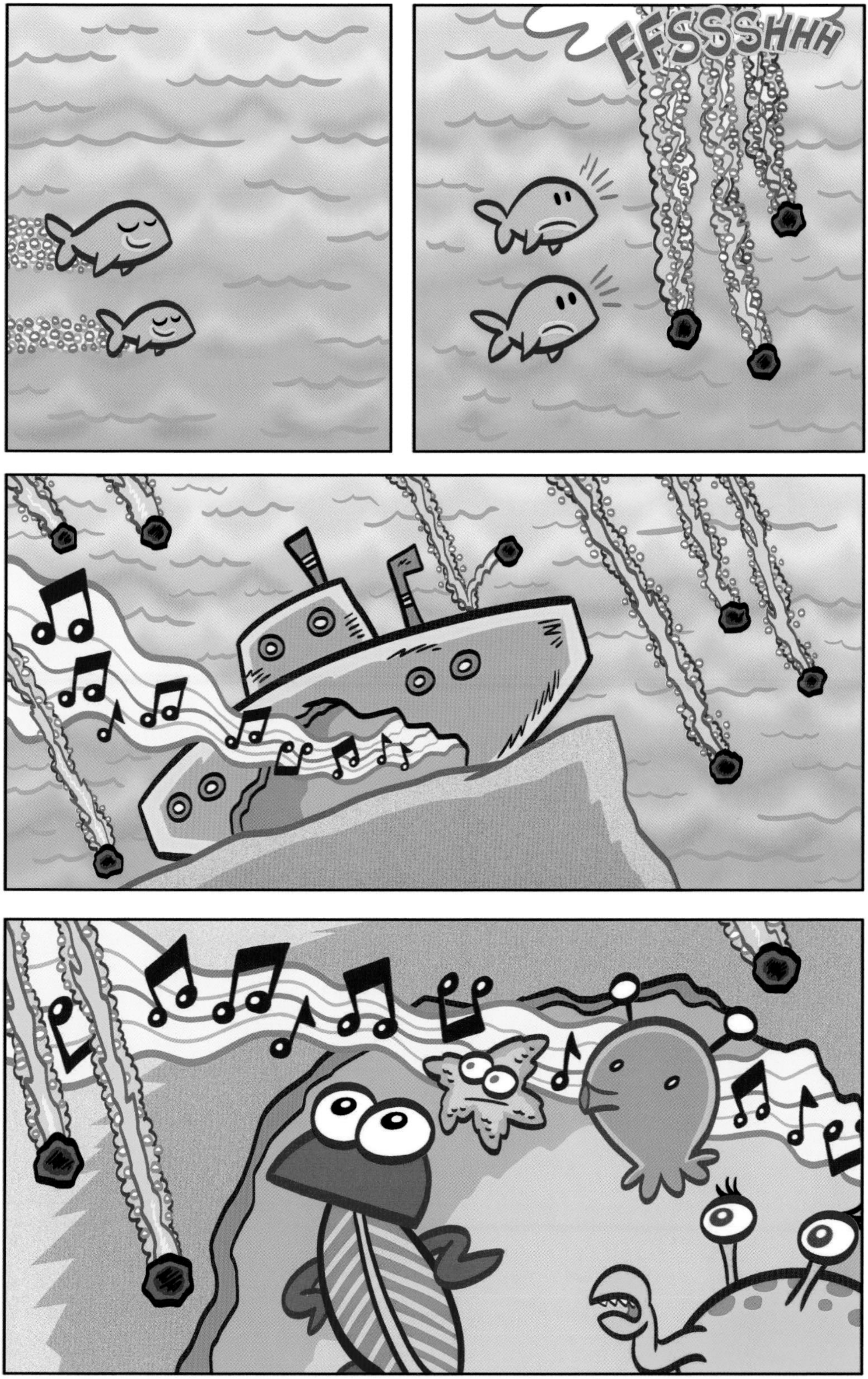
FFSSSHHH

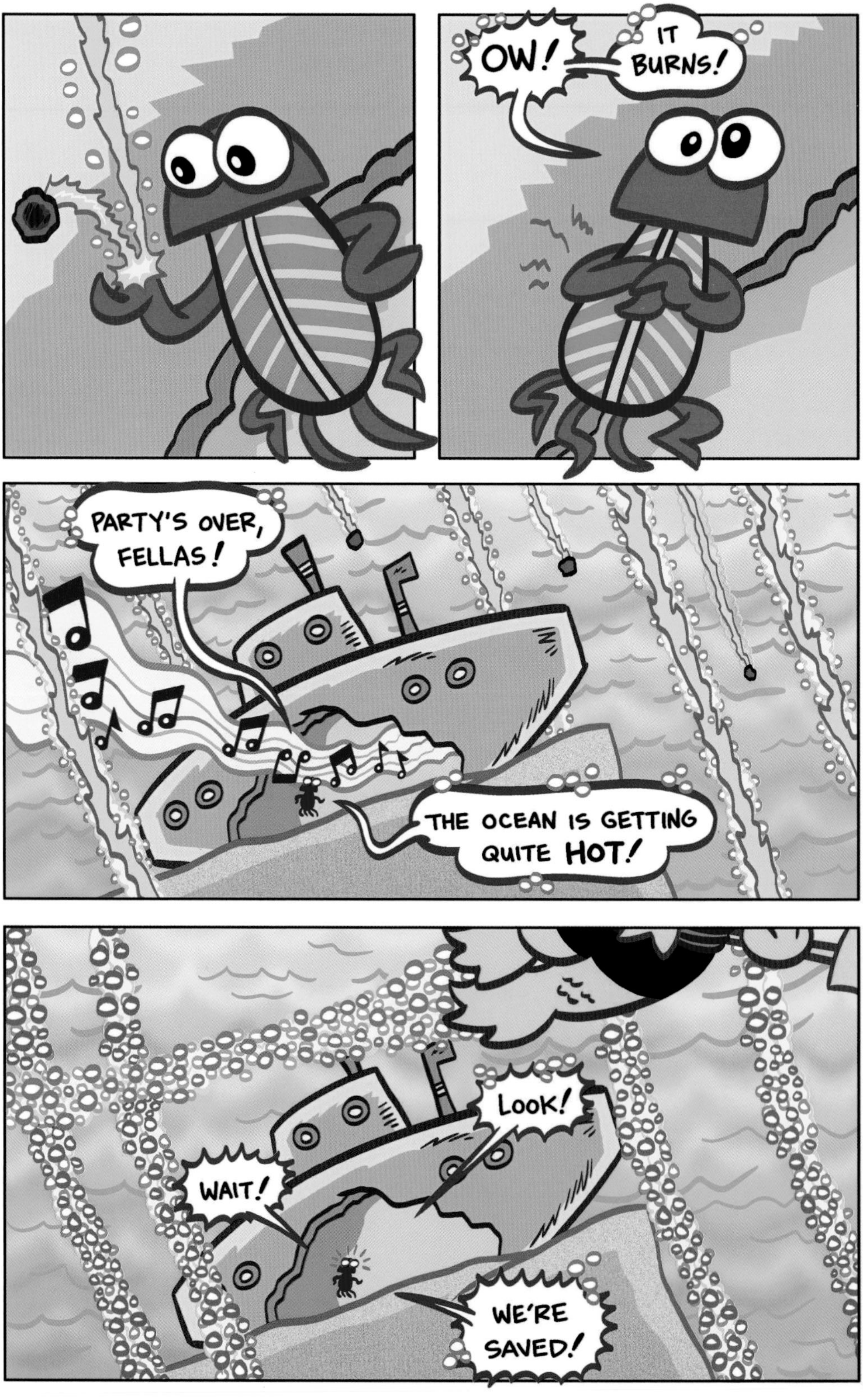
OW!
IT BURNS!
PARTY'S OVER, FELLAS!
THE OCEAN IS GETTING QUITE HOT!
LOOK!
WAIT!
WE'RE SAVED!

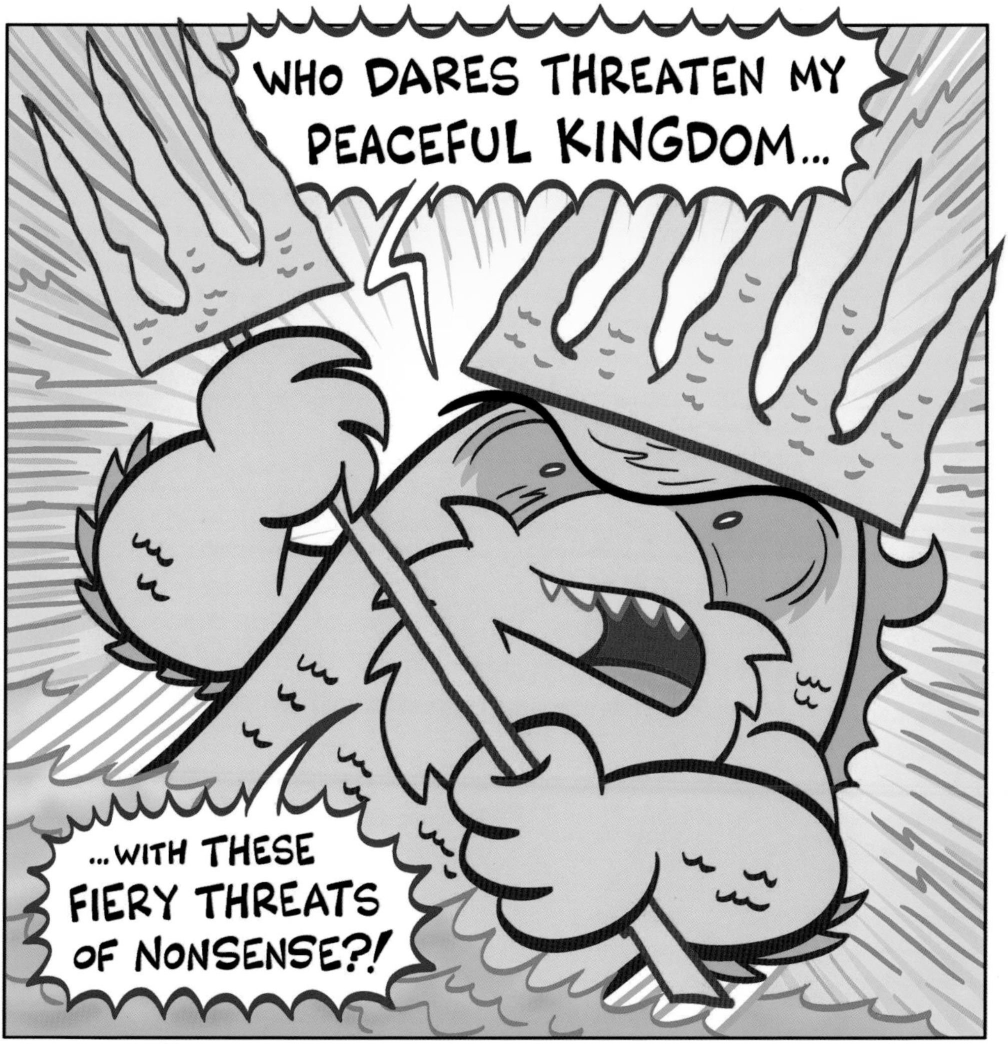
WHO DARES THREATEN MY PEACEFUL KINGDOM...
...WITH THESE FIERY THREATS OF NONSENSE?!

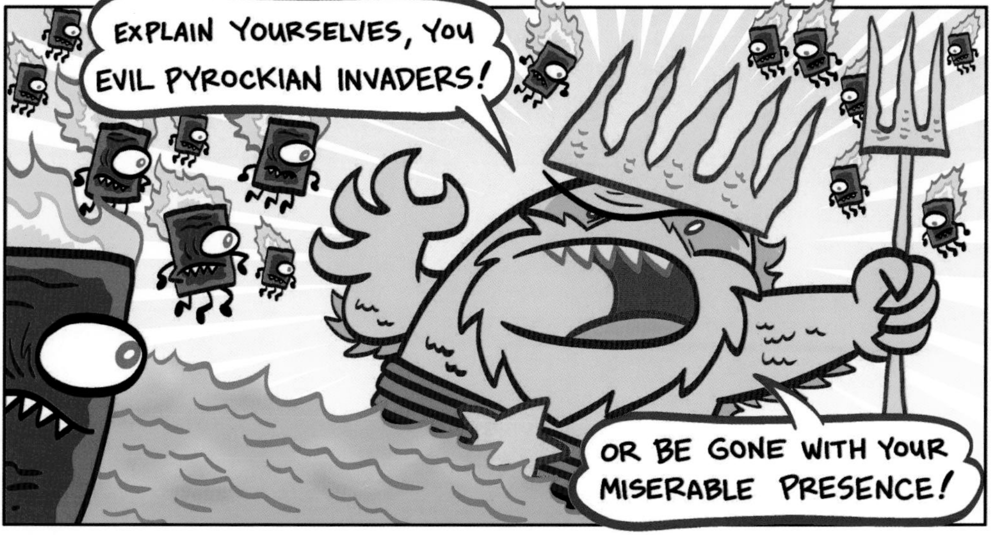
EXPLAIN YOURSELVES, YOU EVIL PYROCKIAN INVADERS!
OR BE GONE WITH YOUR MISERABLE PRESENCE!

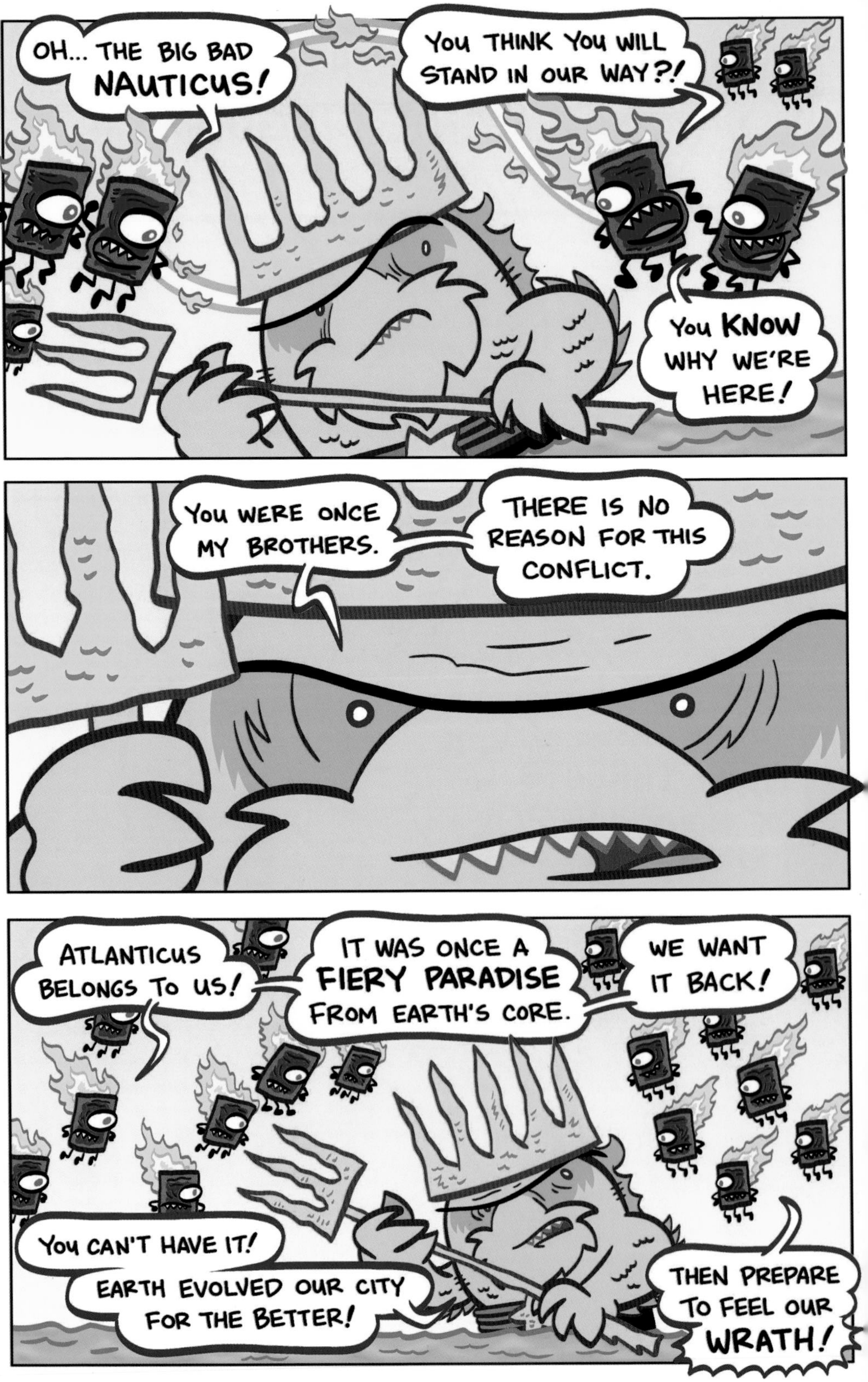
OH... THE BIG BAD NAUTICUS!
YOU THINK YOU WILL STAND IN OUR WAY?!
YOU KNOW WHY WE'RE HERE!
YOU WERE ONCE MY BROTHERS.
THERE IS NO REASON FOR THIS CONFLICT.
ATLANTICUS BELONGS TO US!
IT WAS ONCE A FIERY PARADISE FROM EARTH'S CORE.
WE WANT IT BACK!
YOU CAN'T HAVE IT!
EARTH EVOLVED OUR CITY FOR THE BETTER!
THEN PREPARE TO FEEL OUR WRATH!

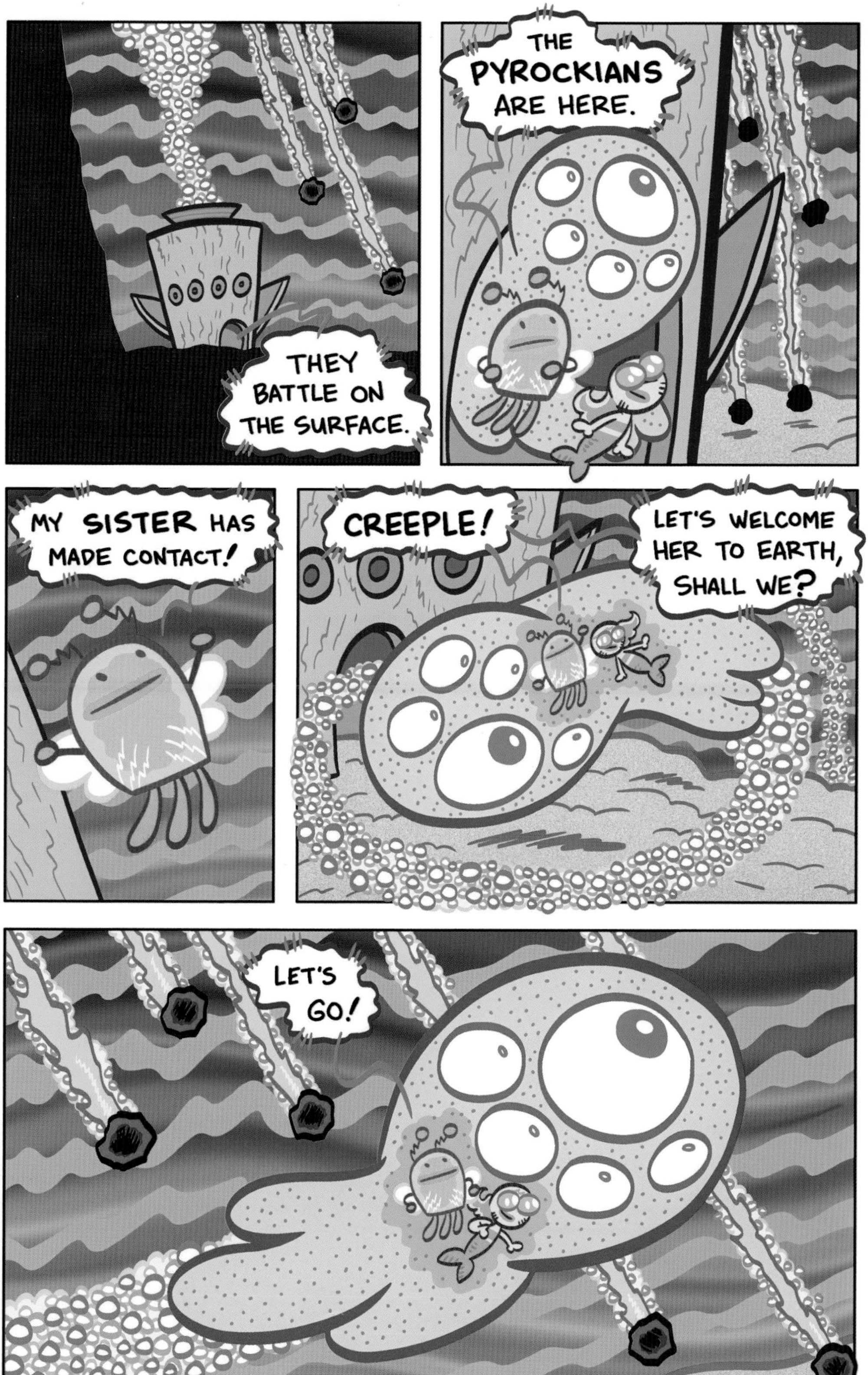
THEY BATTLE ON THE SURFACE.
THE PYROCKIANS ARE HERE.
MY SISTER HAS MADE CONTACT!
CREEPLE!
LET'S WELCOME HER TO EARTH, SHALL WE?
LET'S GO!

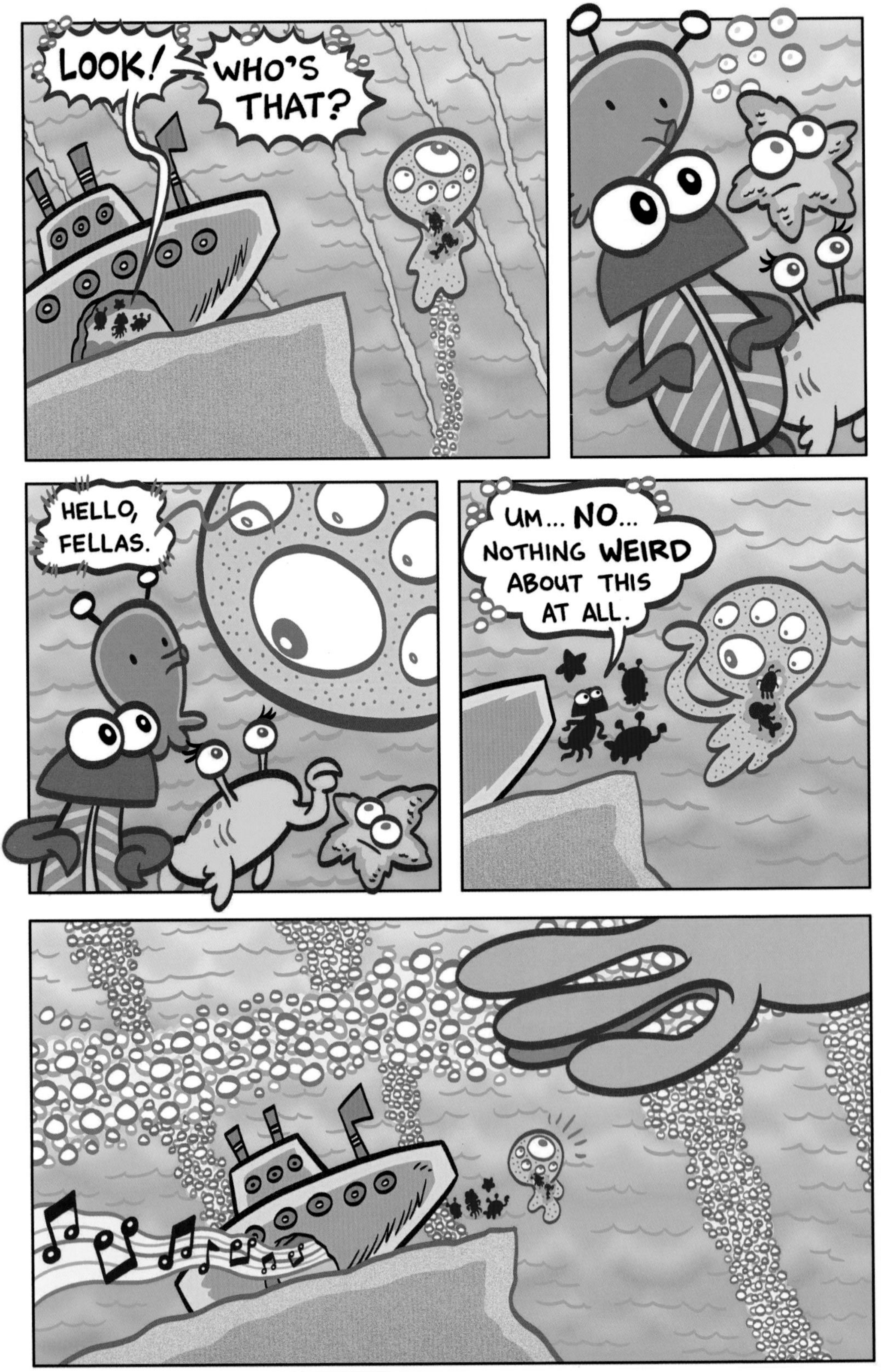
LOOK!
WHO'S THAT?
HELLO, FELLAS.
UM... NO... NOTHING WEIRD ABOUT THIS AT ALL.

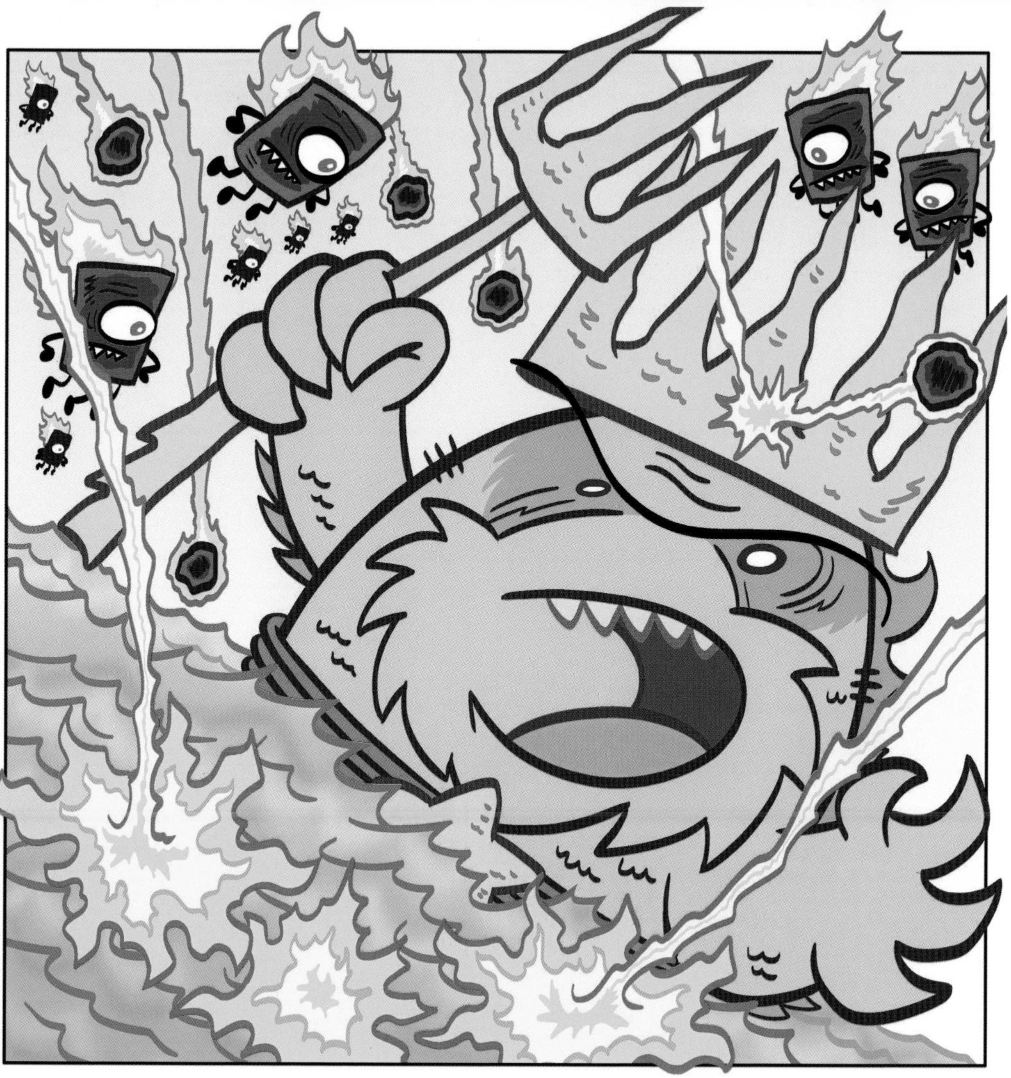

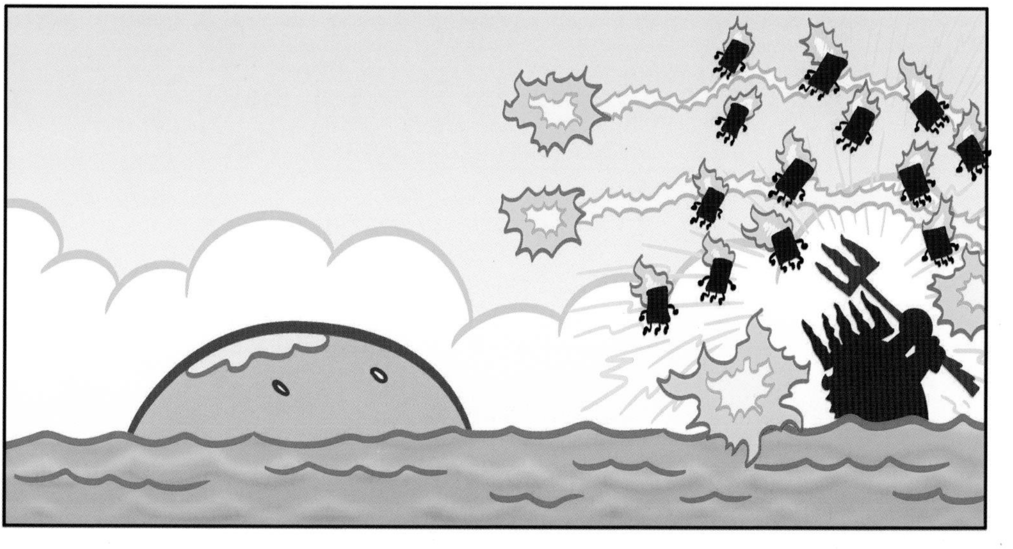

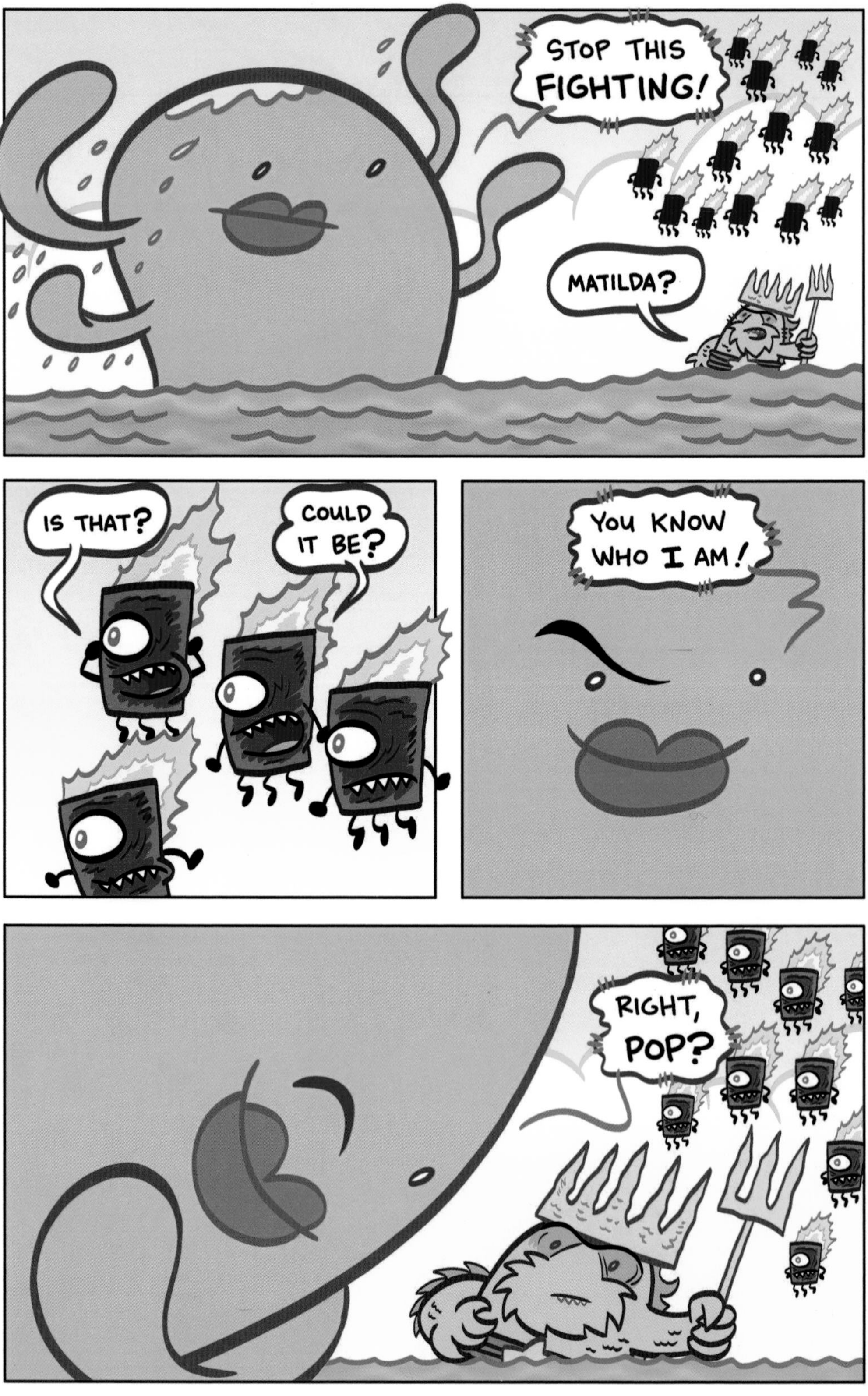
STOP THIS FIGHTING!
MATILDA?
IS THAT?
COULD IT BE?
YOU KNOW WHO I AM!
RIGHT, POP?

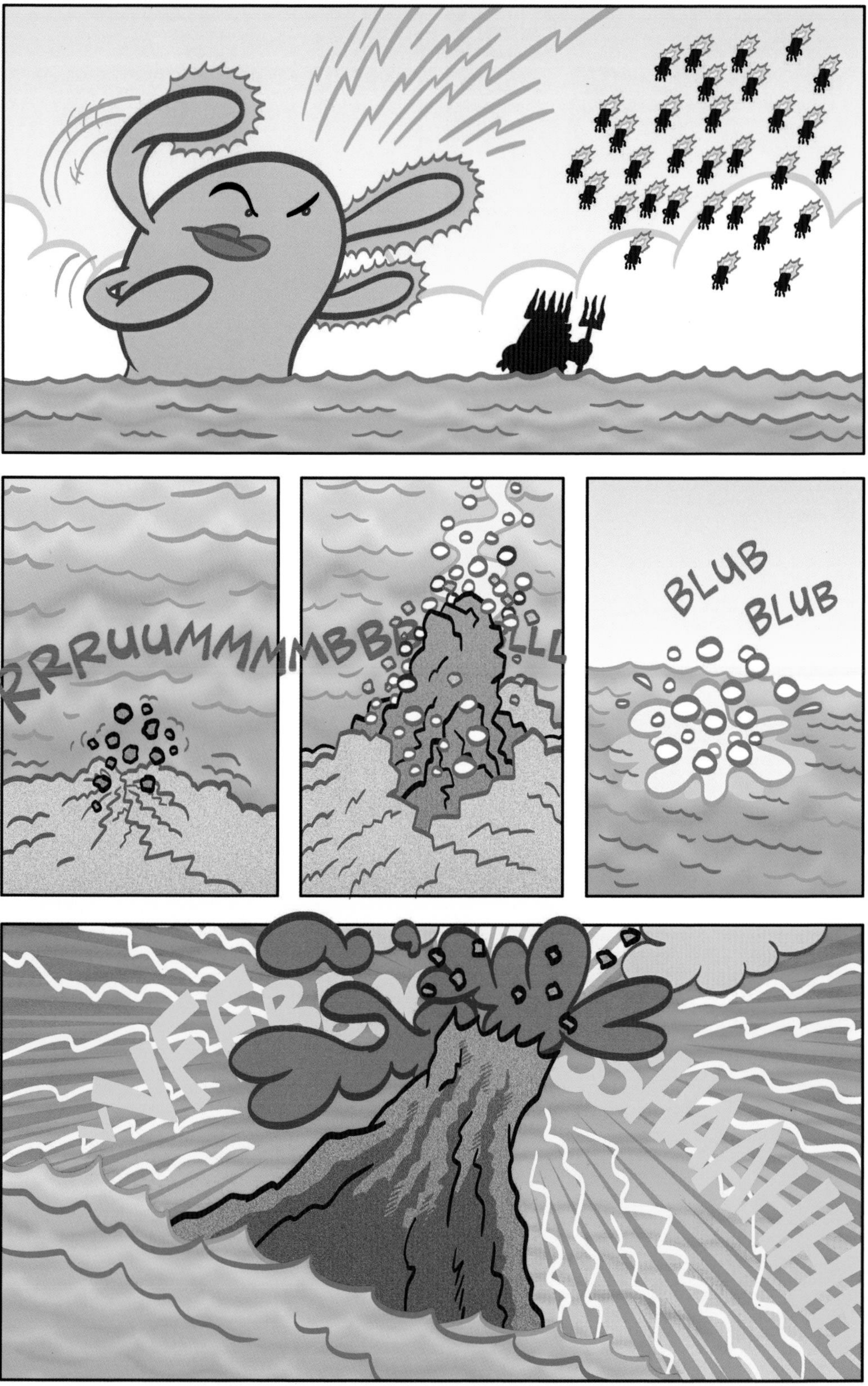
RRRUUMMMMBB
BLUB
BLUB

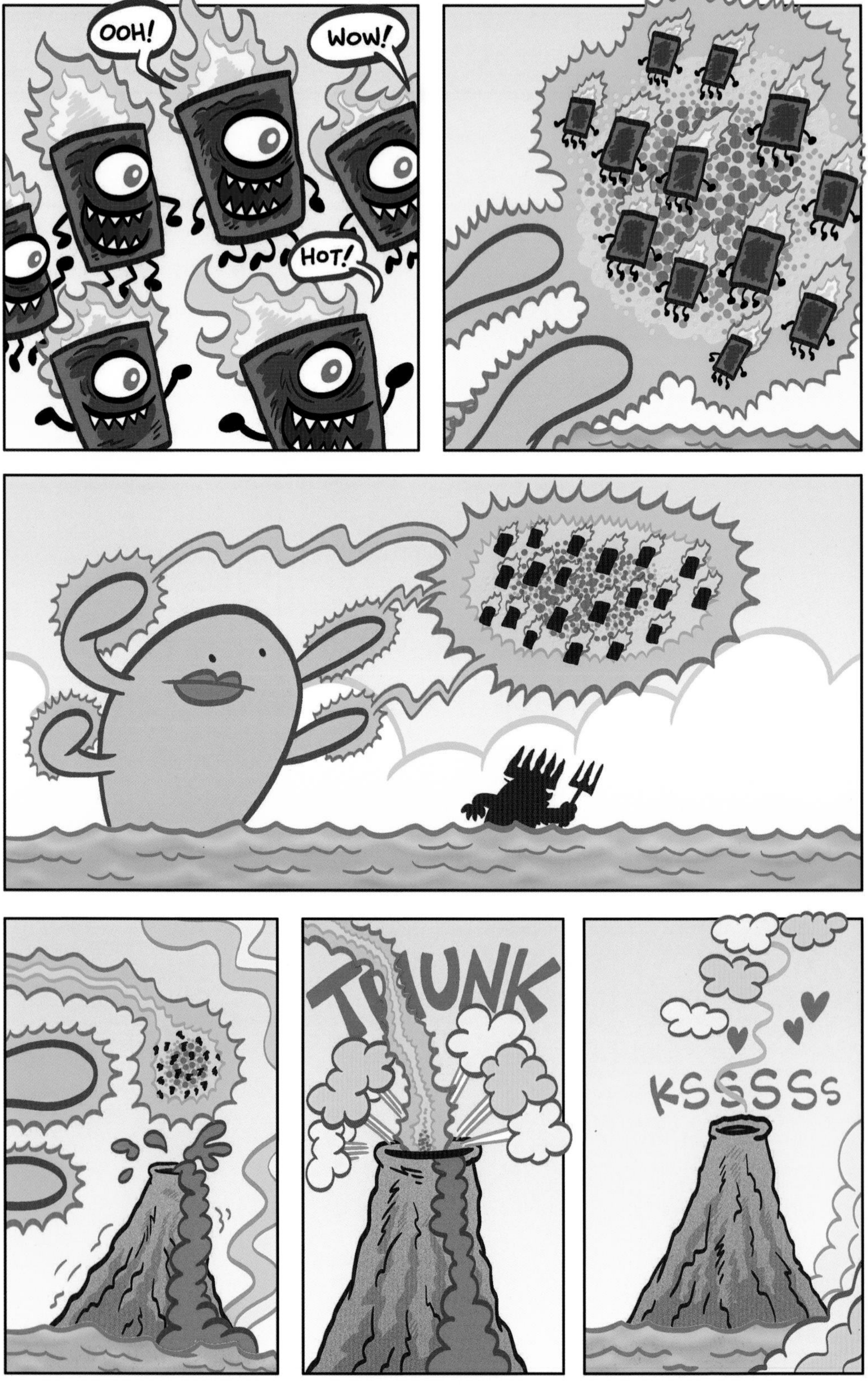
OOH!
WOW!
HOT!
THUNK
KSSSSs

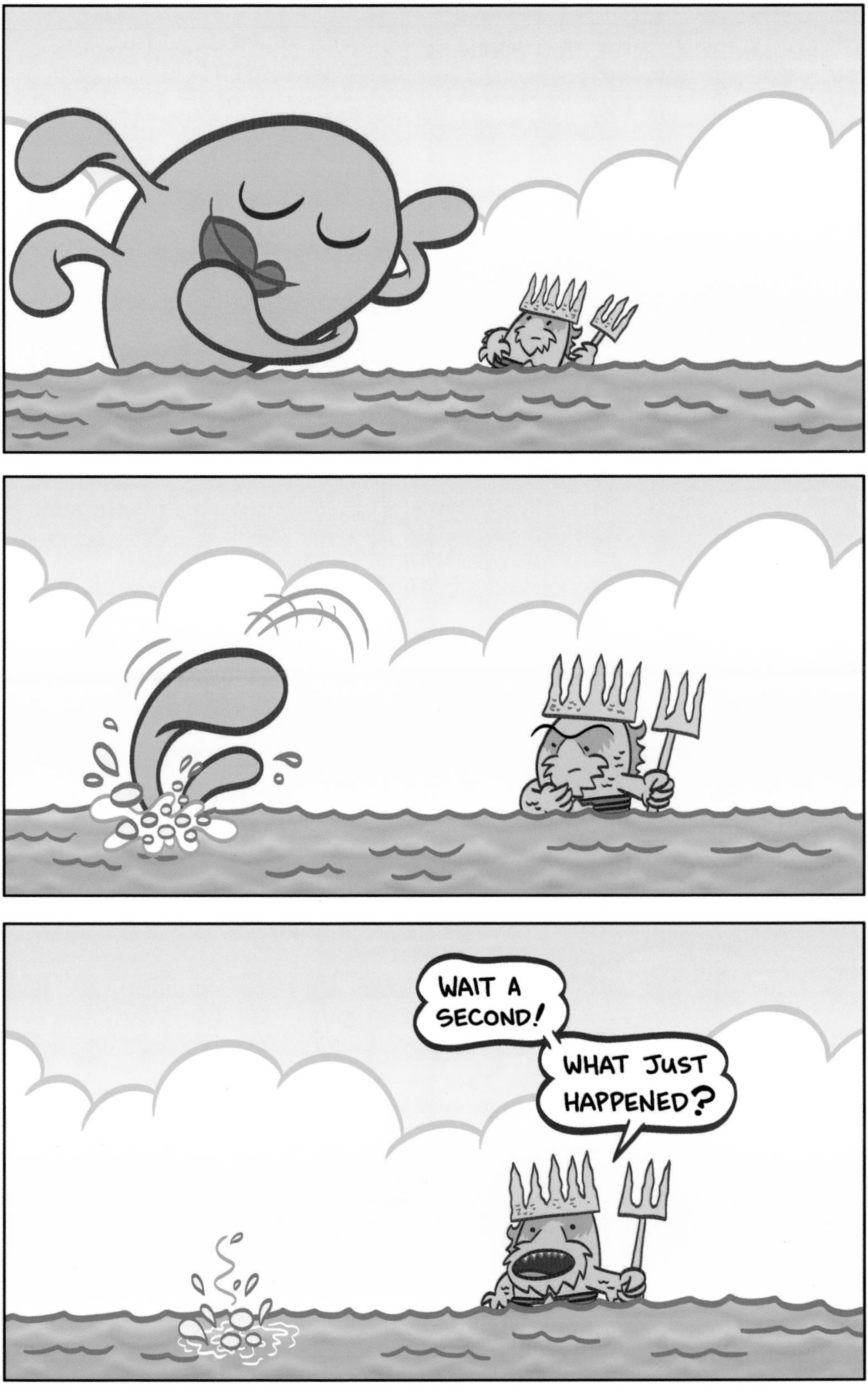
WAIT A SECOND!
WHAT JUST HAPPENED?

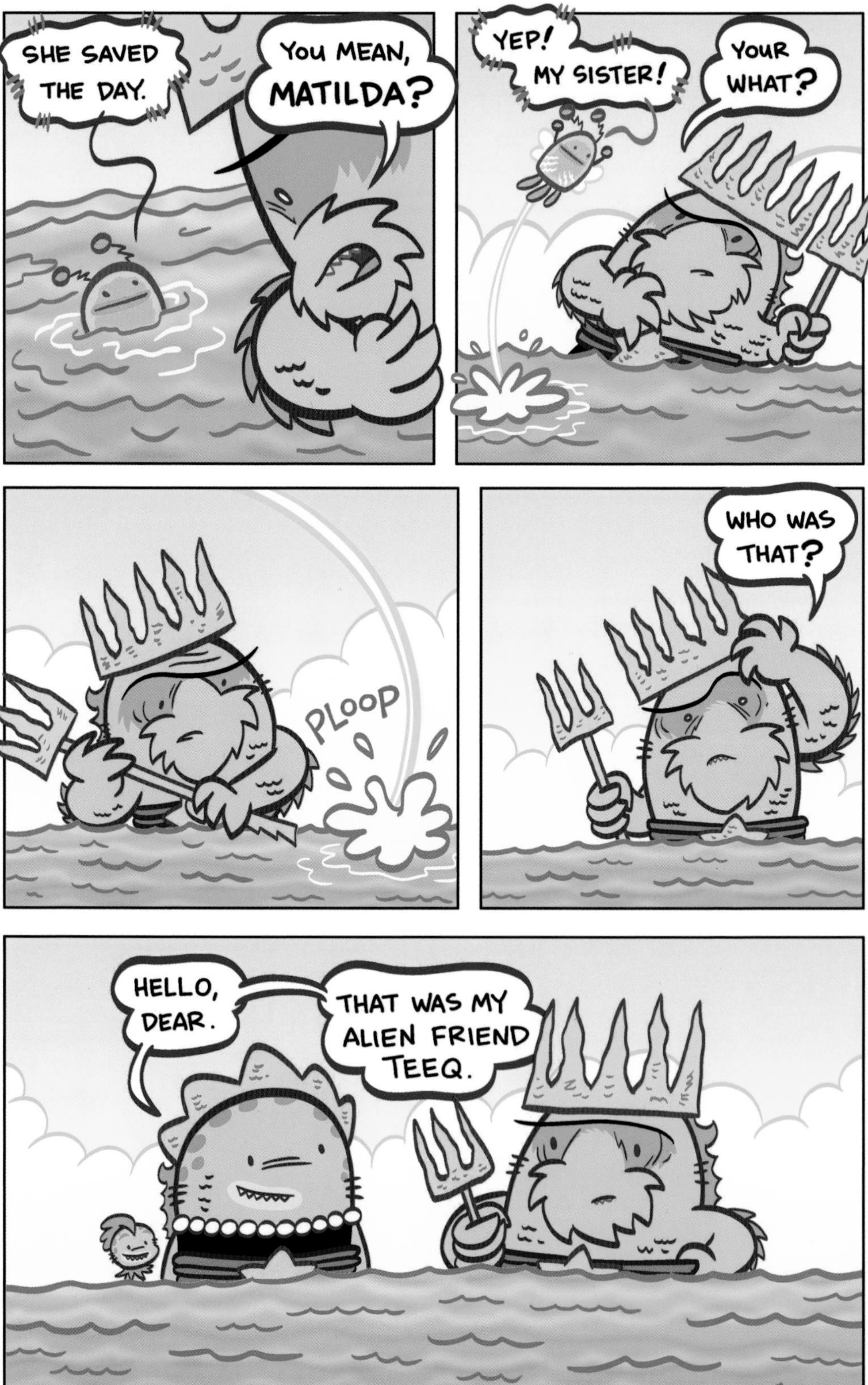
SHE SAVED THE DAY.
YOU MEAN, MATILDA?
YEP! MY SISTER!
YOUR WHAT?
PLOOP
WHO WAS THAT?
HELLO, DEAR.
THAT WAS MY ALIEN FRIEND TEEQ.

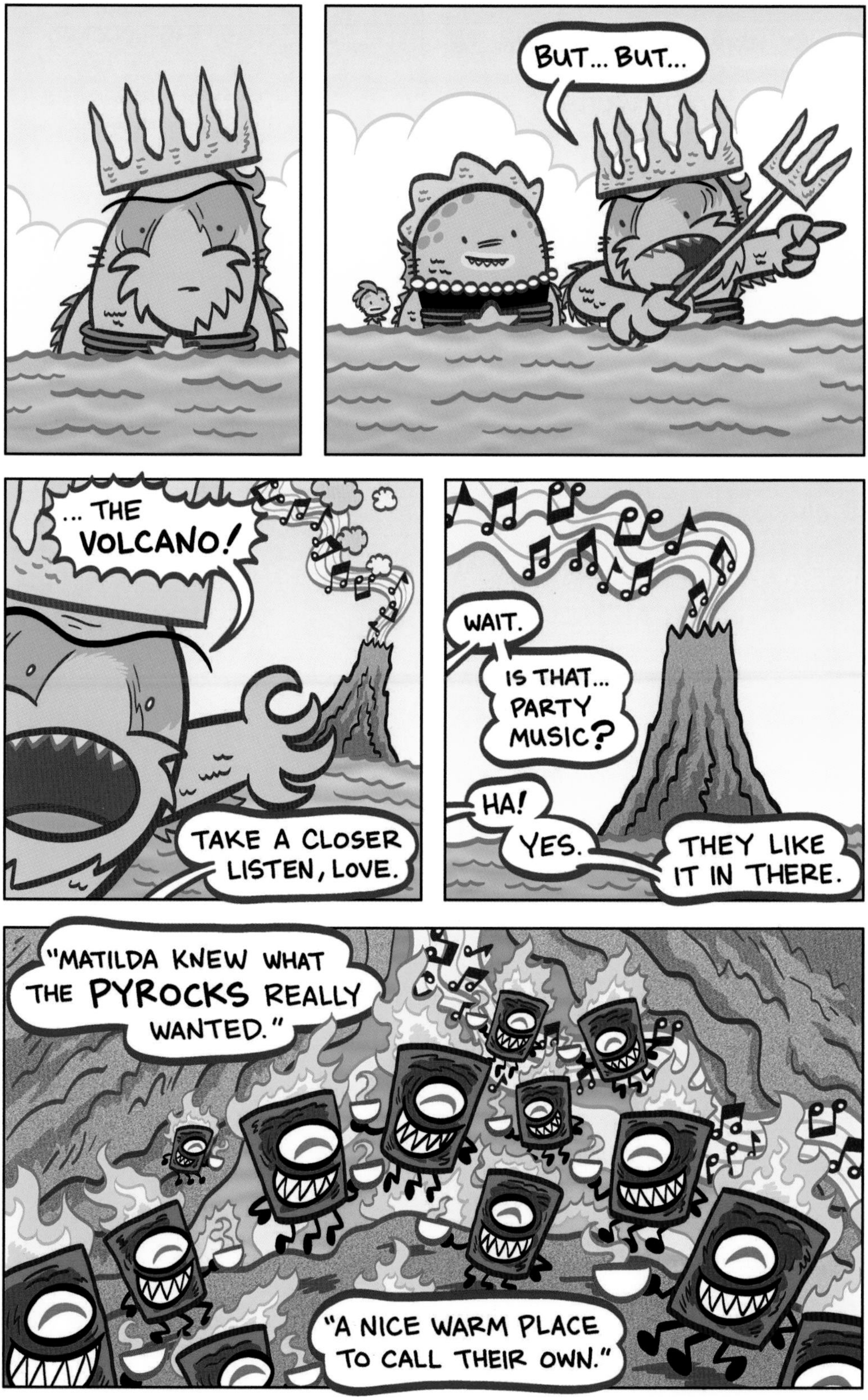
BUT... BUT...
... THE VOLCANO!
TAKE A CLOSER LISTEN, LOVE.
WAIT.
IS THAT... PARTY MUSIC?
HA!
YES.
THEY LIKE IT IN THERE.
"MATILDA KNEW WHAT THE PYROCKS REALLY WANTED."
"A NICE WARM PLACE TO CALL THEIR OWN."

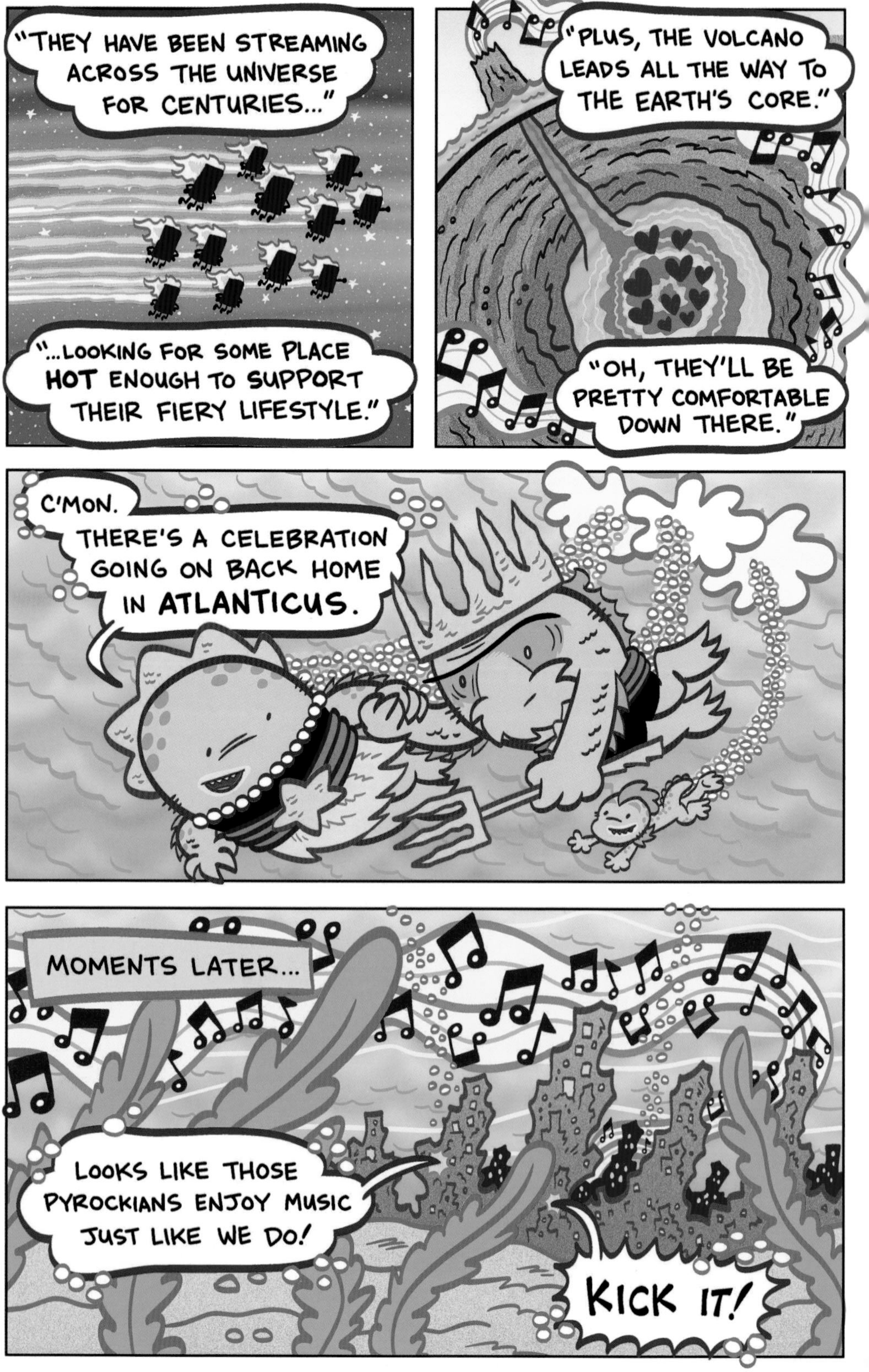
"THEY HAVE BEEN STREAMING ACROSS THE UNIVERSE FOR CENTURIES..."
"...LOOKING FOR SOME PLACE **HOT** ENOUGH TO SUPPORT THEIR FIERY LIFESTYLE."
"PLUS, THE VOLCANO LEADS ALL THE WAY TO THE EARTH'S CORE."
"OH, THEY'LL BE PRETTY COMFORTABLE DOWN THERE."
C'MON.
THERE'S A CELEBRATION GOING ON BACK HOME IN **ATLANTICUS**.
MOMENTS LATER...
LOOKS LIKE THOSE PYROCKIANS ENJOY MUSIC JUST LIKE WE DO!
KICK IT!

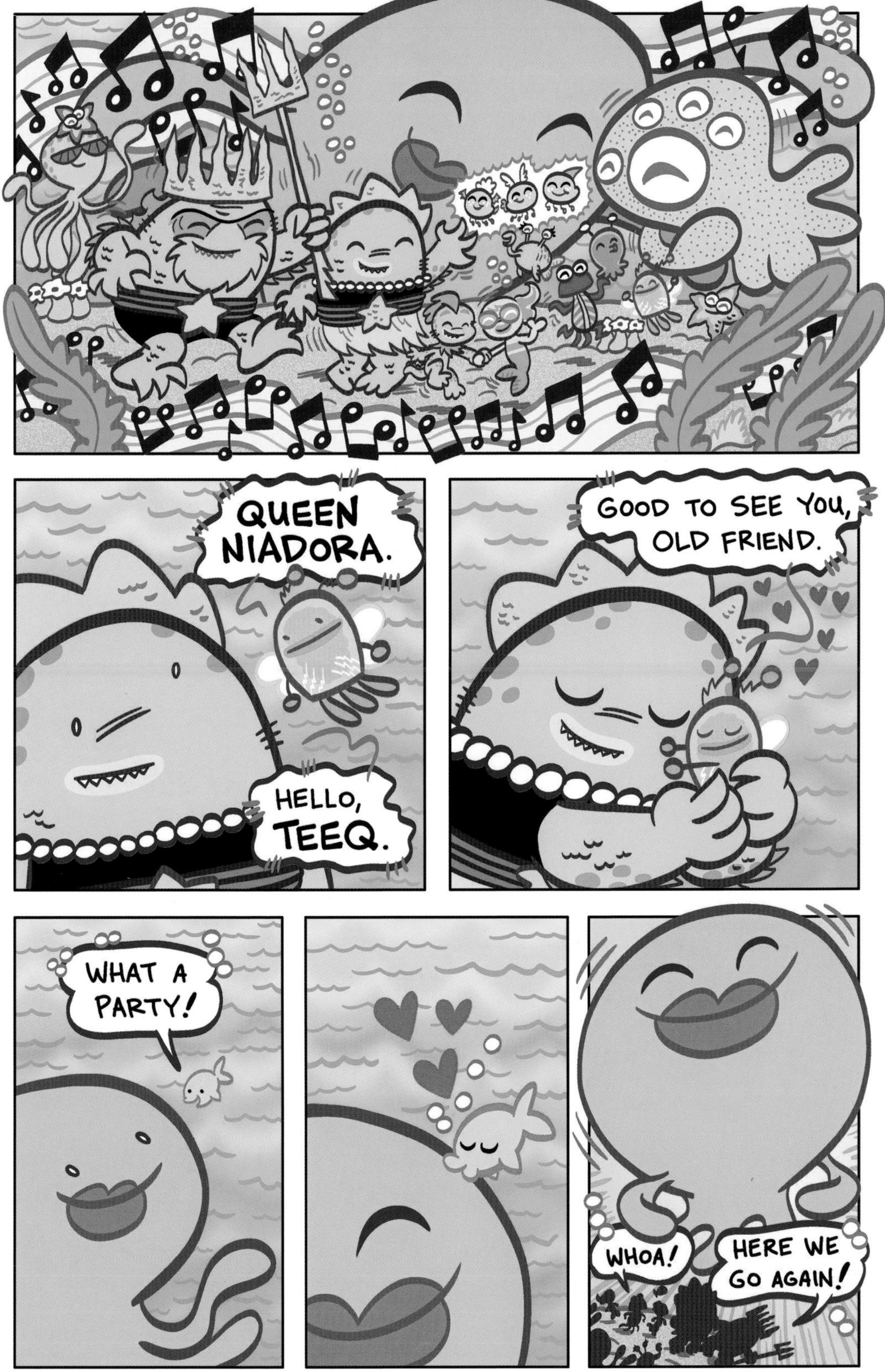
QUEEN NIADORA.
HELLO, TEEQ.
GOOD TO SEE YOU, OLD FRIEND.
WHAT A PARTY!
WHOA!
HERE WE GO AGAIN!

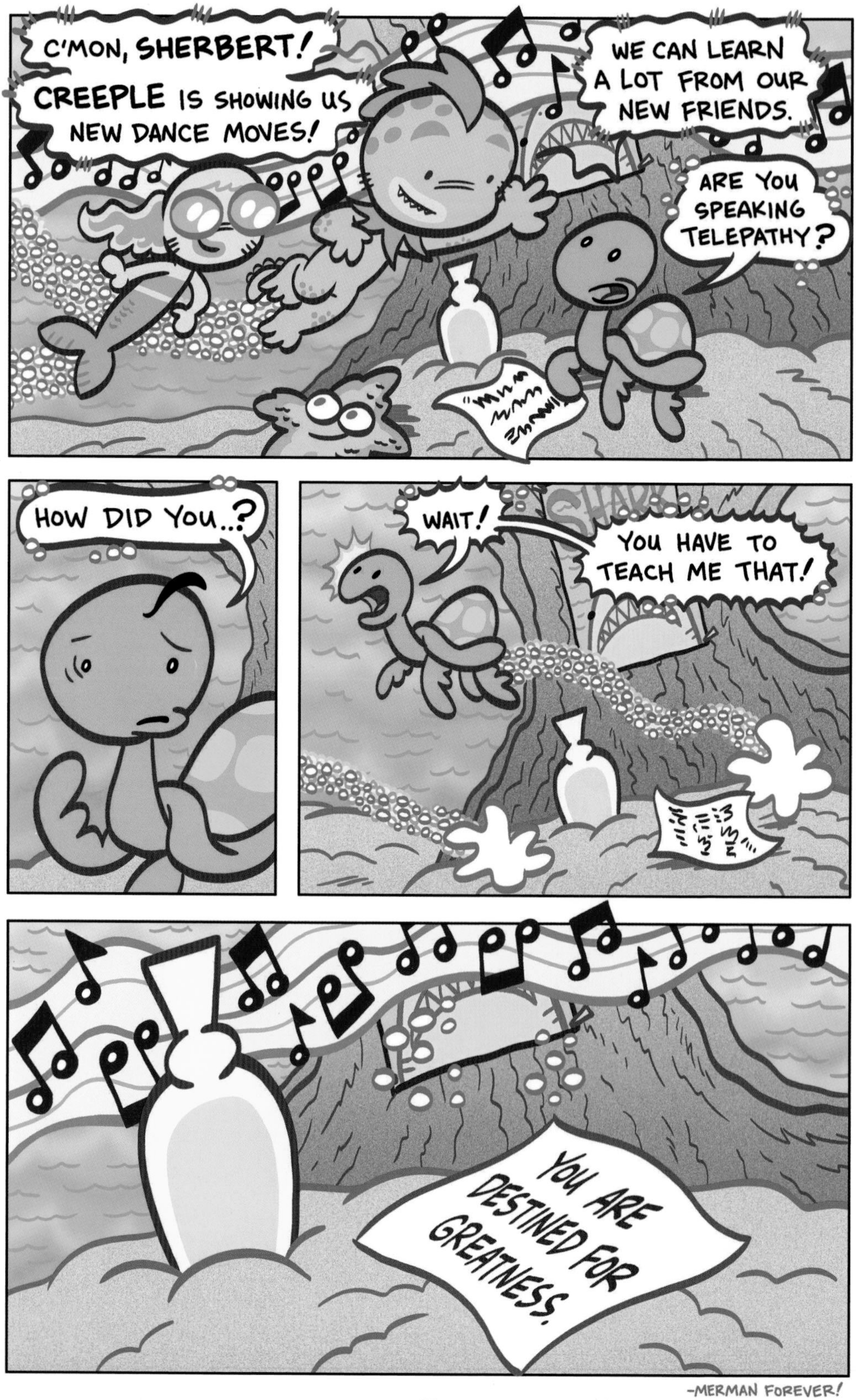
C'MON, SHERBERT!
CREEPLE IS SHOWING US NEW DANCE MOVES!
WE CAN LEARN A LOT FROM OUR NEW FRIENDS.
ARE YOU SPEAKING TELEPATHY?
HOW DID YOU..?
WAIT!
YOU HAVE TO TEACH ME THAT!
YOU ARE DESTINED FOR GREATNESS.

-MERMAN FOREVER!

WATCH OUT FOR PAPERCUTZ

Aw, yeah! Welcome to the grooviest graphic novel ever featuring an aquatic little green guy, GILLBERT #1 "The Little Merman," by Art Baltazar, from Papercutz, those fishy folks dedicated to publishing great graphic novels for all ages. I'm Jim Salicrup, the Editor-in-Chief and erstwhile stowaway on a yellow submarine, and I'm here to tell you a little bit about GILLBERT and Papercutz...

As already noted, GILLBERT is the creation of cartoonist Art Baltazar, a creator who has had great success creating comics for all ages. Let me interrupt myself to clarify exactly what I mean by this "all ages" stuff. Usually "all ages" is used as a euphemism for "just for kids." When we say it at Papercutz, we mean "all ages," as in we hope that someone as young as two (who will need someone to read the graphic novels to them) or as old as 102, and everyone in between, will enjoy our graphic novels. That's our goal. Do we always succeed? You tell us. Seriously, that's why we provide our contact info in that "Stay in touch!" box at the bottom of the page. Obviously some of our titles are enjoyed by more younger fans than others, but that's okay too. At Papercutz we publish a wide variety of graphic novels, some feature incredibly popular characters such as THE LOUD HOUSE, THE SMURFS, HOTEL TRANSYLVANIA, TROLLS, and many more, while others will feature characters you may have never met before, such as ERNEST & REBECCA, ARIOL, THE SISTERS, ANNE OF GREEN BAGELS, MANOSAURS, and many more. But they all respect your intelligence and are never written down to "kids." I've been lucky enough to not only hear from countless children who love Papercutz, but many adults as well. I believe that's because a good story is a good story, and a good story will appeal to everyone, which brings us back to Art Baltazar...

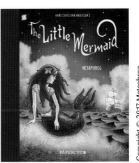

HANS CHRISTIAN ANDERSEN'S
The Little Mermaid
METAPHROG
PAPERCUTZ

I've been a big fan of Art's work for years, and I can't believe it's taken this long to get Art to create a new series for Papercutz. That may be because he's been writing and drawing so many other great comics (such as TINY TITANS, to name just one!), he's just been too busy. But we're nothing if not patient at Papercutz, and we think GILLBERT was worth the wait, and we hope you do too.

GUMBY
50 SHADES OF CLAY
PAPERCUTZ

And speaking of waiting, while you wait for the second GILLBERT graphic novel—coming soon—may I suggest checking out another undersea graphic novel from Papercutz? It's a beautiful adaptation of HANS CHRISTIAN ANDERSEN'S THE LITTLE MERMAID by Metaphrog. Hey, if you enjoyed "The Little Merman," you'll like this non-Hollywood-style version of the classic tale. Oh, and there's another Papercutz graphic novel featuring a groovy little green guy, which even has a great cover by Art Baltazar, called GUMBY #1 "50 Shades of Clay." On the following pages, we're offering an exclusive excerpt—that just happens to take place partially undersea. We hope you like it, and check out the GUMBY graphic novel which features lots more stories with the lovable clayboy.

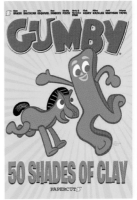

Gee, my fingertips are getting a little pruney, maybe it's time I return to the surface. But I do hope you return for GILLBERT's next great graphic novel, coming soon from... Papercutz!

Thanks, Jim

STAY IN TOUCH!

EMAIL:	salicrup@papercutz.com
WEB:	papercutz.com
TWITTER:	@papercutzgn
INSTAGRAM:	@papercutzgn
FACEBOOK:	PAPERCUTZGRAPHICNOVELS
FAN MAIL:	Papercutz, 160 Broadway, Suite 700, East Wing, New York, NY 10038

Head under the sea with Gumby and the gang in this special preview of GUMBY #1 "50 Shades of Clay"!

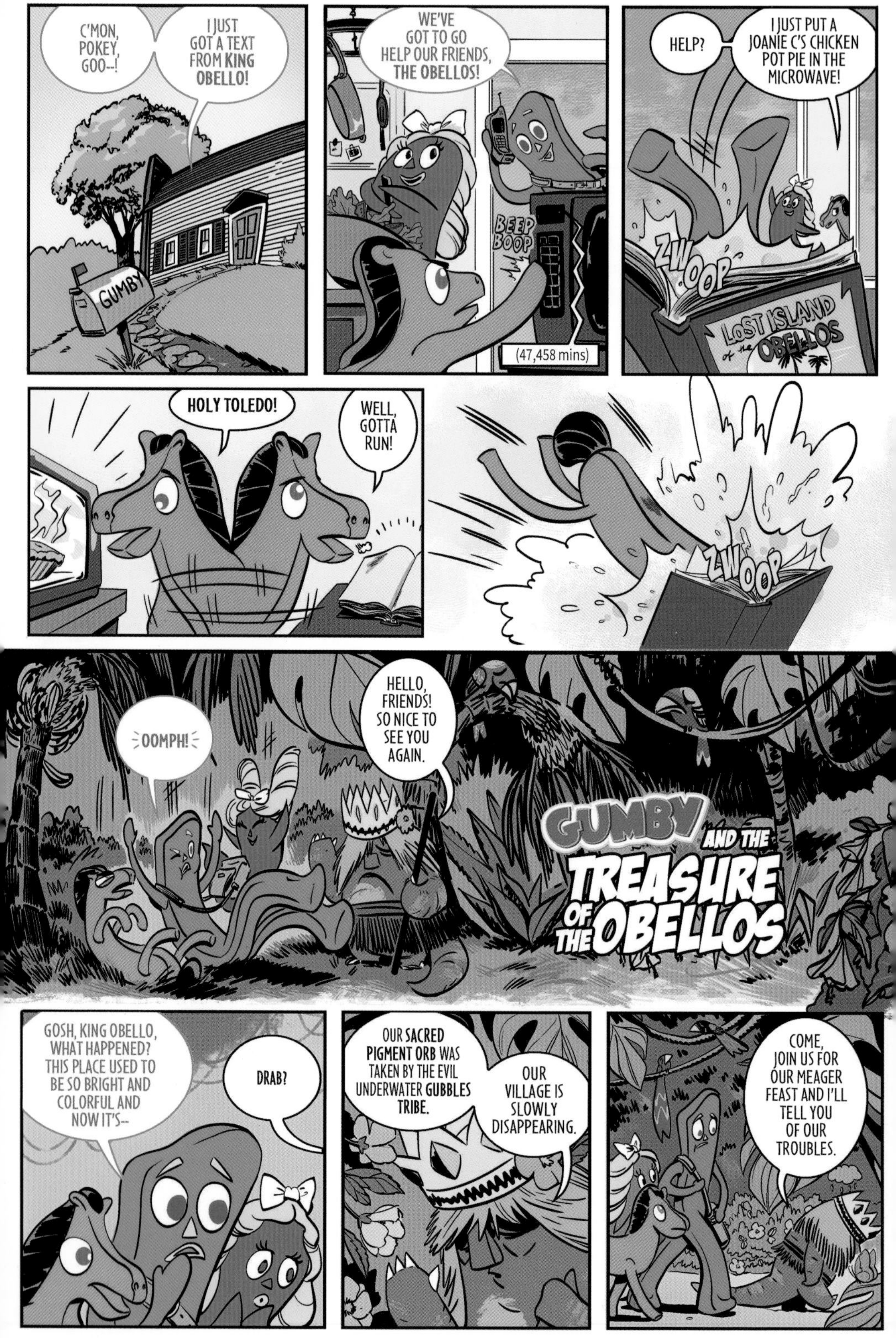
C'MON, POKEY, GOO--!
I JUST GOT A TEXT FROM KING OBELLO!
GUMBY
WE'VE GOT TO GO HELP OUR FRIENDS, THE OBELLOS!
BEEP BOOP
(47,458 mins)
HELP?
I JUST PUT A JOANIE C'S CHICKEN POT PIE IN THE MICROWAVE!
ZWOOP
LOST ISLAND of the OBELLOS
HOLY TOLEDO!
WELL, GOTTA RUN!
ZWOOP
OOMPH!
HELLO, FRIENDS! SO NICE TO SEE YOU AGAIN.
GUMBY AND THE TREASURE OF THE OBELLOS
GOSH, KING OBELLO, WHAT HAPPENED? THIS PLACE USED TO BE SO BRIGHT AND COLORFUL AND NOW IT'S--
DRAB?
OUR SACRED PIGMENT ORB WAS TAKEN BY THE EVIL UNDERWATER GUBBLES TRIBE.
OUR VILLAGE IS SLOWLY DISAPPEARING.
COME, JOIN US FOR OUR MEAGER FEAST AND I'LL TELL YOU OF OUR TROUBLES.

By Veronica and Andy Fish

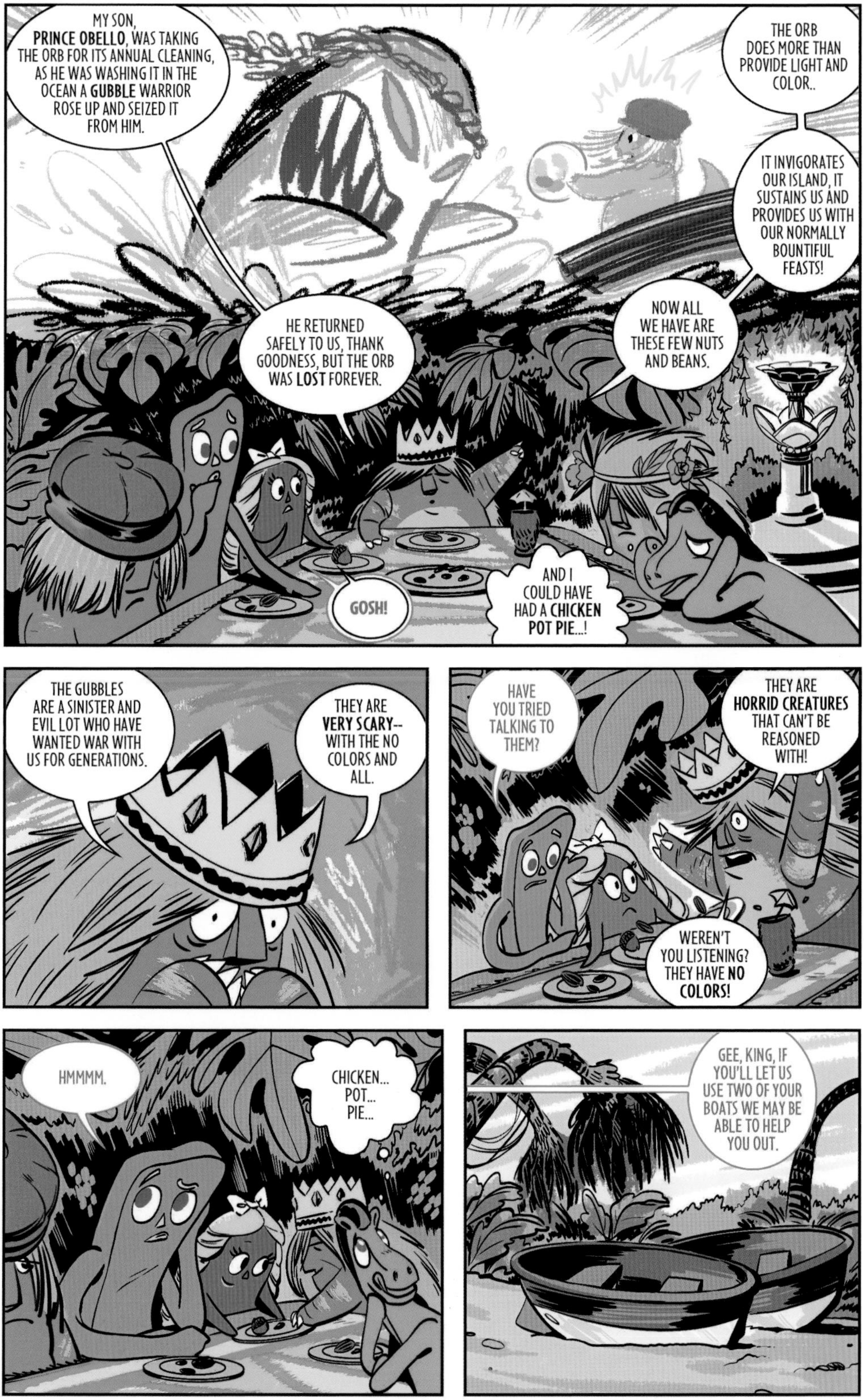
MY SON, PRINCE OBELLO, WAS TAKING THE ORB FOR ITS ANNUAL CLEANING, AS HE WAS WASHING IT IN THE OCEAN A GUBBLE WARRIOR ROSE UP AND SEIZED IT FROM HIM.
THE ORB DOES MORE THAN PROVIDE LIGHT AND COLOR..
IT INVIGORATES OUR ISLAND, IT SUSTAINS US AND PROVIDES US WITH OUR NORMALLY BOUNTIFUL FEASTS!
HE RETURNED SAFELY TO US, THANK GOODNESS, BUT THE ORB WAS LOST FOREVER.
NOW ALL WE HAVE ARE THESE FEW NUTS AND BEANS.
GOSH!
AND I COULD HAVE HAD A CHICKEN POT PIE...!
THE GUBBLES ARE A SINISTER AND EVIL LOT WHO HAVE WANTED WAR WITH US FOR GENERATIONS.
THEY ARE VERY SCARY-- WITH THE NO COLORS AND ALL.
HAVE YOU TRIED TALKING TO THEM?
THEY ARE HORRID CREATURES THAT CAN'T BE REASONED WITH!
WEREN'T YOU LISTENING? THEY HAVE NO COLORS!
HMMMM.
CHICKEN... POT... PIE...
GEE, KING, IF YOU'LL LET US USE TWO OF YOUR BOATS WE MAY BE ABLE TO HELP YOU OUT.

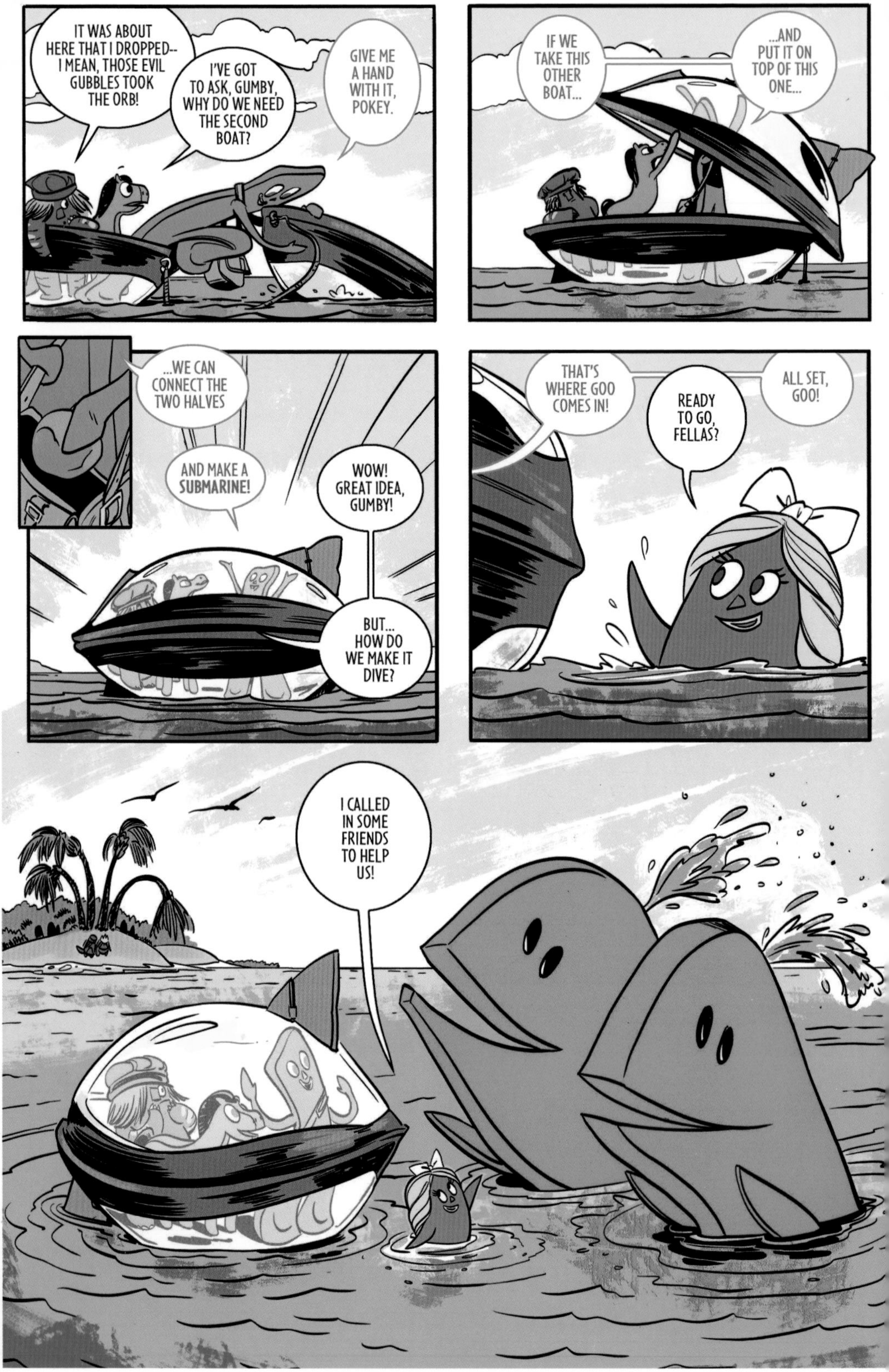
IT WAS ABOUT HERE THAT I DROPPED-- I MEAN, THOSE EVIL GUBBLES TOOK THE ORB!
I'VE GOT TO ASK, GUMBY, WHY DO WE NEED THE SECOND BOAT?
GIVE ME A HAND WITH IT, POKEY.
IF WE TAKE THIS OTHER BOAT...
...AND PUT IT ON TOP OF THIS ONE...
...WE CAN CONNECT THE TWO HALVES
AND MAKE A **SUBMARINE!**
WOW! GREAT IDEA, GUMBY!
BUT... HOW DO WE MAKE IT DIVE?
THAT'S WHERE GOO COMES IN!
READY TO GO, FELLAS?
ALL SET, GOO!
I CALLED IN SOME FRIENDS TO HELP US!

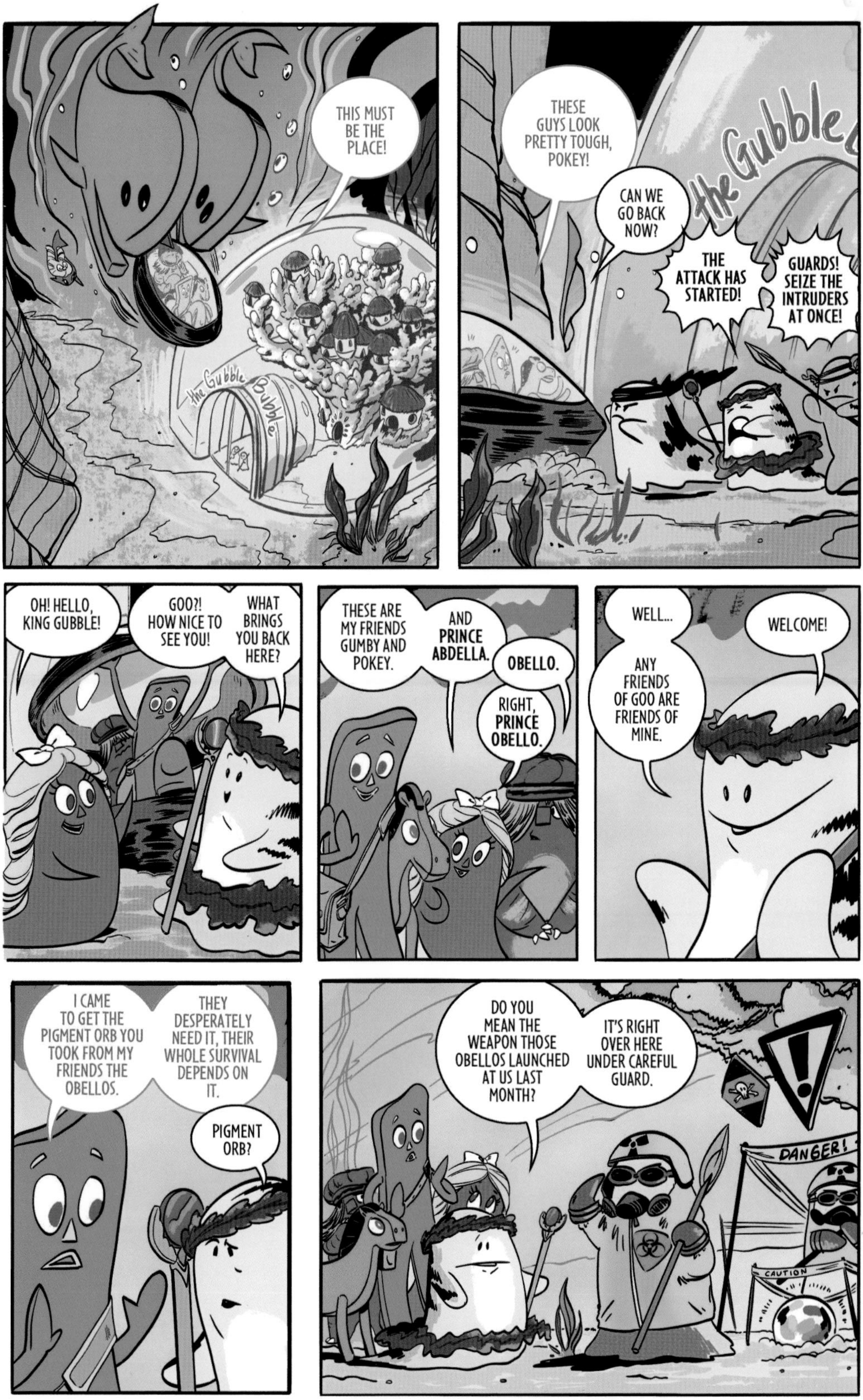
THIS MUST BE THE PLACE!
the Gubble Bubble
THESE GUYS LOOK PRETTY TOUGH, POKEY!
CAN WE GO BACK NOW?
the Gubble
THE ATTACK HAS STARTED!
GUARDS! SEIZE THE INTRUDERS AT ONCE!
OH! HELLO, KING GUBBLE!
GOO?! HOW NICE TO SEE YOU!
WHAT BRINGS YOU BACK HERE?
THESE ARE MY FRIENDS GUMBY AND POKEY.
AND PRINCE ABDELLA.
OBELLO.
RIGHT, PRINCE OBELLO.
WELL...
ANY FRIENDS OF GOO ARE FRIENDS OF MINE.
WELCOME!
I CAME TO GET THE PIGMENT ORB YOU TOOK FROM MY FRIENDS THE OBELLOS.
THEY DESPERATELY NEED IT, THEIR WHOLE SURVIVAL DEPENDS ON IT.
PIGMENT ORB?
DO YOU MEAN THE WEAPON THOSE OBELLOS LAUNCHED AT US LAST MONTH?
IT'S RIGHT OVER HERE UNDER CAREFUL GUARD.
DANGER!
CAUTION

Can't we all just get along? Find out in GUMBY #1
"50 Shades of Clay" available now wherever books are sold!

MORE GREAT GRAPHIC
NOVEL SERIES AVAILABLE FROM PAPERCUTZ™

THE SMURFS #21

THE GARFIELD SHOW #6

BARBIE #1

THE SISTERS #1

TROLLS #1

GERONIMO STILTON #17

THEA STILTON #6

SEA CREATURES #1

DINOSAUR EXPLORERS #1

SCARLETT

ANNE OF GREEN BAGELS #1

DRACULA MARRIES FRANKENSTEIN!

THE RED SHOES

THE LITTLE MERMAID

FUZZY BASEBALL

HOTEL TRANSYLVANIA #1

THE LOUD HOUSE #1

MANOSAURS #1

THE ONLY LIVING BOY #5

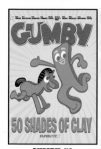

GUMBY #1